VICTORS & LORDS

Historical Fiction Published by McBooks Press

BY ALEXANDER KENT
Midshipman Bolitho
Stand into Danger
In Gallant Company
Sloop of War
To Glory We Steer
Command a King's Ship
Passage to Mutiny
With All Despatch
Form Line of Battle!
Enemy in Sight!
The Flag Captain
Signal–Close Action!
The Inshore Squadron
A Tradition of Victory
Success to the Brave
Colours Aloft!
Honour this Day
The Only Victor
Beyond the Reef
The Darkening Sea
For My Country's Freedom
Cross of St George
Sword of Honour
Second to None
Relentless Pursuit

BY R. F. DELDERFIELD
Too Few for Drums
Seven Men of Gascony

BY DAVID DONACHIE
The Devil's Own Luck
The Dying Trade

BY C. NORTHCOTE PARKINSON
The Guernseyman
Devil to Pay

BY V. A. STUART
Victors and Lords
The Sepoy Mutiny

BY CAPTAIN FREDERICK MARRYAT
Frank Mildmay OR
   The Naval Officer
The King's Own
Mr Midshipman Easy
Newton Forster OR
   The Merchant Service
Snarleyyow OR
   The Dog Fiend
The Privateersman
The Phantom Ship

BY DUDLEY POPE
Ramage
Ramage & The Drumbeat
Ramage & The Freebooters
Governor Ramage R.N.
Ramage's Prize
Ramage & The Guillotine
Ramage's Diamond
Ramage's Mutiny
Ramage & The Rebels
The Ramage Touch
Ramage's Signal
Ramage & The Renegades

BY JAN NEEDLE
A Fine Boy for Killing
The Wicked Trade

BY W. CLARK RUSSELL
Wreck of the Grosvenor
Yarn of Old Harbour Town

BY RAFAEL SABATINI
Captain Blood

BY MICHAEL SCOTT
Tom Cringle's Log

BY A. D. HOWDEN SMITH
Porto Bello Gold

BY NICHOLAS NICASTRO
The Eighteenth Captain

Victors & Lords

V. A. STUART

The Alexander Sheridan Adventures, No. 1

MCBOOKS PRESS
ITHACA, NEW YORK

Published by McBooks Press 2001
Copyright © 1964 by V. A. Stuart
First published as *Like Victors and Lords* in Great Britain
by Robert Hale Limited, London 1964

Cover painting: *The Battle of Sebastopol, after 1855* by Jean Charles Langlois
Courtesy of Musée des Beaux Arts, Caen, France,
UK/Bridgeman Art Library.
Frontispiece: from *Gardiner's School Atlas of English History,* London, 1891.

Library of Congress Cataloging-in-Publication Data
Stuart, V. A.
    Victors and lords / by V.A. Stuart.
        p. cm.
    ISBN 0-935526-98-6 (alk. paper)
    1. Great Britain—History, Military—19th century—Fiction. 2. Great
Britain—History—Victoria, 1837-1901—Fiction. 2. Balaklava (Ukraine),
Battle of, 1854—Fiction. 4. Crimean War, 1853-1856—Fiction. I. Title
PR6063.A38 V54   2001
823'.914—dc21   2001045006

Distributed to the book trade by
LPC Group, 1436 West Randolph, Chicago, IL 60607
800-626-4330.

Additional copies of this book may be ordered
from any bookstore or directly from
McBooks Press, 120 West State Street, Ithaca, NY 14850.
Please include $3.50 postage and handling with mail orders.
New York State residents must add sales tax.
All McBooks Press publications can also be ordered by calling
toll-free 1-888-BOOKS11 (1-888-266-5711).
Please call to request a free catalog.

Visit the McBooks Press website at www.mcbooks.com.

Printed in the United States of America
9 8 7 6 5 4 3 2 1

To Robert Meikle of Perth whose grandfather
charged with the Royal North British Dragoons
(Scots Greys) at Balaclava.

⇛ • ⇚

. . . They rode like victors and lords,
Thro' a forest of lances and swords
In the heart of the Russian hordes,
They rode or they stood at bay . . .

"THE CHARGE OF THE HEAVY BRIGADE AT BALACLAVA"
OCTOBER 25TH, 1854
ALFRED, LORD TENNYSON

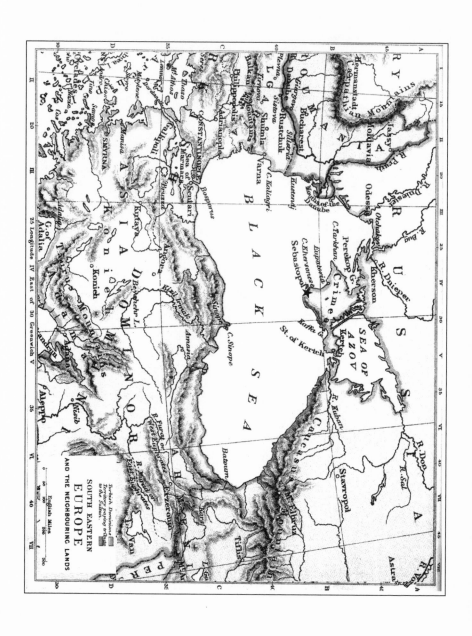

SOUTH EASTERN
EUROPE
AND THE NEIGHBOURING LANDS

Turkish Dominions
Territory paying tribute
to the Sultan.

English Miles
0   50 100   200   300

AUTHOR'S NOTE
➹➹➹ • ❦❦❦

With the exception of the hero and heroine and their relatives,
all the characters in this novel really existed and their actions are
a matter of historical fact. Their opinions, too, are in most cases
widely known, and where they have been credited with remarks
or conversations (as, for example, with the fictitious characters)
which are not actually their own words, great care has been taken
to make sure that these are, as far as possible, in keeping with their
known sentiments.

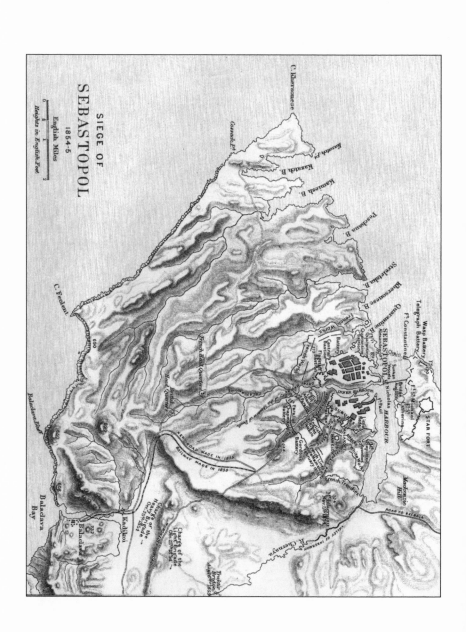

SIEGE OF
SEBASTOPOL

1854-5

English Miles

Heights in English Feet

PROLOGUE

❯❯❯ • ❮❮❮

ON A WARM August morning in the year 1846, the Royal Borough of Windsor was gay with flags and bunting. Crowds had been gathering from an early hour, attracted by the prospect of a military review, which was to be held that afternoon in the Great Park, in honor of His Royal Highness Prince Albert's twenty-seventh birthday.

Aware that the queen herself was to be present with her royal consort, people began to assemble outside the castle and along the processional route, so that very soon every vantage point was occupied and the pavements lined, six-deep, with spectators. Many made their way to the gates of the cavalry barracks where, in addition to the squadron of Household Cavalry which would furnish the Sovereign's Escort, it was rumored that the Earl of Cardigan's famous "Cherry Pickers"—the 11th Hussars—had spent the night.

The regiment had recently returned from Dublin. Renowned both for the magnificence of its uniforms and the precision of its drill, the 11th was a great crowd-puller on such occasions, and had been missed during its three-year tour of duty in Ireland. Although Prince Albert had ceased to be colonel-in-chief on his appointment to the Grenadier Guards four years before, the Cherry Pickers were still known as Prince Albert's Own and would have a special part to play in the afternoon's spectacle. The majority of those milling about the barrack gates had gone there hoping merely for a glimpse of the Hussars in their fabulous cherry-coloured pantaloons but a few, rowdies and trouble-makers for the most part, had other intentions.

They stood in a small, muttering group, apart from the rest, grimly awaiting the expected appearance of the regiment's commanding officer, so that they might boo and shout insults at him, for the Earl of Cardigan was universally disliked and a recent scandal had once more aroused public opinion strongly against him.

By noon, when the regiments of Foot were starting to converge on the park from bivouac and barrack, the pavements were so densely packed by cheering spectators that the troops lining the processional route and the blue-uniformed constables of Sir Robert Peel's police force found difficulty in holding them back. But there were few incidents, even among those outside the cavalry barracks, where trouble had been anticipated and extra police were on duty. True, there were shouts and catcalls, when a closed carriage drove up and someone hurled a stone at its rear window but, when it disappeared across the parade ground, even the rowdies fell silent. The crowds on the whole were happy and good humored, eager to demonstrate their loyalty to their young queen and anxious, too, as a wave of patriotic fervor swept them, to prove to the not always popular Prince Albert that on this, the occasion of his birthday, they bore him no ill-will.

The streets echoed to the stirring strains of martial music and to the rhythmic tramp of marching men. As they watched the splendid spectacle of England's military might flowing towards them, rank upon rank, scarlet and gold, tartan and tossing plumes, in a perfectly ordered river of brilliant colour, the citizens of Windsor cheered lustily. Voices rose above the shrilling of the fifes and the beat of drums, above the music of the ever-changing marches played by the military bands—eager, excited voices, calling for the royal personage in whose honour all this pageantry had been set in motion.

"Long live Prince Albert!"

"God bless his Royal Highness!"

"Let's give him three cheers . . . come on, lads, make it a good'un. Three cheers for the Prince . . . hip, hip, hurrah!"

The cheers rang out. No one, it seemed, could hold for long aloof from the crowd's pride and pleasure or remain unaffected by their mounting enthusiasm. Yet, in one of the windows of a graceful Georgian house overlooking the processional route, a young girl stood, face pressed against the glass and eyes tightly closed as she wept with anguished abandon.

She was a pretty, auburn-haired girl of about seventeen, dressed in the height of fashion in a green brocade gown, whose elegant cut emphasized the slim loveliness of her still childish figure and stamped her, for all her youth, as a lady of quality. Few of the passers-by on the pavement below, had they chanced to look upwards at the window in which she stood, would have failed to recognize her as the Lady Charlotte Mowbray, eldest and most beautiful of the four daughters of a distinguished soldier of the Peninsular War—General the Earl of Dunloy, until recently Her Majesty's Lord Lieutenant of Ireland.

Some of them, indeed, who had witnessed the arrival fifteen minutes earlier of a tall young man in the frock coat and top hat of a civilian, might even have guessed the reason for her tears, for Lady Charlotte Mowbray's engagement to Lieutenant Alexander Sheridan, of the 11th Hussars, had been announced a few months previously in *The Times.* And a great many people in Windsor that day had heard of Lieutenant Sheridan in connection with the latest Cardigan scandal. . . .

Lady Charlotte herself was, however, unconscious of the crowds below her. In spite of the noise and the commotion, she was conscious of little save the silent, brooding presence of the man who waited in the room behind her, for whom now—although they had once been so close—she could find no words. She wished wretchedly that he had not come, wished that she had not allowed her stepsister Emma, a mere child of fourteen, to persuade her, against her better judgement, that it was her duty to receive him.

Emmy with her precocity, her absurd passion for justice, her ludicrous and entirely unreciprocated devotion to her elder sister's fiancé . . . Charlotte bit her lower lip, feeling it quiver rebelliously. She did not need Emmy to tell her where her duty lay or what she must do. It was evident that she could not marry Alex Sheridan in his present circumstances. But she was willing to wait until he should have demanded a fresh hearing of his case and had had his commission restored to him—as it must be, if the truth were told.

"Alex," she whispered brokenly, "Alex, please . . . we cannot part like this. We must not!"

Only by the slight contraction of a muscle at the angle of his grimly set jaw did Alex Sheridan betray the fact that he had heard her. He made no response to her plea and Charlotte's throat ached with tears.

A company of Foot Guards, brave in their immaculate scarlet, the black bearskins meticulously aligned, passed under the window at that moment, to be greeted with loud applause from the watching throng. Charlotte saw them as a confused blur of colour through her tears and watched them go without interest, not troubling to raise her head. Even when the Guards were followed by a detachment of kilted Highlanders, swinging smartly along behind their magnificently uniformed pipe band, the weeping girl scarcely noticed them and the crowd's noisy expression of approval left her unmoved.

Only when the sound of pipes faded into the distance, yielding to the measured clip-clop of trotting horses, did she rouse herself sufficiently to pass a hand across her tear-filled eyes. A little half-stifled cry escaped her as she saw and instantly recognized the officer who now came into view, clad in a glittering blue and red Hussar uniform and riding a fine blood chestnut, draped with a crested shabraque.

Even if she had not seen him many times before in Phoenix Park, Dublin similarly attired and mounted, she would have experienced no difficulty in guessing the identity of that arrogant rider, Charlotte thought wryly, for his appearance fitted his reputation. In any dress, James Thomas Brudenell, Earl of Cardigan, cut an impressive and elegant figure, but in uniform and on horseback, he was possessed of an eye-catching magnificence few could equal. A man of over fifty now, the years had robbed him of few of his youthful good looks and he sat his horse with the easy, natural grace of an accomplished horseman. He rode confidently at the head of his regiment, a smile curving his lips beneath the flowing, carefully trimmed moustache which, like the luxuriant, ginger whiskers, was as yet untouched with grey. The thick rows of gold lace which adorned his brief jacket gleamed in the sunlight and the richly braided, fur-trimmed pelisse, slung by its cords from one shoulder, moved gently as he rose in the saddle, head held high when the crowd—recognizing him, as Charlotte had done—shouted his name.

The shouts were critical and uncomplimentary, even abusive. What cheers there were—and they were few—were reserved for the squadron trotting at his back, a solid phalanx of blue and cherry red and gold, set off by the shining coats of the well-groomed, perfectly matched chestnuts on which the men were mounted.

Lord Cardigan gave no sign that he'd heard the shouts or was aware of the offensive nature of the crowd's comments. But his smile faded when one of the spectators, bolder than all the rest, evading the attempt of a constable to restrain him, planted his thin, ill-clad body in the path of the earl's startled charger and, grabbing the reins, hurled a spate of words into his face.

From the window, fifteen feet above, it was impossible for Charlotte to hear what the shabbily dressed stranger had said, but the people flocking the pavement heard his cry and, with one accord, they took it up, chanting it in derisive unison, their mood swiftly changing and their earlier good humor forgotten.

"Lieutenant Sheridan!" they shouted. "Where is Lieutenant Sheridan today, your lordship? Why is *he* not on parade?"

In a brief struggle with two husky constables, the man who had stepped from the pavement was overpowered. But, although the Peelers bore him off, the shouting continued unabated.

"Lieutenant Sheridan fired a shot . . . and now he's copped the perishing lot!" It was a couplet which had been going the rounds and Charlotte said, the colour draining from her cheeks, "Do you hear them, Alex? They are singing that rhyme about you."

The man in the shadows behind her broke his self-imposed silence at last. His voice was weary as he answered. "Yes, I hear them. But it will do no good, you know—my case is closed. It is best forgotten."

"Is it?" Charlotte challenged reproachfully. "Oh, Alex, why do you say that?"

"Because it has all happened before," Alex Sheridan returned, with flat finality. "That is why, Charlotte."

He came to stand beside her, a tall, slim scarcely recognizable stranger in the unaccustomed grey frock coat of a civilian, his face pale and taut with strain. For an instant, his gaze went to the street below and his blue eyes, bright with an emotion Charlotte could not analyze, followed the retreating backs of the trotting Hussars. There was pride and an odd wistfulness in his voice as he added softly, "They look well, do they not? And I see that Phillip is riding that new mare of his—the one he bought in Moy."

"Is he? I had not observed it." Charlotte dismissed the subject of her brother indifferently but, with unexpected obstinacy, Alex returned to it. "Phillip is a fine fellow, with all the makings of a first-rate officer. And he is popular. He gets on with everyone— even Cardigan likes him. You should be proud of him, Charlotte."

"I am proud of him. But . . ." Charlotte's lower lip quivered and she felt the tears starting again to her eyes as she looked into the face of the man beside her. It was a handsome, boyish face but already bitterness and disillusionment had marred its good looks and the lines etched about mouth and eyes were not those normally to be seen in the countenance of a man of scarcely five and twenty.

Lord Cardigan seemingly did not age, but Alex Sheridan had added ten years to his appearance during the past few months. She bit her lip and, greatly daring, put out a hand to touch his arm. "It is *you* I am thinking of now . . . I can think of no one else. If only you would fight back, Alex—if only you would appeal against Lord Fitzroy Somerset's decision! You heard the crowd just now. Public sympathy is on your side and they sing that couplet everywhere. If you were to lodge an appeal, is it not possible that you might be reinstated, in another regiment, as Captain Reynolds was? After all, Lord Cardigan is constantly attacked in the newspapers, people know him for what he is and he's detested—the more so since his separation from his wife. And—"

"No." Alex cut her short, his tone curt, brooking no argument and discouraging pity. "It is quite useless for me to appeal. I told you . . . my case is closed. It cannot now be reopened."

"But Captain Reynolds had his case reopened. Why should not you?"

"The two cases are quite different. Reynolds was tried by court martial and cashiered . . . I was not. In any event, he's had to wait nearly two years before being gazetted to the 9th Lancers. I could not afford to wait for so long." Alex avoided her gaze. "Please, Charlotte, I did not wish to discuss this matter. It is all over and done with—I could do no more, even if I wanted to. And I do not."

"Because you are afraid, Alex?" Charlotte accused.

"Afraid! Afraid of what, pray?"

"Afraid to fight against the injustice that was done you . . . even for my sake?"

He reddened, stung by this accusation. "Say rather that I have experienced the futility of trying to fight against it. When one has neither influence nor money, one's hands are tied and one loses faith in one's cause."

"Then why have you come here?" Charlotte demanded, with a swift flash of anger. "If you have lost faith in your cause and if you do not intend to fight to redeem yourself, then I cannot marry you, Alex. I . . . I should not want to and you can scarcely expect it. You cannot ask me to honor a promise I made to you in such . . . such different circumstances."

Alex Sheridan expelled his breath in a long, pent-up sigh.

"I am not seeking to hold you to your promise of marriage now," he told her stonily. "But I had hoped . . . that is, Philip and Emmy urged me to come because—" he broke off and took her hand gently in his. Her fingers were ice-cold against his palm and she turned her head away, refusing to look at him. "Charlotte, I love you with all my heart! You know that, do you not?"

She gave him no answer. In the street below, a squadron of Heavy Dragoons went clattering by, the sun striking dazzling reflections from their plumed helmets. The 5th, Alex saw, and he stared after them miserably, the barrier of silence once more between himself and Charlotte, holding them apart, in spite of their two linked hands. Would she never understand, he wondered despairingly, could she not try to understand the lengths to which he had been driven and the bitter humiliation he had suffered at Lord Cardigan's hands before, finally, he had rebelled? He knew that she could not when she said at last, her voice a small, chill whisper of sound in the shadowed room, "Was it for love of me that you sacrificed your career in the 11th, Alex?" Her eyes met his then and again they accused him. "I was in love with you when I consented to marry you. I was happy to think that I should have as my husband an officer of my brother's regiment, whom he respected and admired. But all that is changed now and *you* have changed it, not I."

"Yes," he conceded tonelessly, "I have changed it."

"Then why," Charlotte asked for the second time, "*why* have you come? Why did you choose to come today—because you knew that my father would not be here? Or was it Emmy's idea . . . did *she* persuade you?"

"Emmy?" Alex shook his head. "Oh, no, Emmy did not have to persuade me . . . and I have your father's permission to call on you. He said that I might come in order to talk to you and to . . . to acquaint you with my future plans. You see . . ." He hesitated, uncertain how to tell her what he had decided to do and then, aware that there was no escape, said regretfully, "I am to sail for India at the end of this week, Charlotte. It breaks my heart but I . . . that is, I venture to hope that—"

"For . . . *India?*" Charlotte put in. She stared at him in shocked disbelief, the last vestige of colour gone from her cheeks. "You cannot mean that, Alex . . . you cannot!"

"Charlotte my dearest love. . ." he drew her to him and felt her tremble in his arms as they closed about her. "I do mean it. God forgive me, it's what I have been trying to tell you ever since I arrived. I am leaving England for good, Charlotte. My uncle has procured me a cornet's commission in the Bengal Native Cavalry, in the service of the East India Company. My passage is booked to Calcutta in the S.S. *Ripon* . . . she sails on Friday."

"But must you go to India? Must you, Alex? India is half the world away and you will be gone for years. I shall never see you again. . . ." Charlotte shivered, as realization of what his going would mean to her came swiftly and disturbingly. Until this moment she had not visualized losing him irrevocably and the knowledge that she might do so hurt much more than she had imagined it would. So long as he remained in England, even if she were not officially betrothed to him, there was always the chance that his case might be reopened. Her father was not without influence—if he interceded with Lord Fitzroy Somerset or perhaps approached the duke himself on Alex's behalf . . . She said, her voice choked with sobs, "Oh, Alex, I beg you not to go. If you love me, please cancel your passage."

Alex heard the pain in her voice and released her abruptly.

"My love, I must go. Do not make it harder for me." The echo of her pain was in his own voice but he went on resolutely, "I am a soldier and soldiering is my life—it is all I know and understand. In India, in the Company's service, I can become a soldier again. What else can I do, Charlotte?"

When she did not answer him, he moved away from the

window and from her and started restlessly to pace the room. His back turned towards her, he continued in a low, expressionless voice, seeking to make the reasons for his decision comprehensible to her. "I have sold my commission in the 11th, as I was commanded to by Lord Fitzroy Somerset. My military career in this country is at an end. The alternative to selling out was, as Phillip must have told you, to stand trial by court martial."

"But Alex"—Charlotte had recovered her composure— "would you not have been better off now, if you had elected to stand trial?"

"I was offered no choice," Alex stated flatly. "In any event, the result would have been a foregone conclusion. Cardigan would have seen to it that I was cashiered."

"But at least if you had stood trial, you could have defended yourself against his charges, could you not?"

"No, my dearest." He shook his head despairingly. "I had no defense."

"No defense! But everyone in the regiment knows how Lord Cardigan treated you!" Charlotte protested indignantly. "Surely you could have called witnesses to prove that he provoked you beyond endurance?"

Alex sighed. Was this not precisely the course which the military secretary had feared he might follow, if afforded the opportunity of a court martial? It would not have saved him, of course but—had he done so—he might have brought Cardigan down with him. He had been bitter enough to want this but . . . he said, with weary resignation, "It was made clear to me, when I first requested a trial, that I should not be permitted to call any of my brother officers as witnesses. Nor should I have asked any of them to speak in my defense."

"Why not, Alex? They were your friends . . . Phillip is your friend still, is he not? He assures me that he is and he holds no brief for Lord Cardigan, of that I am certain."

"Charlotte my dear," Alex told her quietly, "to have called Phillip to speak in my defense might well have ruined him too, in spite of the regard Cardigan has for him. You must understand . . ." He halted and came to stand looking down at her from beneath furrowed brows. "For any officer to challenge another to fight a duel is a breach of the Articles of War. It is quite unpardonable, whatever may have led up to it. My guilt was never in doubt—I could not deny it. Furthermore the man from whom I demanded satisfaction was at that time my commanding officer."

"But you did not fight with Lord Cardigan, Alex," Charlotte objected. "There was no duel."

"No," Alex returned grimly, "but that was scarcely my fault. I issued the challenge, in writing and in full awareness of the consequences. I had stood all I could stand and I lost my temper. But that is no excuse, Charlotte—rather is it a condemnation. No British regiment would accept me now if I did apply for another commission, since it's widely known that I attempted to call Cardigan out, while I was serving under him. I'm finished in the British army, my love—did not Phillip tell you so?"

"He endeavored to tell me," Charlotte admitted reluctantly, "but I did not believe him, I could not. I was certain that you would be given another chance. If you are not, then it is a cruel injustice . . . because you were not the only one. There were others, Alex."

"Yes," Alex agreed. His face darkened. "There were a great many others. I should have heeded their example, it was before me for long enough . . . I knew what to expect." He resumed his restless pacing of the floor.

❦

It was true, Alex Sheridan reflected wryly, that his had been by no means the only case of its kind in which his late commanding officer had been involved . . . and it would not be the last, for Lord Cardigan's record as a regimental commander was one of the worst in the British army. In 1834, as Lord Brudenell, he had been removed from command of the 15th Hussars as a direct result of his mistreatment of one of its officers, Captain Augustus Wathen. A court martial had upheld Wathen and, in its findings, censured his lordship severely.

Yet less than two years later, the wealthy peer had been permitted to purchase the lieutenant-colonelcy of the 11th, which was then a Light Dragoon Regiment stationed in India. Despite a storm in the House of Commons, when the appointment was gazetted, it was not revoked. At a time when the official price for a cavalry command was in the region of £6,000, it was rumored that Lord Brudenell had paid £40,000 for that of the 11th and his anxiety to seek active military employment was, in consequence, regarded sympathetically at the Horse Guards. It was held that he had learned his lesson and the storm abated when a number of distinguished and high-ranking officers came forward to testify, in glowing terms, to his lordship's character and military accomplishments.

But these were not so apparent to the officers and men of his new regiment—of whom he had been one Alex recalled—when, after assuming command, Lord Brudenell spent a short time with them in Cawnpore. However, he succeeded his father as Earl of Cardigan in August 1837, so that it was not until the following year, when the regiment returned to England and was posted to Canterbury, that its lieutenant-colonel revealed himself in his true colours. It was then very soon evident that the system of command he practiced had not changed; since it stemmed from his own arrogance, Alex thought with bitterness, he knew no other.

The effect on his unfortunate regiment was disastrous. The 11th had served with distinction in India for seventeen years and, officered by experienced professional soldiers, possessed an exemplary record. But this was soon lost under Lord Cardigan's command, during the first two years of which—when the regimental strength was 335 rank and file—no less than 105 courts martial were held and over 700 punishments ordered. Discipline became notoriously harsh. Extra drills, inspections and parades were a daily occurrence and minor misdemeanors were treated with the utmost severity, without regard for rank or length of service. Arrests, floggings and charges of insubordination were as commonplace as public insults and reprimands, delivered before the whole regiment or in mess, in front of the assembled officers.

Any of Lord Cardigan's officers who crossed, or otherwise displeased him, were subjected to a merciless persecution, calculated to break the spirit of even the most courageous. It had been all too easy to incur his lordship's displeasure, as he had found to his cost . . . Alex sighed, his mind shrinking from the unpalatable details which he now wanted to erase from it. He did not want to discuss what had happened with Charlotte; he did not want to speak to anyone of what lay between Cardigan and himself. The experience had been too traumatic, the memories had been too recent and too humiliating for him to recall them without shame.

Yet . . . his hands clenched at his sides. He could not forget. Others besides himself had suffered the same tyranny and many had, like himself, been driven at last to rebel against their commander . . . so many, indeed, that it seemed unbelievable that their united protests could continue to be ignored by the army authorities. But they were ignored or, at any rate disregarded in all but a few instances, when they could not be hushed up. In spite of countless rumors and scandals concerning his conduct and repeated public demonstrations against him, the Earl of Cardigan remained in command of the 11th, wielding so powerful an influence in high places that, it seemed, his position was unassailable. Whatever he did, the Horse Guards and the twin ramparts of rank and wealth protected him from the consequences of his actions. And, no doubt, these would continue to do so, Alex told himself, his mouth hardening into a tight, resentful line, for as long as the system of promotion by purchase was maintained in the British army. Certainly while aristocratic connections and the possession of money were considered greater military assets than merit, then junior officers who lacked both were expendable. This was a lesson he had learned and would remember. . . .

As he had said to Charlotte, he had had the example of others before him. But he had not heeded it and, looking back, he knew that faced with the same situation again, he would still have acted as he had. There were some insults no man could swallow and still call himself a man. He had done what honor demanded, however futile his act of defiance had been and however high the price he was compelled to pay for it. But the price was high . . . Alex's mouth relaxed in a mirthless smile. He had at least been allowed to retain the value of his commission; he had not been cashiered and broken, as he had fully expected he would be. He had simply been ordered to sell out and the military secretary, Lord Fitzroy Somerset, had evidently hoped that, by showing him this clemency, another public scandal involving his commanding officer might be avoided.

This, he was cynically aware, was the sole reason for the clemency accorded him. The Harvey Tuckett affair and the Reynolds court martial had led to so fierce a storm of criticism

against Lord Cardigan that those who controlled the army's destiny had been afraid lest, on his account, it be repeated. And so
he had escaped comparatively lightly but nevertheless he was
ruined, and he had achieved nothing except his own downfall.
The story had got about—he had no idea how—and now he was
a marked man, a pariah to whom the British army would never
again open its ranks. He was black-listed as an insubordinate
young officer, who had dared to defy his regimental commander,
and not one of his military superiors had the slightest desire to
investigate the reasons which had led up to his insubordination.
An investigation would have given him the chance to defend his
actions and this at all costs—since it must lead to renewed criticism of Lord Cardigan—the Horse Guards had sought to prevent.
They had not been entirely successful, Alex decided, judging by
that performance in the street just now, and by the *Globe*'s pub-
lication of the derisive couplet, in which his name was mentioned.
Yet by condemning him unheard, they had enforced his silence;
by offering him a generous-seeming compromise, Lord Fitzroy
Somerset had avoided any repetition of the Wathen court martial. He wished that he could have afforded to refuse the
compromise and glanced then at Charlotte, for whose sake he
had believed, at the time, that he would be accepting it.

She was so beautiful, he thought, his heart contracting as his
gaze rested on her small, tear-wet face and bent head . . . so young
and sweet and gentle, this girl whom he loved and had once pur-
posed to marry. In the gracefully draped gown she had donned
in order to receive him, she looked even lovelier than he had
remembered. Green had always suited her—it was a colour which
brought out the highlights in her glorious auburn hair and accen-
tuated the creamy whiteness of her skin, lending it, despite her
tears, a subtle radiance that defied description.

Alex took a pace towards her. He longed, in sudden desperation, to take her once again into his arms and hold her to him
. . . to promise with his lips on hers that, for him, there would be
no one else, however long the parting between them, however far
away from her his destiny might lead him. But even as he reached
out his arms to her, he hesitated.

Charlotte asked, without turning her head, "What is it, Alex?"

"It does not matter, Charlotte. I . . . " he mumbled something
unintelligible even to his own ears and went back to his measured pacing of the room, feeling like a prisoner, caught and held
within the narrow confines of a cell from which it was impossible to break free.

He had no future, he reminded himself. He was going into
exile, from which there might be no return. How could he beg
her to wait for him, as he had intended when he came here,
when he could not tell her for how long she might have to
wait? The East India Company, he was aware, did not entertain
applications for home leave from any officer with less than ten
years' service.

Ten years! Alex was conscious of sick despair. He had no right,
in his present circumstance, to attempt to bind her to him . . .
unless she herself expressed her willingness to remain bound to
him. It had been on this understanding that he had been permitted to see her today. He had given his word, both to her father
and to Phillip, that he would take his final leave of her now if
this were Charlotte's wish. Neither had insisted that their engagement was to be broken and neither had suggested that their
parting was to be irrevocable, if Charlotte wanted it otherwise.

But marriage was out of the question for them now—she had
told him so and he himself was painfully aware of the fact. He
could not take her with him when he sailed; India was a hard

country for British women, the hazards of its climate only off-set by the provision of a well-appointed house and numerous servants, which were expensive. He had only the price of his commission behind him and a small allowance, made grudgingly by his elder brother to enable him to pay his mess bills in the 11th. This would stop when he joined the Indian army; he could scarcely expect or ask his brother to continue it. And a cornet's pay would not be enough on which to support a wife—least of all one who, like Charlotte Mowbray, had always been accustomed to wealth and position.

In any case, Charlotte had expressed no desire to accompany him . . . he looked at her, his face tense and questioning. Only Emmy had believed that her sister would agree to join him in India when, if they ever did, his prospects improved. Only Emmy had been confident that Charlotte would wait for him, forever if need be—and Emmy was a child with a child's touching faith in all humanity. He had been a fool to listen to her and to allow himself, against all reason, to hope. The parting must come now and, for Charlotte's sake, it must be final. She was young—too young, perhaps, to love him as he loved her. She would forget him once he had gone out of her life and it was better so, for both of them.

The decision made and his emotions under stern control, he crossed to her side. "Charlotte my dearest," he said, making no move to touch her, "I have to say goodbye to you."

Charlotte gave no sign that she had heard him. In the street below, the cheering rose to a thunderous crescendo and Alex guessed, without looking down, that this excited outburst heralded the appearance of the queen herself. The queen, regal and gracious, driving in an open carriage, surrounded by her escort of Household Cavalry . . . his heart lifted. It was a sight he had seen before and one which, in the past, had never failed to stir him deeply. But now he did not take the single step that separated him from the window from whence—perhaps for the last time—he might again have witnessed it.

Instead he stood in silence watching Charlotte, seeking to close his heart and mind to her appeal. Her face was turned from him, so that all he could see was her slender body in the graceful green dress and the back of her head, with its shining crown of hair, transformed to flame-bright beauty by the sunlight streaming in through the window. He knew that the exquisite picture she made, framed between the heavy velvet curtains which hung on either side of her, would remain imprinted on his memory for the rest of time . . . although this, too, was a sight he might never see again. She did not speak until the cheering had died to a faint, far-off murmur and then she said, her voice low and devoid of feeling, "You are really going to India, then? You had made up your mind to go before you came here?"

"Yes, I had," Alex admitted. The spell was broken and he was aware of a strange physical numbness creeping over him. "It is the only course open to me, Charlotte. Indeed, I am fortunate that the East India Company is willing to accept me. But for the fact that my uncle is a member of the Court of Governors and has given a lifetime of service to the Company, my application for an Indian army commission might well have been rejected and—"

Charlotte interrupted him, with a hint of impatience. "If you go, Alex, I cannot wait for you. I . . . oh, the very thought of living in India is abhorrent to me. I could not face it . . . the climate, the hardships, the kind of social life I should be compelled to live out there. And your position, the fact that you . . ." her voice trailed off into silence but the implications of all that she had left unsaid were as plain to him as if she had spoken the words aloud.

She would not like having to be presented, as his wife, to the wives and daughters of the queen's commissioned officers whom she would meet in Calcutta and Delhi. . . .

Alex flushed wretchedly, the knowledge that, even in India, she might feel ashamed to bear his name striking him with the force of a physical blow. It wrought havoc with his last despairing hopes and he said, with what dignity he could muster, "I understand, Charlotte. I do not expect you to wait or to consider that you are under any obligation to me in the circumstances."

Her lips parted in a revealing sigh of relief but there was still a suspicion of moisture in her eyes as, turning to face him, she asked, "Is this really the only course open to you? Is there no other, even if you feel compelled to leave England for a time?"

He spread his hands in a gesture of resignation. "I thought of the possibility of selling my sword in Spain or Austria. But I have no contacts, I know of no one who would recommend me."

"It did not occur to you to ask my father?"

Alex's colour deepened and he shook his head. "India offers me the opportunity of an honorable career, in the service of my country, without asking for favours. That is what I want."

"And you will take it," Charlotte reproached him, "even if it means that we may never see each other again?"

He eyed her somberly, having to steel himself to answer her because even now, he realized, she would not be completely lost to him if he were to change his mind. But she wanted him as he had been, not as he was and that was impossible. The eligible young Hussar officer who had courted her so ardently was dead—as dead as if the fatal duel to which he had challenged Lord Cardigan had been fought and a bullet from a duelling pistol were lodged in his heart. He said, with defensive coldness, "To my infinite regret, Charlotte, I must."

"Then . . ." Charlotte held out her hand to him. On its palm lay the small pearl and sapphire ring which he had given her when Lord Dunloy had consented to their betrothal. "This is yours, Alex. And there are letters . . . a few I kept, which I will destroy."

"Please," Alex begged, "will you not keep the ring? I should like you to have it."

She looked down at the ring, an odd little smile playing about her lips. "To remind me of you? But I do not wish to remember you, Alex."

"Charlotte . . ." he began hoarsely but she gestured him to silence. "There is no more to be said." She placed the ring in his hand and stepped back, out of his reach. Head held high, she went towards the door and Alex gazed after her, his pain a living thing, tearing at the shattered remnants of his control.

Charlotte paused by the door and glanced back at him, "I will tell them to show you out," she informed him, with a chill politeness that was unbearably hurtful. Her fingers closed about the bell rope and she pulled on it firmly. "I fancy Emmy may wish to bid you farewell. I shall tell her that you are leaving." Then, as if it were an afterthought, she added tonelessly, "Good-bye, Alex. I wish you well in your new life, even though I cannot share it with you. And I trust that you will find what you seek in India."

"What I seek?" he echoed dully.

"An honorable career in the service of your country, was it not? And happiness . . . with someone else, since I cannot give it to you." Her words were deliberately intended to provoke him. Alex's control snapped and he was beside her, gathering her to him, holding her in his arms.

"Wait, Charlotte, I beseech you! We must not part on such terms, with bitterness between us. I love you . . . believe this, at least, and try to find it in your heart to forgive me. I do only what I am compelled to do, I give you my word." His mouth found hers and, for a moment, she clung to him in surrender, her lips soft and yielding under his. Then with a breathless, "Let me go, Alex . . ." she averted her face, her body suddenly limp and unresponsive, her arms falling to her sides. He released her, as she had bidden him and she turned to him, in a passionate blaze of anger.

"If you loved me you would not run away like a whipped cur! You would stay in England and vindicate yourself—for my sake, Alex, if not for your own. But you will not!"

"Because I cannot, Charlotte . . . if only I could."

"It is because you will not," Charlotte said, as if he had not spoken, "that I can never forgive you." Her eyes met his, scorn and contempt in their grey-green depths and then were lowered. "Go to India, I do not care! If you were the last man in all the world, I would not marry you now, Alex. Ask Emmy . . . she can see no fault in you. Perhaps she might wait for you, if you asked her to . . . you are still a hero to her, if not to me." As swiftly as it had flared up, her anger faded and she said sadly, "I could have loved you, if you had let me. But you did not, so it is not my fault." She gave him no chance to reply. The door closed behind her and Alex was alone, staring dazedly at the small, jewelled talisman in his hand. From the Great Park, muted by distance, came the sound of gunfire as the cannon fired a Royal Salute. He heard it but did not raise his head.

Emmy came to him, as he was preparing to leave. She came running, her thin, earnest little face alight with hope but, at the first glimpse of his expression, her eager smile vanished.

"Oh, Alex, did our plan fail?" She studied him with troubled brown eyes. "Charlotte has told me nothing, save that you are leaving and that you sail on Friday for India."

"Yes," Alex confirmed, "I sail on Friday, Emmy."

"But . . ." she caught sight of the ring in his hand. "Is your engagement broken? Charlotte was upset but I thought, I had hoped . . . Alex, will she not wait for you, after all?"

He shook his head. "It is my doing, Emmy child, not hers."

"*Your* doing? Oh, surely not—" she stopped herself, lest she offend him. "I am so sorry. Perhaps you should not have come."

"Perhaps I should not."

"Poor Alex," she said pityingly, "I am truly sorry."

He knew that she was and did not resent her pity. Emma O'Shaughnessy was Charlotte's stepsister, the daughter of Lord Dunloy's second wife, a charming young Irish widow whom he had married during his term of office in Dublin. She had entered the vice-regal household in order, originally, to act as governess to the three Mowbray girls and the marriage had shocked them almost as much as it had delighted Dublin society when it had first been announced. But Constance O'Shaughnessy was of good family, the widow of a naval captain, and the girls, as well as Phillip, had swiftly succumbed to their new stepmother's charm. They now accepted her, as they accepted her daughter Emmy, as members of the family, regarding both with a warm, if faintly condescending affection.

Emmy at fourteen was a leggy, coltish child, whose dark colouring and elfin features offered small promise of future good looks. But she possessed considerable charm and a lively intelligence and, for her age and sex, was remarkably well educated. Her desire for learning was insatiable. In an attempt to satisfy it, she read any and every book on which she could lay hands, seeking no guidance save her own avid thirst for knowledge. Throughout the time he had known her, she had been a constant source of astonishment to Alex because of the breadth and nature of her interests and her extraordinarily retentive memory. She cared little for such feminine matters as dress or appearance and had once confided to him that, had it not been for the fact that she had had the misfortune to be born a woman, she would have chosen, of all things, to study medicine.

Her one talent—and the only one recognized by her family—was her ability to ride. Emmy was a startlingly brilliant horsewoman, and, young as she was, could handle any animal they gave her, however wild and intractable. Alex had made her acquaintance when she was eleven, largely as the result of her prowess on horseback, and they had been firm friends ever since . . . a friendship which had led, in due course, to his meeting with Charlotte.

He smiled down at her sadly, remembering. His betrothal to Charlotte had been, for Emmy, the fulfillment of a cherished dream. The child worshiped her beautiful stepsister and the thought that Alex was to marry her had been cause for immense satisfaction on Emmy's part, since it had been she who had introduced them to each other and not—as many people imagined —Charlotte's brother Phillip. And it had been Emmy's idea that he should come here today, she who had prevailed upon Charlotte to receive him and she, too, who had sought and obtained Lord Dunloy's consent to his visit, Alex thought, feeling the muscles of his throat tighten. Now the dream was over, for Emmy as well as for himself. . . .

"I failed you," he apologized, with weary contrition. "You did everything in your power to plead my cause, Emmy, and I'm grateful. But it was no use. As you say, perhaps it was a mistake for me to come here. I should have known what Charlotte's feelings would be."

"You could not have known," Emmy offered consolingly. "And you had to take your leave of her, Alex. I am sorry Mamma was not here, she might have been able to plead your cause better than I could." He was silent and she watched him with pensive gravity. "It has hurt you very much, has it not?" she suggested gently. "It has hurt Charlotte too. Because she loves you—I *know* she does."

"But not enough to face life with me in India, apparently." Alex's tone was bleak. Emmy cast him an uneasy glance but came at once to her stepsister's defense.

"It was too drastic a step for her to contemplate, Alex. India is so far away and the news that you were going there must have come as a shock to her, because she did not expect it. Charlotte had hoped that you would demand a fresh hearing of your case, you see. She was certain that, if you did so, you would have your commission restored to you. I endeavored to explain to her that this was not possible but she would not listen to me."

"*You* endeavored to explain to her? Emmy child, what do you know of such matters?"

"A little," Emmy assured him. "I consulted some of my step-father's military manuals and read the Articles of War. You were guilty of a breach of Article 60. . . ." As ably as any lawyer, she gave him chapter and verse, quoting Article 60 at some length. "It lays down, does it not, that 'any officer who shall give, send, convey or promote a challenge to any other officer to fight a duel or who shall upbraid another for refusing a challenge shall be liable to be cashiered.' You could have no defense, Alex. But Charlotte does not understand that. In time she may come to understand, to realize that you had no alternative. Now she is hurt and disappointed, believing that you could vindicate your-self but you are afraid to try. Later on, perhaps, she may—"

"No!" Alex uttered the single word vehemently. He added, with deep and anguished conviction, "Our parting is final, at her wish, Emmy. Charlotte will never marry me now and whether I go or stay will make no difference."

"She will never marry you? Are you sure of that?"

"I am quite sure, child." Alex glanced at the clock on the ornate marble mantelpiece and from it to Emmy's pale, troubled little face. "The streets should be starting to clear now. I think I had better take my leave, don't you?" He put his arm around her, as he had done many times in the past, and gave her an affectionate hug. "Do not look so sad, Emmy dear. It is not the end of the world, you know, simply because I am going away."

"I shall miss you," Emmy whispered, "I shall miss you so much. Oh, Alex, take care of yourself! I *wish* you hadn't to go. . . ." She had not shed a tear until this moment but now, Alex saw with compunction, she was weeping.

"Tears . . . for me, Emmy?" he teased her gently. "Come now, it is not like you to cry. And I am not worth your tears, so let us dry them, shall we? Take my handkerchief, it is larger than yours. Here . . ." he offered it to her, forcing a smile.

"I'm sorry." Obediently she mopped at her eyes. "I did not mean to cry but I . . . I cannot help it. I hate you to go, Alex."

Alex took both her hands in his and bent to kiss her cheek.

"Emmy my dear, surely it is I who should be weeping, not you? I am the one who will be lonely—a stranger in an alien land, soon to be forgotten, even by you."

"I shall never forget you," Emmy said. She blinked back her tears and faced him bravely. "Alex, I am not beautiful, as Charlotte is and I know how deeply you love her. But I . . . I am not a child any more, I am almost fifteen. If it would be of the smallest comfort to you, if it would ease your loneliness even a little, I would gladly . . . I mean I would do anything, I—" she broke off in sudden shyness, her cheeks flaming.

Alex looked down at her, startled and conscience-stricken, as he recalled Charlotte's parting words to him. *"Ask Emmy, she can see no fault in you,"* Charlotte had said, with bitter scorn, *"Perhaps she might wait for you . . . you are still a hero to her. . . ."* But Emmy was a child, whatever she might claim to be—a trusting and, for all her avid reading of the books in her stepfather's library, an inexperienced, vulnerable child. Dear heaven, he reproached himself, what had he done in his thoughtless self-pity? He had not taken Charlotte's taunt seriously but the small face upturned to his was very serious indeed and he wondered in some dismay how, without hurting her feelings, he could prevent her making the avowal she was evidently about to make. He shrank from wounding her pride as his own had been wounded—it was the last thing he wanted to do and yet . . . "Emmy," he began, helplessly, "you must not concern yourself with my troubles. They're of no account—"

Before he could say any more or, indeed, think of anything more to say, she interrupted him, still pink with embarrassment, "I'll wait for you, if Charlotte will not, Alex. I will even marry you when I'm old enough, if you wish. There are not many unattached girls in India, are there?" She smiled up at him innocently. "I told you once that I did not intend to marry . . . and I did not. But with you, of course, it would be different. We've known each other for a long time and, in any case, it would not be for some years, would it?"

"No," he managed, "I should not be able to afford to marry for several years, Emmy. But—"

"You can send for me," Emmy pointed out, "when you have advanced in the East India Company's service and need a wife to keep house for you and entertain your friends and fellow officers. I believe that I should like to live in India . . . it would be a splendid adventure. And I should like to see the Taj Mahal and Delhi and Fatepur Seekri . . . I have read so much about them. And also Cawnpore, where the 11th were stationed. You would take me to all those places, would you not, so that I could see them for myself?"

How could he destroy so bright a dream, Alex asked himself and stifled a sigh. Time would destroy it, he did not doubt but now he could not take it from her.

"Thank you, Emmy my dear," he responded, matching her gravity, "This is most generous of you and I shall look forward keenly to the prospect of exploring India with you, in a few years' time. That is, of course, if you do not change your mind about marrying me. If you should, or if you meet anyone more worthy of you than I am, then you must tell me so at once."

"Oh, but I should never do that, Alex—you are the only man in whom I am likely to be interested." Emmy spoke with certainty, her young voice vibrant and warm. Talking excitedly of the future, she accompanied him to the hall and there lifted her cheek for his kiss, quite reconciled to their parting, since now it was not to be forever. "I wish, for your sake, that I were more like Charlotte, Alex," she said solemnly. "But even though that is not possible, I will be a good wife to you, I promise. Farewell, dearest Alex . . . and do not be lonely. I shall be waiting for you and I shall wait for as long as it is necessary. You may trust me . . . there will be no one else and I shall not fail you."

"I know that, Emmy," Alex assured her. His lips brushed her bony little cheek and then, unable any longer to keep up the pretense, he took his leave abruptly.

Five days later, he sailed for Calcutta.

CHAPTER ONE

❯❯❯ • ❮❮❮

THE SUN was setting in a blaze of crimson splendor when a small band of horsemen numbering, with pack animals, about sixty, made their way at a steady jog-trot along the Bulgarian bank of the River Danube. Behind them the shell-scarred walls and battered redoubts of the fortress city of Silistria faded into the distance and were swiftly lost to sight in the gathering darkness.

The little force rode cautiously and in silence, with scouts spread out ahead and on either flank, for this had lately been hostile country and Cossack patrols had been reported in the area, despite the Russian retreat. It was the first week of July in the year 1854 and the siege of Silistria—aptly called the Citadel of the Danube—had been raised ten days before, amid scenes of terrible carnage. Leaving an estimated thirty thousand dead behind them and with Prince Menschikoff, their commander-in-chief, severely wounded the Russians, under General Luders, were in full flight across the river. The stubborn Turkish defense had thwarted their attempt to capture the city which, had it succeeded, might well have been the prelude to an advance through the Balkans and a threat to Constantinople itself.

The silent horsemen had all played a part in the raising of the siege. All save two of them were Turkish irregulars dressed in the barbaric motley of Bashi-Bazouk costume and armed with scimitars, pistols and flintlock carbines—the latter of ancient pattern, but set in silver and even at long range, of surprising accuracy.

The Bashi-Bazouks kept a respectful horse's length behind

their two leaders, who were British officers clad, less resplendently, in Indian army uniforms. The younger of the two was a slim, fair-haired man in his early thirties, whose insignia proclaimed him a captain. His sensitive, high-boned face was deeply tanned and clean shaven, except for a pair of side-whiskers and a moustache, trimmed more closely than the fashion of the day dictated. In repose, his face wore an expression of almost forbidding aloofness, which was only dispelled when his rare smile revealed the humour that lay hidden behind the habitually grave, defensive façade.

One of several Indian army volunteers in the garrison of Silistria, his uniform was the French grey and silver of the East India Company's native light cavalry, over which he had donned a heavy, dark blue cloak. Both the cloak and the silver-laced jacket beneath it showed signs of wear, and the cloak bore the mark of a sabre cut across the left shoulder, which had been roughly and inexpertly mended—mute evidence of the ferocity of the fighting in which its owner had recently taken part.

During the siege, the tall captain had acquitted himself well and had acquired a reputation for courage and sound judgement among the Turkish leaders. The rank and file, always adept at assessing the qualities of a fighting man, had put him down as a skilled professional soldier, who took his profession seriously and cared for little else. In this estimate they were not far wrong, for Alex Sheridan had changed a great deal in the eight years he had spent in India.

He himself was aware of most of the changes and did not regret them. His life as an officer in the East India Company's service had been both eventful and rewarding and had taught him much about himself and his fellow men. His brother officers in the two regiments in which he had served—if they were aware of the circumstances which had caused him to sell his commission in the British army—had displayed no curiosity but had simply accepted him as one of themselves. With them and with the native sowars he had led, Alex had found a comradeship that, under Lord Cardigan's command, had been wholly lacking in the 11th Hussars.

In action against the Sikhs, prior to the conquest and annexation of the Punjab, he had proved himself a soldier, in their eyes and in his own. He had earned commendations for gallantry at Chilianwala. and Gujerat and his brevet captaincy, awarded at the end of the year-long campaign, had set the seal of success on his career in the Company's army. His Indian service had brought him, as a welcome addition, the friendship of the man who now rode at the head of this small cavalcade beside him.

Alex smiled to himself in the darkness, as he glanced at his companion. Colonel William Fergusson Beatson was a Scotsman from Fife, the youngest of four brothers. He was a big man of magnificent physique, upon whom his fifty years sat lightly, although he had packed into them more fighting and greater experience of war than most men of his age. He had come to Turkey at the invitation of another distinguished Indian army veteran, General Cannon, who, as Behram Pasha, had been appointed to a command in the Ottoman army soon after the Turkish declaration of war.

William Beatson had come with a considerable reputation. A soldier since the age of sixteen, when he had been commissioned as an ensign in the East India Company's 2/25th Native Infantry, he had fought under Cannon's command in the Carlist War in Spain in 1836, rising to the rank of lieutenant-colonel. On his return to India he had successively commanded Shah Shuja's Contingent, the Bundelkhand Legion and the Nizam of Hyderabad's

Cavalry as well as the Company's 65th Native Infantry.

The Turks had not been slow to recognize his merit. Omar Pasha, the Turkish commander-in-chief, had appointed him a brigadier-general and put him in over-all command of the untrained Bashi-Bazouk cavalry, with which he had already performed so many feats of valor and daring that he had become something of a legend in Turkish military circles. He was held in such high esteem by the fierce Moslem horsemen he commanded that he had managed to instill into them a remarkable measure of discipline to which, as a race, they were not usually amenable. It was said that they would follow him anywhere and William Beatson had given proof of this when he had fought his way into Silistria at the head of a small body of Bashi-Bazouks, against appalling odds, thus opening the way for the city's relief by the infantry, under General Cannon. The final desperate battle had been fought on 22nd June and the Russian withdrawal had begun two days later.

Alex had been overjoyed to meet the older man again. He had originally volunteered for service in Turkey at the Bashi-Bazouk leader's behest, intending to join him in his present command, but the speed and suddenness of the Russian advance had wrought havoc with his original plans. He had gone instead to Silistria, with a number of other Indian army officers who had assisted in its defense, and it had been almost three months before the fortunes of war had reunited him, within the walls of the beleaguered fortress, with the man he had come to seek. Since then the two had remained together and Alex had been well satisfied with his change of service until, with news of the arrival of the British Expeditionary Force in Bulgaria, a strange restlessness had seized him, born of the knowledge that his old regiment formed part of the Light Cavalry Brigade.

With the raising of the siege, the opportunity to rejoin the British army had presented itself and Colonel Beatson had persuaded him to seek leave of absence from the Turks and accompany him to Varna, where Lord Raglan had established his headquarters and the Cavalry Division was based. Both men were hopeful of obtaining useful employment under the British command, if for no other reason than by virtue of the experience each had gained in action against the Russians. But Beatson, in addition, intended to offer Lord Raglan the services of his Bashi-Bazouk cavalry, backed by a recommendation from the Duke of Newcastle. He had obtained permission from the Turkish High Command to enlist and train as many irregular regiments as might be required, in order to make good the known British deficiency in this arm.

He, at least, Alex was confident, could count on being given a British command or, failing this, a staff appointment. Of his own chances he was much less hopeful, for he was aware that the Earl of Cardigan was now a brigadier-general, in command of the Light Cavalry Brigade. They had parted on the worst possible terms eight years ago and Lord Cardigan was reputed to possess a long memory . . . he expelled his breath in a brief sigh. From time to time, he had had news of Cardigan, in letters from Phillip Mowbray and other friends in his old regiment and, from these, it did not seem likely that the passing of the years had mellowed or softened his onetime commanding officer. That bridge, however, could be crossed when he came to it. The part he had played—together with Nasmyth and Bullard and poor young James Butler, his fellow Indian army volunteers—in the defense of Silistria, had gained him the notice of Omar Pasha. He carried a letter in his pocket, which contained the Turkish commander-in-chief's estimate of the value of the work he had done.

There were others besides Cardigan who might find a use for his services—Lord Lucan, the cavalry divisional commander, perhaps, or General Scarlett of the Heavy Brigade. Or Sir Colin Campbell, that fine Indian campaigner, who was at the head of the Highland Brigade and might remember him, for they had fought together at Chillianwalla. It was foolish to allow himself to become despondent. One of these surely would find a place for him so that he might once again fight with men of his own race and creed and blood beside him . . . he sighed again and this time Colonel Beatson heard it.

"Alex . . ." he turned in his saddle, breaking the silence they had maintained since leaving the fort. "You are very pensive, are you not?" His deep voice sounded amused. "Could it be that your thoughts are following the same trend as my own? Are you planning our next campaign, with British soldiers under our command?"

Alex permitted himself a wry smile. "No, not exactly, sir. I was weighing up our chances of being given any sort of command in the British Expeditionary Force . . . and finding them, I am afraid, somewhat slight. Lord Raglan—"

"Ah!" The colonel shrugged. "I, too, have been thinking about our coming audience with his lordship, on which, for both of us, so much depends. Tell me, Alex my friend . . . you have met the commander-in-chief, have you not? I seem to remember your telling me once that you had done so."

Alex hesitated and his smile faded. It was many years since he had allowed his mind to dwell on the memory of that last interview with the then military secretary who, two years ago, had been created Baron Raglan. "If, sir," he answered reluctantly, "you consider that a summons to attend his lordship at the Horse Guards, in order to receive a severe official reprimand, constitutes meeting him, then . . . yes. I have met him. But I retain no very pleasant recollections of the occasion, since it resulted in the termination of my service with the 11th Hussars."

It had also led, in the fullness of time, to his parting from Charlotte Mowbray, Alex recalled, feeling the old, familiar ache in his throat when he thought of her. It had led to his parting from Charlotte, of whose subsequent betrothal—to an officer of the 11th, who had been one of his closest friends—he had learned from a year-old copy of *The Times,* when waiting to go into action against the Sikh guns at Chilianwala. Emmy O'Shaughnessy had sent him the newspaper. Her handwriting had been on the wrapper, so that it must have been she who had despatched it to him . . . but her letters had told him nothing and, soon afterwards, without explanation, they had ceased.

Looking back, he wondered, as he had wondered often in the past, whether the shock of reading that announcement had been responsible for the foolhardy recklessness he had displayed during the disastrous battle. He was not by nature reckless but that day, he knew, he had counted his life of little value and had wanted to lose it, if he could do so honorably. Ironically he had not only lived, he had distinguished himself, and had earned the gratitude of William Beatson for saving the life of a young cousin of his, who had been cut off and his horse shot under him, when the ill-fated cavalry charge had been routed.

Now, for Beatson's sake, he had enlisted in the Turkish service and was on his way to Varna. The wheel would turn full circle, perhaps, when he met the officers of his old regiment in their camp at Devna and shook the hand of Arthur Cassell to whom, by this time, Charlotte must be married. . . .

Alex drew himself up, suddenly aware that Colonel Beatson's eyes, alert and shrewd, were fixed on his face, searching it in the dim light, as if seeking the answer to a question he had not voiced.

He waited and the colonel said thoughtfully, "It was, I suppose, as a consequence of the duel you fought with the Earl of Cardigan that you were summoned to the Horse Guards?"

"I did not actually fight a duel with Lord Cardigan, sir," Alex corrected and saw a swift smile flit across the colonel's bearded lip.

"But you issued a challenge—you called him out, did you not? Or have I been misinformed in the matter?"

"You have not been misinformed, sir," Alex admitted. "Although"—he eyed his senior inquiringly—"I do not know from what source you obtained your information."

Colonel Beatson grunted. He replied, with studied casualness, "I met some of the officers of your old regiment at Scutari and heard the story from one of them, who seemed very pleased and interested, when I told him that you were in Silistria. A young major in the 11th Hussars who, it seems, has lost touch with you . . . he recently succeeded to his father's title as Earl of Dunloy."

"You met Phillip Dunloy?" Alex made an almost visible effort to control his excitement at this news. It was a long time since he had last heard of or from Phillip. . . . "He's still with the regiment, then?"

"Indeed, yes. And he had his wife and sister with him—they were both guests of the British ambassador, Lord Stratford de Redcliff, I believe. Two exceptionally charming young ladies and in great demand socially . . . but of course you must know them?"

"Yes," Alex agreed tonelessly. "Although Dunloy was not married when I was with the 11th." He hesitated, pale and suddenly tense. "His sister, sir . . . did you speak to her, can you tell me her name? Phillip has three sisters, you see, and I was . . . that is, I knew one of them rather well. Also his stepsister, Emma O'Shaughnessy, who was a child of about fourteen the last time I saw her."

"Alas, no, Alex, I can't help you." William Beatson spoke with genuine regret. "I was only in Scutari for a few days and the British advance parties had been there for little longer. The bulk of the transports were still unloading when I left. But"—his tone became dry—"there was a great deal of social activity going on. Embassy receptions and the like. It was at one of these that I met your friend Lord Dunloy and talked to him. He pointed the two ladies out to me but I did not stay long enough for him to introduce me to them. There was talk of all the ladies who accompanied the army making their headquarters at the Hotel d'Angleterre at Therapia for the duration of the war. The ambassador has his summer residence there . . . it is a pleasant spot, I understand. Only one or two went on to Varna, or so I heard . . . and they did so contrary to official orders."

"I see." Alex's momentary excitement died. Even if Charlotte was in Turkey, even if she had braved the official ban and gone to Varna with the army, she would have done so on her husband's account. In any case, that part of his life was over—a closed book, never again to be reopened. He had no desire for it to be reopened, he told himself, and forced a note of indifference into his voice as he said, "I did not realize that you had been to Scutari, sir. Or, indeed, that you had made any previous contact with the British Expeditionary Force."

"Oh, yes, I was there, Alex. To tell you the truth . . ." Colonel Beatson sighed. "I went there on Omar Pasha's account, in the hope of arranging an early conference with the British High Command. But I found those concerned were more interested in wining and dining with the French than in making plans for the conduct of the war. Lord Raglan was too occupied with other matters to see me and had, in any event, only just arrived. The other British generals seemed disposed to make plans for a military parade in the Sultan's honor but that was all to which I was able to commit them. So"—he shrugged his massive shoulders—"I returned to Shumla, where I have been of some use, perhaps. Certainly of more than I should have been had I remained any longer in Constantinople, escorting parties of delectable young English ladies on trips up the Bosphorus!" His voice held the contempt of the fighting man for such unmilitary diversions and it was again dry as he went on, "The British army has brought its womenfolk with it in unprecedented numbers, you know . . . and not only the rank and file. Half the aristocracy in the country seem to be serving in the Guards or the Cavalry. None has had any experience of war and most of them have permitted their wives to accompany them. It is fantastic!"

"I imagine it must be, sir," Alex said, but without surprise, for he did not find it hard to imagine. It was almost forty years since Waterloo, which was the last occasion that the British army had fought on European soil, and only the most senior of its present commanders had been in action under the great duke. They included Lord Raglan, of course but . . .

"The atmosphere," William Beatson told him disgustedly, "when I was in Scutari at the beginning of May, was that of London at the height of the season. The officers were too busy with their social activities to take any interest in maintaining discipline and the troops, when not on duty, spent their time getting drunk and whoring. I believe it was the same in Malta and Gallipoli. . . . Let us hope, now that they have got as far as Varna, that they will make an effort to take the war seriously. If they do not then I, for one, can forsee trouble with our Turkish allies."

Alex piously echoed this hope. The British and French armies had come to Bulgaria with the avowed intention of marching to the relief of Silistria. Their long delay in making any attempt to do so had left the Turks in a position where they had been forced to act alone and, as a result, they had incurred very heavy casualties. He knew that feeling ran high among the Turkish soldiers and, in particular, among those who had garrisoned the stricken city, to whom their allies' lack of action was utterly inexplicable. He himself had been puzzled by the delay and Colonel Beatson's description of conditions in Constantinople and Scutari increased his bewilderment. But he offered no comment and the colonel returned to more personal matters.

"Alex," he said bluntly, "why did you challenge Lord Cardigan? Surely you knew what the outcome would be?"

Taken by surprise at this question, Alex stiffened. He answered it, however, as honestly as he could. "He had driven me to the limit of my endurance, sir. Perhaps had I realized what the outcome was eventually to be, I should have held my hand. But"—he shrugged resignedly—"even now I am not convinced that I should or *could* have done so. I had seen others driven, as I was, to seek satisfaction from Cardigan and fail. He made a practice of insulting certain of his officers in public, sir, and then claimed his privilege, as commanding officer, to avoid being called upon to withdraw the insults or making them good. I demanded that he waive his privilege in my case, sir . . . in writing. But he refused and—"

"*Certain* of his officers?" Colonel Beatson put in, frowning. "What do you mean by that, Alex?"

Alex's expression hardened. "His lordship wanted the 11th to be officered by gentlemen of his own class, sir, well connected and possessed of substantial means. After seventeen years in India, most of our officers were professional soldiers, who were dependent on their army pay for the most part and who could not afford to buy promotion or hunt three days a week and entertain lavishly. Cardigan wished to be rid of them, in order to make way for officers of his own choosing, who could afford to do all these things. He had changed us from Light Dragoons to Hussars, sir, our uniform had been redesigned . . . His Royal Highness the Prince Albert had been appointed our colonel-in-chief. The 11th was considered smarter than the Guards, sir, and there weren't enough commissions available to meet the demand for them. His lordship set out to make them available by forcing our so-called 'Indian' officers to sell out or exchange into other regiments. If they did not do so willingly, then pressure was brought to bear on them."

"Pressure, Alex?" Colonel Beatson's brows lifted.

"For want of a better word, sir . . . or an uglier one. It amounted, in some cases, to deliberate persecution."

"Did it amount to that in your case, my friend?"

"In mine and in others, I consider that it did, Colonel," Alex said forcefully. "The others were my friends, to whom I felt a certain loyalty. They had served in the regiment for many years and . . ." he bit his lower lip, a swift anger blazing momentarily in his eyes. "When I challenged Lord Cardigan, I expected, of course, to be tried by court martial and cashiered. But I believed that I should be afforded the opportunity to draw official attention to conditions in the regiment under Lord Cardigan's command . . . they were past all bearing, sir. I had not any adequate defense, the court would have been bound to find me guilty . . . but I had justification and I think I could have proved that I had, if I had been given the chance. But instead I was ordered to sell out and the whole matter was officially hushed up . . . by Lord Raglan, sir. As Lord Fitzroy Somerset, he was then military secretary."

"Dunloy said you were a fool—and then admitted that if he had had the courage, he would have done the same in your place."

William Beatson spoke thoughtfully. "I don't consider you a fool, Alex. How did Lord Cardigan drive you to the limit of your endurance? You've never told me, have you?"

"No, Colonel." Alex was silent, feeling the hot blood rushing to his cheeks. Finally he said, "I had endured his tyranny for years. I loved the regiment, it was my life and I was determined that he should not force me to exchange or sell out. But matters came to a head, in the end, when I refused to obey an order he had issued, because I felt it to be unjust. Cardigan reprimanded me in front of the assembled regiment on morning parade and when I still refused to obey the order, he lost his temper and struck me across the face with his empty glove. . . ."

Alex shuddered, reliving the scene. He had refused to administer a flogging to a man of his squadron for some trifling misdemeanor and, heedless of his own vulnerability, had endeavored to plead the man's cause and Lord Cardigan had rounded on him furiously. He might have suffered the blow with the glove without reply but then had come the final deliberate and quite unforgivable insult. Cardigan had made a sneering reference to his betrothal to Phillip Mowbray's sister, implying that he had taken advantage of the fact that Phillip was a brother officer in order to ingratiate himself with the Dunloys. This had been more even than he could stomach. He had gone to his quarters in the grip of an anger so intense that he had been powerless to control it and, in a letter intentionally modeled on the one written by Richard Reynolds, some years before, he had issued his fatal challenge. That had been madness, of course—with Reynolds' example before him, he had known what would be the result. Cardigan's answer had been to place him under close arrest and apply for his court martial.

Ironically Phillip had been the officer charged with his custody

and Phillip had reproached him for his loss of temper and his suicidal gesture of defiance. But then, Alex reflected bleakly, Phillip
had not heard the words Lord Cardigan had flung at him concerning his betrothal to Charlotte and he was, in the circumstances
the last person to whom they could be repeated. . . .

"And . . ." Colonel Beatson prompted, from beside him.

He smiled gravely. "In addition, sir, his lordship offered me a
personal insult that left me with no choice but to call him out.
Unfortunately few people heard it, for he lowered his voice but
the whole regiment saw him strike me." Alex's smile faded. "I
haven't thought of the affair for years but all too soon, I fear, I
am likely to be reminded of it, when brought face to face with
the noble gentleman again. I can only hope that I have altered sufficiently in my physical appearance as to avoid recognition . . .
at all events until after I have put in my request for employment. Otherwise I may regret having left the Turkish service so
precipitately."

"We may both regret that, my friend," the colonel told him.
"They say . . ." He jerked his horse to a standstill, holding up his
hand. Behind him, the Bashi-Bazouks came obediently to a halt.
The track ahead of them rose steeply, narrowing into the neck of
a rocky, tree-lined gorge which twisted down towards the river.
Colonel Beatson signaled to the dark-faced leader of the troop
and the man instantly set spurs to his horse and made off in pursuit of the scouts.

The two officers waited, listening intently and straining their
eyes into the darkness ahead. But there was no movement, no
sound, save for the faint echo of hoofbeats, as the leader of
the Bashi-Bazouk troop breasted the slope on his sturdy, half-
shod horse.

In a little while he returned, as swiftly and silently as he had departed, with one of the scouts riding at his heels. A wolfish smile played about his mouth as he approached the waiting officers and his voice shook with suppressed excitement as he said briefly, in his own language, "Cossacks, Lord! They camp at the summit of the hill with but half a dozen sentries posted to give them warning of attack."

The colonel studied the little he could see of the hillside with speculative eyes. "How many are they?" he asked evenly.

The troop leader spread his hands. "Perhaps five score, O Mighty One. Perhaps a few more than that, it is hard to tell. But our men have the sentries covered. In the darkness, they will be neither seen nor heard . . . and the rest of the Cossacks sleep."

"Where are their horses?" Beatson asked.

It was the scout who answered and he, too, was smiling.

"Lord, the horses are tethered at a little distance, with two men watching over them. It would be simplicity itself to cut them loose, once the sentries have been disposed of and then"—his voice rose exultantly, as he glanced at the eager faces of the men clustered about him—"we could go amongst them with our knives!"

A fierce murmur of approval greeted this suggestion. The Bashi-Bazouks' hatred of the Russians was proverbial and, looking from one to another of the savage, hawk-faces of the men composing the troop, Alex wondered whether Colonel Beatson would be able to control them. Their respect for him amounted almost to veneration, it was true, and usually they obeyed his commands without question . . . but this was the sort of action they liked. A sudden attack, under cover of darkness, on a sleeping enemy, and that enemy a Cossack—Alex knew that it would not be easy to restrain them, even for William Beatson.

They waited, out of deference to him but it was evident that they were all impatient to be gone. Already one or two were fingering the knives in their belts and each face wore the same lustful, wolfish smile that the troop leader's had worn, when he had first reported the presence of the Cossack *sotnia*. The Bashi-Bazouks were bloodthirsty, primitive warriors, whose instinct was to fight and kill, regardless of strategy, and none now remembered the purpose of his mission or cared about its fulfillment, when the chance of battle had been offered.

"Lord," the troop leader pleaded urgently through tightly clenched teeth, "is it not a good plan? May we not ride at once?"

Alex became aware of sharp prickles of apprehension coursing up his spine and of a dryness in his mouth that always came, just before he was called upon to go into action. Both ceased, when he was actually in the thick of battle, but he had never been able to overcome either sensation during those tense moments of waiting which were the prelude to an attack.

He possessed, he was well aware, too vivid an imagination and, as he listened intently for the colonel's answer, he found himself picturing the Cossack bivouac on the rock-strewn hillside and mentally assessing the odds against their small, lightly armed force. They would have the initial advantage of surprise, of course, and he did not doubt the scout's boast that the sentries could be disposed of and the horses cut loose without a sound to disturb the sleepers but . . . there was a hollow ache of anxiety in the pit of his stomach. Cossacks slept lightly, with their weapons beside them and . . .

"Lord," the troop leader cried again, "Lord, may we not attack the accursed Cossacks?"

Very slowly but with finality, Colonel Beatson shook his head.

For a moment, Alex feared that the Bashi-Bazouks were about to challenge their commander's decision. They stared at him in mute dismay, unable to comprehend his refusal, reluctant to believe that he had rejected their black-browed leader's request. A camp of sleeping Cossacks at their mercy and they were being ordered not to attack. . . . They started to murmur angrily among themselves.

"Hast thou a better plan, Great One?" the troop leader asked sullenly. For answer, Beatson gestured towards the unseen head of the defile, through which lay the track they had been following. He ordered, without raising his voice, "Go thou thither, Arif, and report to me all that thou seest. Go with caution and make no sound."

The troop leader hesitated for an instant, as if about to protest. Then, thinking better of it, he bowed his head in token of submission and made off in the direction the colonel had indicated. Silence followed his departure and Alex, warned by Colonel Beatson's expression, made no attempt to break it.

When the dark-faced Arif returned, he was crestfallen and subdued.

"Well?" Beatson demanded, his voice rasping.

"Lord, thou art the wisest among us," Arif acknowledged humbly. "Thine eyes saw through the darkness, where mine did not." He glanced at the men, crowding about him, and gestured towards the head of the defile. "A host is gathered on the river bank engaged, though it is night, in crossing the river with guns and horses. Had we attacked the Cossack post, we would have raised a hornet's nest about us."

The colonel regarded him unsmilingly. "Then send out scouts again—we will strike westward across the hills. Take six men with thee and, as thou goest, cut loose the Cossacks' horses. But raise not thy voice and lay not a hand on any save the sentries, or I will take thy rank from thee. Dost thou understand?"

The troop leader's salaam was respectful.

Within twenty minutes, he was back, waving his hand to indicate that the way was now clear. He rejoined the troop with his six men as Colonel Beatson gave the order to trot. The little party rode on towards the hills, the scouts spread out ahead of them as before, and Alex found his tongue at last.

"How did you know, sir?" he asked, in English.

"I did not know," the older man confessed, with disarming frankness. "But there is a ford at that point and it seemed to me an obvious place to choose for a crossing. The Russians are anxious to save their guns, so . . ." he smiled. "Besides, did not Arif say that the Cossacks slept?"

The simplicity of his reasoning was impressive and Alex echoed his smile.

The moon rose as the little troop descended the far side of the range of hills and found themselves once more on a narrow track which led through flat cultivated land, in the direction they sought. The excitement of their brief encounter with the Russians died down and they slowed to a walk, the men fumbling in their pouches for the provisions they carried and ate, habitually, in the saddle.

"Tell me about Lord Raglan, Alex," William Beatson requested unexpectedly. "I'm aware that you have only met him once and that the occasion is probably one you'd prefer to forget but . . . I should like to know what impression you formed of him. How is he, as a man? I've heard about him, of course, and I know that he enjoyed the personal friendship of the great duke—who did not bestow his regard lightly—over a period of many years."

"He became the Duke of Wellington's military secretary in

1810, sir," Alex supplied, "and was with him throughout the Peninsular campaign. He married the duke's niece—"

"Yes, yes . . . these are facts anyone can find out," the colonel interrupted. "I want to know more than the bare details of his career. Describe him to me as you saw him . . . and be frank, Alex. You know that I shall not betray your confidence."

Alex's brows came together. Almost against his will, he found himself returning in memory to the austerely furnished room overlooking Whitehall in which, eight years before, Lord Raglan had received him. He had gone to the Horse Guards that day confident that, if nothing else, he would be given a hearing and the chance to state his case. Instead . . . he stifled a sigh. Cardigan's hand had reached him, even there; Cardigan's influence had been apparent in the manner in which the military secretary had dealt with him. There had been no vindication, no escape, no justice and he wondered, looking back, why he had expected any of these things, when the dice had been so heavily loaded against him. And yet, against all reason, he had expected to be heard. To be sacrificed, of course—he had not sought to escape retribution—but not to be sacrificed in vain. Not, God help him, to be condemned unheard, as he had been. . . . He sighed again, regretfully. Across the years, Lord Fitzroy Somerset's opening words came to him. The military secretary had looked up and smiled, he remembered, a mild mannered man with the appearance, not of a soldier, but of some gentle scholar or kindly Father Confessor. His voice, too, had been mild and not unsympathetic when he said, "Lieutenant Sheridan, the honor of your regiment demands, I fear, the sacrifice of all personal feelings in this unhappy affair. Both yours and my own. . . ."

Stung afresh by the memory, Alex increased his pace, kneeing his horse impatiently, as if thus to put it behind him. But it was useless—a futile, abortive attempt to escape the torment of his own thoughts. He knew that he had not forgotten, would never be able to forget the injustice which had been done to him that afternoon in Whitehall, eight years before. His feelings and not Lord Raglan's had ultimately been sacrificed . . . and not only his feelings. His honor, his career, even his marriage to Charlotte Mowbray—all these had been disregarded by the smiling, serene-faced soldier-prelate, who had spoken so glibly of honor but who, it seemed, knew no other interpretation of it than his own. His own or, perhaps, that of his military superiors. . . . Suddenly sick with bitterness, Alex gave vent to an angry exclamation.

"Alex my dear fellow . . ." Colonel Beatson's deep voice brought him abruptly back to the present. He drew rein and waited. "I am sorry," the colonel went on, "if my question has revived bitter memories for you. The opening of an old wound is always painful but sometimes, in order to effect a cure, it is necessary to open it."

"I fancy you may be right, sir," Alex agreed, without conviction. But he felt his anger drain out of him. It had all happened a long time ago. The past was over and he was no longer a boy but a man—a soldier of proven worth and ability. "I bear no personal grudge against Lord Raglan, Colonel," he said quietly. "He was the soul of courtesy in his dealings with me and, at the time, I was convinced that the action he took in my case went against his own inclinations. It was dictated from above and he had no choice in the matter. Within the bounds imposed on him, he treated me generously. Indeed . . ." He fell silent, uncertain of how much he could say, even now and even to Colonel Beatson. He trusted the colonel implicitly but, until now, he had never spoken to anyone of his interview at the Horse Guards. The keeping of his own counsel had become second nature to him and the habit of years was not easily broken. At last he said, "Sir, you have asked me to give you my impression of his lordship and this, I confess, I do not find easy to do. I was labouring under a sense of deep resentment during my interview which may cloud my judgment. I felt that the official attitude, which Lord Raglan expressed to me, was unjust and—"

Colonel Beatson emitted a short laugh. "When," he asked, still smiling a little, "does a soldier expect justice, Alex?"

"He is entitled to a hearing, surely? He is entitled to hope for an opportunity to vindicate himself"—Alex's temper flared— "when he can do so, when he can prove that he's right!"

"Then least of all," his senior stated calmly.

"You really believe that? Oh come, sir, you cannot—it is taking too cynical a view."

"I believe what over thirty years of soldiering have taught me. You expected a hearing, you say—you were prepared to suffer trial by court martial, so that you might justify yourself by bringing Lord Cardigan down with you—"

Alex shook his head. "So that I might justify myself by telling the truth, sir," he amended.

"When that truth must have been irreparably damaging to a man of Cardigan's importance! You were a trifle naïve, weren't you?"

"You think so, Colonel?" Alex returned stiffly.

Beatson threw back his handsome, leonine head, with its mane of sun-bleached hair and laughed again. This time his laughter was loud and full-throated, holding genuine amusement. The Bashi-Bazouk horsemen at his back, hearing his guffaws, joined in them, without having the least idea of what had amused their leader. It was enough for them that he laughed. Alex remained somewhat resentfully silent, feeling affronted, until a muscular brown hand came out to grip his arm and Colonel Beatson said, his voice warm and sympathetic, "Alex, my dear fellow, I laugh that I may not weep. Once, long ago, I also cherished ambitions and a belief in justice. I am much happier now that I have abandoned my ambitions and no longer look for justice. You might do worse than follow my example."

"Do you not think I did, sir . . . also a long time ago?"

"No, I do not think you did entirely—otherwise that old wound of yours would not have opened so easily when I probed it." Beatson relaxed his grip on his companion's arm. He went on gravely, "Consider the High Command of the British Expeditionary Force, which we are about to join, Alex. Their ages average more than sixty—the Duke of Cambridge is, of course, an exception, but then he has royal connections. Apart from His Royal Highness, Lord Lucan, at fifty-four is the youngest of the divisional commanders. None of them has been in action since Waterloo . . . few, in fact, have seen any action at all since they were subaltern officers. Sir Colin Campbell, who has a lifetime of fighting behind him and whose record you and I both know is second to none . . . Sir Colin has only been given a brigade, although he commanded a division in the Punjab. This, my dear Alex, is an army officered entirely by the aristocracy, commanded by men who have bought their promotion with money, not with experience of war, with but few exceptions." He sighed. "And you have the Guards, the most aristocratic of all, with their iniquitous system of double ranks. A Guards captain ranks as a colonel in any mixed force . . . do you realize that?"

"I do, sir, yes."

"Then of what use for a professional soldier to be ambitious? He has little chance in the British army."

"Is the Company's system any better?" Alex countered. "Promotion by seniority means that our generals average nearer seventy than sixty, does it not? They are old men before they even command a regiment."

"But they are wise old men," William Beatson argued. "Men who have learned their trade in battle, men who have charged against an enemy at the head of their troops. Not men who have only commanded troops on field days and exercises and at Royal Reviews . . . and who have left all routine training in the hands of their noncommissioned officers. I was shocked by the sheer inefficiency of many I met in Scutari, Alex. Commands in this force should have been given to some, at least, of the Company's officers, who are skilled and conscientious soldiers. To John Jacob, for instance . . . he is one of the finest cavalry leaders in the world. Had *he* been in Lord Raglan's place, I warrant the British army would not have remained idle in Constantinople and at Varna, leaving us in Silistria to fight off the Russians as best we might, unaided."

"Perhaps so, sir," Alex conceded. "But—"

Colonel Beatson ignored the interruption. He continued, his tone faintly satirical, "No doubt Lord Raglan was, once again, obeying the orders he had received from a higher source! Or, as Omar Pasha suggests, he may be influenced by the French. Marshal St Arnaud is said to have refused to send more than one French division to Varna, initially—despite his promise that Silistria was to be relieved with all possible despatch!" He turned in his saddle, eyeing Alex searchingly in the dim light. "Alex, my friend, I need a clue to Raglan's character, so that I may know best how to make my approach to him, when the time comes. That was why I wanted you to tell me what, from your knowledge of him, was your opinion of our commander-in-chief—

I had no more personal reason for asking, I do assure you. And although you may not have known him well, at least you have met him and you've served in the British army, which I have not. I simply wish to hear your impression of him, whether prejudiced or not."

"Then I shall do my best to enlighten you, sir," Alex promised. He chose his words carefully, endeavouring to free them of all bias. "His lordship is a fine-looking man, possessed of much refinement and charm. He is always very popular with his staff, by all accounts . . . even I, meeting him in the circumstances I did, found him gracious and considerate. I felt that he sincerely regretted what he was compelled to do to me. Yet"—he frowned—"this is not easy to explain, sir. But had it not been for the fact that he was in uniform when he received me, I do not believe that I should have taken him for an officer of high military rank."

"For what would you have taken him, then?"

"Oh . . . a politician, a diplomat, perhaps. Or even a priest. By this I am not implying any lack of military qualities but rather that his manner seemed to accord oddly with his high military rank."

"Pray continue," Colonel Beatson encouraged. "You interest me very much indeed, Alex."

Alex hesitated, again searching for the right words. "Well, sir," he said at last, "I felt that he was less a leader of men, less a disciplinarian, if you will, than a savior of men's souls. Yet even this impression was a contradictory one, for he has a splendid reputation for courage in the field. It is said of him that after Waterloo, when his right arm was amputated, he called out very coolly that his arm was to be brought back to him, so that he might remove a ring he especially valued from one of the fingers."

The colonel smiled. "Yes, I have heard that story. But let us

hope—for all our sakes and not least for the sake of British pres-
tige—that he does not try to conduct *this* war according to the
principles which governed the fighting at Waterloo! It will take
more than an impenetrable British square to defeat the Russians."

"He will surely have advisers. Officers on his staff, who have
had experience of modern warfare," Alex suggested.

"That is not what I have heard, I am afraid. Few of Raglan's
staff officers have even attended the senior department of the
Royal Military College . . . and he has, as aides-de-camp, four of
his own nephews, I believe. There is Sir George de Lacy Evans,
of course, commanding the 2nd Division. He fought in Spain
with great distinction but he must be . . . what? Almost seventy,
I think, and—"

"And you yourself, sir," Alex put in. "You have been out here
since the war began—you have been with Omar Pasha and General Cannon. I should imagine that Lord Raglan will consider
any advice you can give him to be of inestimable value."

Colonel Beatson's shoulders rose in an elaborate shrug beneath
the folds of the gaudy native cloak he had draped about himself
against the chill night air. The moon came from behind a cloud
at that moment and it was possible to see his face quite clearly.
Observing the sceptical expression on it, Alex was taken aback.
"Do you doubt that, sir?" he asked incredulously.

"I do, Alex. I'm going to Varna because I see it as my duty to
offer my services to the British army. As I told you before, it
remains to be seen whether my offer will be accepted."

"I cannot conceive that it will be refused, Colonel."

"Can you not?" William Beatson laughed shortly. "We are not
dealing with the Turks now, my friend. I am a mere brevet lieutenant-colonel in the East India Company's Army of Bengal. I
have no aristocratic connections, no influential friends—and my

service has been exclusively with Oriental troops, save for a brief period in Spain. I am, in a word, a mercenary . . . a paid, professional soldier. I do not imagine that advice from me will be welcomed. To be honest, the most I hope from the British commander-in-chief is his acceptance of the offer I intend to make to him of the services, as scouts and skirmishers, of my Bashi-Bazouk brigands." There was a gleam of indulgent pride in his eyes, as he glanced over his shoulder at the men who rode at his heels. "But look at them!"

Alex did so, frowning. The Bashi-Bazouk horsemen sat their small, unclipped mounts like veterans but they rode in no particular order and their weapons were slung, in unsoldierly fashion, about their persons, with a view more to comfort and ease of handling than to uniformity. Forage bags and spare ammunition pouches hung untidily from the necks of their horses, and the men ate as they rode. When the pangs of hunger assailed them, they bit great chunks from the coarse black bread which formed their staple diet, together with grapes and olives, and a handful of onions to flavour the bread. In their tatterdemalion finery, with the exotically embroidered, tinsel-trimmed jackets and waistcoats and the voluminous shawls they wrapped about their heads or wound round their waists, the Bashi-Bazouks looked a motley crew of Oriental ruffians, fit only for ambush and highway robbery, which was their normal trade.

A slow smile, in which understanding and affection were mingled, spread across William Beatson's face, as he turned to Alex once more. "Alex," he said softly, "these men are warriors—do not be deceived by their appearance. Not so long ago, they were cut-throat robbers, plying their trade in the Circassian mountains. If you spent your lifetime trying, you would never teach them to drill or train them to look or behave like conventional soldiers.

Yet I confess I've never commanded troops I respected more. Each man is a rugged individualist, who fights for plunder for himself and for the love of fighting, but he will spend twenty hours in the saddle without complaint. He will ride all day and all night on a crust of bread and go into action at the end of it. If he flees from superior opposition, it will be to attack again, unexpectedly from the flank . . . not because he is afraid. He scorns death, for it is his daily companion and he laughs at fear, since he has known it from birth and must always fight for what he wants, because he is poor and owns nothing. But he is a magnificent fellow for all that, and he fights this war as a volunteer because, to him, it is a Holy War . . . he does not have to be pressed into service. By heaven, Lord Raglan will be guilty of a grave error if he refuses my Bashi-Bazouks! Yet I'm very much afraid that he *will* refuse them."

"Why should he, sir, if you vouch for them and are prepared to train and command them?"

"I told you to look at them, Alex." The colonel's smile was amused. "Can you see them riding knee to knee with your immaculate Cherry Pickers?"

"Well . . ." Alex smiled too, as he glanced behind him once more at the straggling troop. "I can see them making something of an impression on my late commanding officer, when he first sees them. And when he smells them! His lordship has a sensitive nose."

William Beatson chuckled beneath his breath and lapsed abruptly into silence.

Dawn was grey in the sky when one of the scouts came galloping back to the main body. He spoke excitedly to his commander and Alex, roused from a doze, could only make out a fraction of what he said. He looked at Colonel Beatson in mute inquiry and saw that there was a wary brightness in his alert blue eyes. "What is it?" he asked, now fully awakened. "More Cossacks, sir?"

The colonel shook his head. "Believe it or not, Alex, but we are about to rendezvous with the British army. My scout reports that a patrol of light cavalry is bivouacked in a hollow, a mile or so ahead of us. From his description of the uniforms, they are undoubtedly British and I shall be much surprised if the patrol does not include a troop from your old regiment. In fact"—his voice held a hint of mockery—"we may be about to make an impression on your late commanding officer, if this scout's observations are correct."

"You mean that *Cardigan* is with them?" Alex stared at him, the colour draining from his cheeks. "It isn't possible!"

"I rather fancy it is," Colonel Beatson replied evenly.

He called his straggling band to attention and once again his eyes met Alex's. "If, as I should imagine he must be, his lordship is on a reconnaissance, it is conceivable that we may be able to assist him. I propose therefore to offer my co-operation." His eyes, still resting on Alex's face, were narrowed and questioning. "Will you come with me, Alex, or would you prefer to ride on to Varna and await me there? I can let you have an escort, of course. And there is no necessity for *you* to offer Lord Cardigan any assistance, if you do not wish to do so. The choice is yours."

Alex's hesitation was brief. He was far from anxious to meet Cardigan again but . . . this was war. "I'll ride with you, sir," he answered quietly, "and end this journey as I began it." He took his place at the colonel's side and the small party broke into a canter.

They entered the British bivouac unchallenged and a startled sergeant of the 13th Light Dragoons, in his shirtsleeves, came over to inquire their business.

"Take me to your commanding officer," Colonel Beatson ordered. "I am Lieutenant-Colonel Beatson, of the Indian army, serving as a brigadier-general in the Turkish forces of Omar Pasha, which you will please inform him."

The sergeant surveyed him for a moment in open-mouthed astonishment and then, recovering himself, he saluted. "Very good, sir," he assented. "If the colonel will follow me, I will request Lord Cardigan's aide-de-camp to acquaint his lordship of your arrival."

CHAPTER TWO
➢➢➢ • ⋲⋲⋲

ALEX WALKED with Colonel Beatson through the newly awakened camp noticing, without surprise, that Lord Cardigan appeared to be the only occupant for whom shelter had been provided. There were no tents—officers and men had slept, wrapped in their cloaks, on the bare ground—but a small bower, constructed of brushwood, had been contrived, in order to ensure a measure of privacy for the brigade commander during the night. In this, apparently the Earl of Cardigan still slept.

Feeling his gorge rise, Alex waited while the sergeant held a whispered conversation with one of the cloak-wrapped forms and, as he waited, he identified the uniforms of the men moving about the lines of tethered horses. There were, as nearly as he could make out, close on two hundred of them, drawn from the 13th Light Dragoons and the 8th and 11th Hussars. Their horses seemed to be in an extremely sorry state—two or three, tethered close by, were thin and out of condition, their coats staring and their backs rubbed raw. Another half dozen, being led to water, were obviously lame and did not appear able to summon the energy to rid themselves of the cloud of flies, which buzzed viciously about them, settling tormentingly upon their open sores. He watched them, shocked and puzzled, as Lord Cardigan's aide, rousing himself reluctantly, murmured something in an apologetic voice and crossed the intervening space towards the brushwood shelter, inviting Colonel Beatson to accompany him.

Alex was about to follow when an officer in the familiar blue and cherry red of his old regiment came striding towards him. The newcomer studied him for a long moment and then, quickening his pace, came up to him with hand outheld and a delighted smile on his good-looking young face.

"Alex . . . it is Alex Sheridan, is it not? My dear fellow, it's good to see you again after all these years!"

"And you," Alex exclaimed, gripping the proffered hand warmly. "And you, Phillip . . ." he was still holding Phillip Dunloy's hand in his when the Earl of Cardigan, in shirt and overalls, emerged from his shelter. His eyes, bleary from sleep, slid over Alex's face and then rested disdainfully on the massive figure of William Beatson, still shrouded in the folds of the Bashi-Bazouk cloak, which completely concealed his uniform.

"Well, sir?" he challenged thickly. "Who are you, eh? One of the Turkish generals, my aide-de-camp tells me. What can I do for you? Answer me, man . . . I haven't all day. Or don't you speak English, is that the trouble?"

Colonel Beatson bowed with impeccable dignity. He made no move to shed the concealing cloak but he answered, his deep voice sounding quietly amused, "I speak English fluently enough for my purpose, Lord Cardigan. And this—since I am come here from Silistria during the night—is to give you warning of the close proximity of a large body of Russians on this side of the river. It occurred to me that, if you were on a reconnaissance for the British army, it might be information you would be likely to find useful when returning with your report to the commander-in-chief."

"It is not my habit to report troop movement I have not seen for myself," Cardigan replied. "And, as it happens, I am on my way to Silistria now. However, since you're here"—his tone was grudging—"perhaps I had better hear what you have to tell me. Come inside, where these infernal flies are less persistent. I can't offer you any refreshment except a glass of brandy and a biscuit—we've sacrificed comfort for mobility and are carrying few provisions. But I imagine brandy will be acceptable, if you've ridden through the night." He did not wait for Colonel Beatson's assent to his invitation but, taking it for granted, led the way into his shelter. William Beatson flashed a wry glance at Alex and went inside after him.

"Lord Cardigan has not changed," Alex observed.

"No. Did you imagine he would?" Phillip Dunloy's mouth tightened below the line of his up-brushed cavalry moustache. "This reconnaissance, for example, has been madness. Neither men nor horses are fit but Cardigan has driven us without mercy. Already we've lost fifteen of our best horses and I don't doubt that you'll have noticed the condition the rest are in. But"—he took Alex's arm, smiling at him affectionately—"come to my bivouac and let us see if we can find something more substantial than biscuits to offer you with your brandy. We must talk, Alex. It has been a long time since we had sight or sound of each other and I regretted it."

"So have I," Alex confessed, echoing the smile. Of all his old friends, the one he had missed most had been Phillip, and he said as much. Phillip's fingers gripped his arm. "I'd heard that you were in this part of the world," he stated, "from an Indian army officer I met in Constantinople soon after we landed."

"Yes . . . that was Colonel Beatson. He who is now closeted with Cardigan in his sylvan bower. He told me he had met you."

"I thought I had seen him before. But I confess I did not recognize him just now." Phillip laughed. "He was somewhat differently attired on the last occasion we encountered each other, which was at an Embassy reception. Have you both come from Silistria?"

"Yes, we have. I . . ." Alex hesitated, eyeing his onetime friend with a hint of uncertainty. He wanted to ask about Charlotte but the question he had been about to voice died on his lips. It was for Phillip to broach the subject of Charlotte, not himself. He had no right to ask for news of her, no reason even for supposing that it was she who had accompanied her brother and his wife for, as he had told Colonel Beatson, Phillip had several sisters. So he said, with no more than polite interest, "I understand, also from Colonel Beatson, that you've married since we last met, Phillip."

"Ah, yes, indeed I have . . . and I am a most fortunate man, my dear Alex. Sophie is adorable, I assure you." Phillip spoke briefly of his wife, but with evident pride. "I've recently had to send her home, in the private yacht of a friend, for the best of all possible reasons." He flushed. "She is with child and I am delighted, of course. . . ." He motioned Alex to be seated. They settled themselves cross-legged on the ground and he seemed about to say more but finally, thinking better of it, started to search for the flask of brandy he had packed in his kit. When this came to light, he despatched his servant for breakfast and began to question Alex about the siege. They talked of this until their breakfast arrived—a few unappetizing slices of salt pork, cooked several days before but served with due ceremony—and, as they ate they watched, with amusement, the reactions of the smartly uniformed British cavalrymen to the swaggering Bashi-Bazouks of William Beatson's escort.

Phillip studied Arif, the troop leader, with frowning brows and then asked incredulously, "Are *these* the troops you now command, Alex—these savages?"

"Savages, Phillip? Well, they fought with great gallantry at Silistria, I can assure you," Alex defended. He explained the purpose of Colonel Beatson's journey to Varna. "Omar Pasha has promised to furnish a Bashi-Bazouk brigade, under the colonel's command, should Lord Raglan express the desire for their services. The offer has the official sanction of the Duke of Newcastle and—" he broke off at the sight of Phillip's horrified expression. "Why, what is the matter? You seem surprised."

"Oh, for heaven's sake—of course I am!" Phillip exclaimed. "Alex, surely you cannot seriously imagine that Lord Raglan would consider the inclusion of such undisciplined cut-throats in the British Cavalry Division? Why"—he laughed—"we had a visit from a band of them only a few days ago. Led by a woman, if you please . . . a vast Amazon who rejoiced in the name of Fatima. She had the temerity to offer her force to Cardigan!"

"Who refused it, I imagine?" Alex spoke dryly.

"Indeed he did. We had some of the same tribe encamped near our infantry at Varna and I heard it on very good authority that they became a plague, both to our men and the French. They are thieves and barbarians and worse . . . in fact, the French hanged a few of them, I believe, as an example to the rest."

Alex stared at him in disbelief. "The French *hanged* them? But they are our allies!"

"My dear chap, the French are accustomed to dealing with native troops," Phillip retorted. "They have a number of Zouave and Spahi regiments from Algeria attached to them . . . so they should be, should they not? Can't you dissuade your friend Beatson from making such an offer to Lord Raglan? Because he won't entertain it for a moment, I assure you—whatever the Duke of Newcastle may advise from London."

"But Lord Raglan needs light cavalry, Phillip! He has only Cardigan's brigade," Alex objected.

"Perhaps he does. But he does not need them so badly that he must seek for recruits amongst that rabble! Let Omar Pasha keep his Bashi-Bazouks—and control them, if he can. They would be of no use to us and Beatson will only make himself a laughing stock if he suggests they would." Phillip Dunloy dismissed the subject with a disdainful shrug of his slim shoulders. "In any event, you said you were not serving with them, I believe. What is your object in going to Varna, Alex? Are you coming back to us, by any chance?"

"I have been given leave of absence by the Turks and I'm hoping for a staff appointment of some kind, under the British command. In the Cavalry Division, if possible, where my experience may perhaps prove of some slight value."

"A staff appointment? Well, don't ask Cardigan for one," Phillip advised, with a wry grimace. "He'll remember your name, if not your face. I should ride for Varna with all speed, if I were in your shoes, and have the matter arranged before our brigadier-general brings us back from his private war . . . if he ever intends to do so! Lord Lucan would offer your best chance. He's due in Varna soon and is somewhat nominally in command of the division. If you're in Cardigan's bad books, he'll probably welcome you, if only to annoy his brother-in-law by appointing you to his staff, because there's very bad blood between them. Failing him, you could approach General James Scarlett, who commands the Heavy

Brigade, and has been heard to complain that his staff is destitute of battle experience. Well . . ." Phillip raised his drinking horn in smiling salute. "Here's luck to you, Alex! It has been a great pleasure to see you again."

"Thank you," Alex acknowledged, "for your advice and for your good wishes. It seems not unlikely that I shall need both when I reach Varna."

"Yes," Phillip agreed soberly, "I fear that you may. You see—" Again he cut himself short, his smile fading and Alex became aware of a sudden constraint between them, the more hurtful because it was unexpected. They had once been so close, Phillip and he; as close as brothers in the old days and constant companions, having no secrets from each other, trusting each other implicitly. But now, despite the surface cordiality of the words they had exchanged, there was a barrier between them, holding them apart. He sensed that Phillip wanted to tell him something—to give him some item of news or offer another warning, perhaps—and yet was reluctant or afraid to speak his mind. He waited but the younger man said nothing and at last, stifling a sigh, Alex got to his feet.

Was it only the gulf of years which made them strangers now, he wondered, or did it go deeper than that? Could the years destroy a friendship as firm and lasting as theirs had always seemed, even though they had been separated for so long and had communicated with each other so infrequently? He felt the old, familiar bitterness well up inside him and the muscles of his face stiffen.

Why, he asked himself, had he tried to turn back the clock . . . there was never any turning back. He should have learned that partings were final and irrevocable, once time had sealed them.

Out of the tail of his eye, he saw Colonel Beatson emerge

from Lord Cardigan's brushwood shelter, alone. The gaudy cape hung over the crook of his arm now, so that he was revealed in the correct green and gold lace *alkalak* of a British officer of Indian irregular cavalry—in fact, the uniform he wore was that of the Nizam's Cavalry, which he had commanded. He looked, Alex thought, as British as any of the Hussar or Light Dragoon officers in the makeshift camp and, seasoned campaigner that he was, he looked better turned-out than any of them. He walked with dignity and the men drew themselves up and saluted him as he passed, impressed by his personality, although none of them knew who he was nor whence he had come.

Yet, significantly, Lord Cardigan did not do him the courtesy of escorting him to his horse—he had not even troubled to come to the entrance of his shelter to wish the visitor Godspeed. Instead, from its interior, his voice could be heard calling querulously for his aide and then, an instant afterwards, he bellowed a demand for his servant to attend him.

Alex glanced sharply at Phillip, imagining that in this probably lay the clue to the barrier he had sensed rising between them. It was the old barrier which Cardigan had erected all those years before, he decided resentfully, by means of which the 11th's commanding officer had set the so-called "Indian" officers apart from those of his own choice. And—consciously or unconsciously—Phillip now accepted the barrier, perhaps.

He held out his hand and said, with a coldness he could not hide, "Our respective commanders appear to have concluded their conference . . . if such it can be called, when the one so palpably regards the other as beneath his notice."

"Oh, pay no heed to Cardigan," Phillip said easily. "You know what he is like. He treats Lucan, who is his divisional commander, with even less ceremony, I assure you."

"Nevertheless," Alex insisted, his tone still inclined to be cold, "I think I had better take my leave also, Phillip."

"Must you go so soon?" The regret in Phillip's voice banished Alex's momentary anger and because, even now, he could not bear to part from a man who had been his friend on other than friendly terms, he said tentatively, "Yes, but . . . let us hope that this may be only *au revoir* and not farewell. Shall I look for you on your return to Varna? Provided that my quest for employment is successful and I am still there when you return, of course."

"My dear Alex, please do." Phillip grasped his hand impulsively, holding it in both his own. "I should like to see you again, more than I can begin to tell you. I have missed you, but I—" For the third time he bit back whatever it was he had intended to say and two bright spots of embarrassed colour rose to burn his cheeks. He hesitated and then said apologetically, "Alex, there is a question I must ask you."

Alex searched his face with puzzled eyes, at a loss to account for his evident confusion. "Ask me what you will," he invited.

"Then . . ." Phillip's colour deepened. "Alex, are you married? I know so little of what has happened to you, what you have done since you left England. Your letters told me of battles against the Sikhs and of your travels but of little else. They did not mention a wife or suggest that you—"

"Because I have none," Alex answered flatly. "Women have no place in the life I lead, I am afraid. Why do you ask?"

"What of my sister Charlotte?" Phillip pursued. "It is a long time ago, I am aware but . . . you were fond of her, were you not?"

There was so much anxiety underlying the question that Alex, in his turn, paused before replying. He could not have said what instinct warned him to be cautious but he answered with assumed indifference, "Yes, indeed, I was deeply attached to Charlotte,

Phillip." Conscious of the irony of his own understatement, he shrugged and added quickly, lest he betray himself, "But as you say, it was a long time ago. I imagine she will have forgotten me by this time."

"As you have forgotten her?" Phillip suggested, relief in his eyes. "Then I need not have worried!" He expelled his breath in a heartfelt sigh. "Charlotte is in Varna, you see, Alex."

"In Varna? *Now?*" The blood pounded in Alex's veins; he could feel the quickened beat of his heart but he forced himself, somehow, to speak calmly and to maintain his pretended indifference. "You mean she has come with the army? But I understood—"

"That it was forbidden?" Phillip supplied. "Indeed it was, but Charlotte and Emmy—you remember Emmy O'Shaughnessy, our little stepsister, do you not?" Alex nodded dumbly and he went on, a note of almost reluctant pride in his own voice, "The two of them defied Lucan's ban and took ship, unknown to me, I may say, until they arrived, with some of the army women, in a transport. You may imagine what hardships and humiliations they endured, traveling below decks in such company. Some of those women are . . . well, you'll see them for yourself, no doubt. I was quite horrified, when I learned what they had done." Phillip spread his hands helplessly. "I should have prevented them, needless to tell you, if I'd had any inkling of their intentions—but I had not. I imagined them both safe at Therapia as guests of Lady Stratford, at the ambassador's summer residence. After my wife left, they were invited to stay there for as long as they wished, and that is what I had fondly imagined they would do. But Emmy is a madcap, you know, and I am sure that when she heard that Lady Errol and Mrs Duberly had contrived to join their husbands, she prevailed upon Charlotte to endeavor to do likewise. And Lady Errol, of course . . ."

The blood continued to beat an urgent tattoo in Alex's brain. Phillip was telling him of two other officers' wives who had flaunted Lord Lucan's orders but he scarcely took any of it in, could not have repeated their names a moment after he had heard them. Only one name mattered to him, although he had sought for years to forget it. *Charlotte . . .* he drew a shuddering breath, shocked by the intensity of his own emotions.

Charlotte was in Varna, scarcely fifty miles from him. . . . It seemed unbelievable, this fulfillment of his hopeless, so often suppressed longing to see her again. Dazedly he wondered if he were dreaming, fearing that he must be and Colonel Beatson's voice, calling to him a trifle impatiently, failed at first to rouse him, for it sounded as if it were coming from another world. But he recovered himself and started obediently to move in his commander's direction and then, remembering the announcement he had read in *The Times* on the eve of Chillianwalla, his elation faded. He halted and spun round to face Phillip again.

"Phillip," he asked hoarsely, making a desperate effort to steady his voice, "your sister is married to Arthur Cassell, is she not? I read of her engagement to him some years ago. I . . . that is, is he here with you or in Varna?"

Phillip inclined his head. "Yes, they are married, Alex. But Arthur is on Lord de Ross' staff, with promotion to lieutenant-colonel. He was despatched on a mission to buy horses from the Bulgarians—before Charlotte and Emmy arrived. I have no idea for how long he will be gone." His eyes met Alex's speculatively but, if he had noticed anything unusual in his companion's manner, he did not mention it. His tone, however, was guarded as he went on, "Charlotte married him six years ago. She is happy, I think but . . . they have no children, which they both regret."

"I see," Alex managed. "I am sorry, for Charlotte's sake. I imagine, though, that this made it possible for her to accompany you out here." His smile cost him a pang but Phillip echoed it as he fell into step beside him.

"Yes, that's so. Sophie had made up her mind to accompany me when war was declared and I was thankful when Charlotte decided to come with us. My wife is young, you understand, and I felt that if Charlotte was with her, she would be less lonely and unprotected during my necessary absences from her during the campaign. But none of us bargained on Emmy's insisting that she, too, should be included in the party. I put my foot down and refused my consent but Emmy simply ignored me. Believe it or not, Alex, she smuggled herself on board our ship at Devonport in the confusion of departure, claiming that she was my wife's personal maid! And she did not reveal her presence until we had been at sea for several days."

In spite of the emotional turmoil which Phillip's earlier words had caused him, Alex laughed aloud, with genuine amusement. It was typical of Emmy, he thought; once she had set her mind on anything, she did not rest until she had achieved her objective, no matter what obstacles stood in her way.

"You may laugh, my friend," Phillip told him ruefully. "But I wish now that I had sent her home with Sophie. She and Charlotte have put me in a most awkward position—they have no official status, Arthur is somewhere in the wilds of this Godforsaken country, and we're in camp at Devna, which is nine miles from Varna . . . when we aren't on patrol. I don't know what's to be done with them, and that is the truth."

"Then . . . they are alone?" Alex put in, no longer amused but anxious, on Charlotte's account.

"Unfortunately they are. I managed to rent a ramshackle house for them in the town, just before I left to accompany Cardigan on his reconnaissance. But our orders were sudden and unexpected, so that I was compelled to leave before they were properly settled in their new lodging. To be frank, Alex, I am deeply concerned for them. I wonder if you . . . if it would be asking too much of you, that is to say—" Phillip flushed and broke off, frowning, his sentence unfinished.

Alex guessed what was coming and kept himself under rigid control. Colonel Beatson, who had paused to speak to a group of officers, was now mounted, he saw, and judging by his expression, was obviously impatient to be gone. Arif, the Bashi-Bazouk troop leader, catching his commander's eye, signed to the man holding Alex's horse, who came cantering towards Phillip and himself, dragging the animal after him. He could not delay for more than a few minutes longer, Alex knew, and wracked his brains for some plausible excuse, so that he might avoid making the offer which, it was clear, Phillip expected him to make. But he could think of no excuse and, bracing himself, said reluctantly, "Do you wish me to call on your sisters, Phillip, and offer them what assistance I can?"

"My dear fellow, I should be profoundly grateful if you would!" Phillip assented eagerly. "There is sickness in our camp and rumors—which I sincerely trust are unfounded—of cholera among the French. I don't want Emmy to stay and I scarcely imagine that Arthur Cassell will be pleased when he hears that Charlotte has followed him to Varna. Perhaps *you* may be better able to persuade them that they should return to Therapia than I've been up to now. You were one of the few people Emmy always listened to in the old days, I remember." He sighed. "Above all, Alex, I want you to urge them to stay where they are and not to go to the camps . . . whatever Lady Errol or Mrs Duberly are doing. The house I procured for them is in the Street of the Silversmiths. It is not difficult to find, although it is just a pot-holed quagmire, like all the other streets in Varna . . . in spite of its fine sounding name!"

"I shall find it," Alex promised. He took his horse from the man who had brought it for him and again offered Phillip his hand. "You may rest assured that I will do everything in my power to carry out your instructions, Phillip. And"—he said it after only the briefest hesitation "to serve Charlotte as best I may, until her husband returns."

"I am deeply grateful to you, Alex." Phillip Dunloy wrung his hand and then stood aside to allow him to mount, his eyes holding an appreciative gleam as he looked at the magnificent Arab. "That's a fine piece of horseflesh you have there, indeed it is. Well . . . *au revoir,* then. And God go with you."

"With you also, Phillip. I shall look for you in Varna." Alex set spurs to his horse.

Colonel Beatson fixed him with a shrewdly speculative gaze when he rejoined their troop but he said nothing, simply gave the signal to move off to his waiting horsemen. As they clattered up a rocky incline beyond the bivouac, Lord Cardigan reappeared to stand, hand on hip, at the entrance to his shelter, watching them. He was immaculately uniformed now, an arrogant and strik-ing figure in his gold frogged Hussar jacket and the tight fitting cherry coloured overalls that encased his well shaped legs. He did not look his age, Alex thought, nor had he altered a great deal since the last time they had met. The cold blue eyes still held the remembered disdain that they had always held and, as they had done so often in the past, seemed to look through him, as if he did not exist.

They looked through Colonel Beatson, too, and the Bashi-

Bazouk troop . . . Lord Cardigan did not pay them the tribute of a parting salute. He affected neither to see nor to hear their departure but stood smiling to himself, his long, aristocratic nose in the air and the breeze ruffling the flowing, reddish-brown whiskers which adorned his florid but still handsome face. It was as if his thoughts afforded him reason for private mirth or even for self-congratulation, although it was evident that, whatever they were, he did not intend to share them.

William Beatson glanced back at him over his shoulder and said with some exasperation, "Alex, I do not in the least blame you for seeking satisfaction from *that* man . . . whatever the Articles of War lay down. I'd have been tempted to call him out myself, if I'd been compelled to spend much longer in his company. His arrogance is beyond belief."

Alex answered, with restraint, "I am glad that you had the opportunity to meet and judge his lordship for yourself, sir."

"I could have done without it," the colonel confessed. "However"—he turned in his saddle to face his companion—"I did manage to learn one thing from Cardigan that may well prove useful. But if we are to make use of it, Alex, it may mean delaying *your* arrival in Varna by a day or so. Would you have any objection to that?"

There was a coldness in Alex's heart but it vanished and he shook his head decisively. Of what use to hurry to Varna now? Charlotte was married and he had no right even to want to see her in her husband's absence, no hope that she would want to see him. He would keep his promise to Phillip, of course, but a few days' delay could scarcely matter and, selfishly he was aware, he would welcome it. Although there was Emmy—that strange, headstrong, elusive child of whom, in the old days, he had been very fond. He would enjoy meeting Emmy again. . . .

Seeing the headshake, Colonel Beatson laid a hand on his knee. "Cardigan told me," he stated gravely, "that two British naval gunboats have been despatched up the Danube by Admiral Dundas. They are manned by thirty seamen from H.M.S. *Britannia,* all of them volunteers, and they have a platoon of sappers on board, with bridging equipment. The original intention was, I gather, to send them to our assistance at Silistria."

"For which purpose they are too late," Alex suggested dryly.

"True, my friend. But it occurs to me that General Cannon could use them to some advantage, if they could be directed to him. And they should, if Cardigan's estimate of their position is accurate, be less than twenty miles north of us now. If you were to retrace your steps to the river and follow it upstream, you might well be able to intercept them."

"You mean, sir"—Alex looked at him with narrowing eyes— "that I should intercept and redirect them to General Cannon's support, when he endeavors to cross the river from Rustchuk to Guirgevo?"

Beatson nodded. "Exactly. The sappers have bridging equipment with them and Cannon and Ogilvy have only small boats. A pontoon bridge, flung across the river by night, could bring Hussein Pasha's main force into the attack . . . instead of a few thousand men, a whole army. It bears thinking about, does it not, Alex?"

"It does, Colonel, if the gunboats are able to reach Rustchuk in time." Alex was suddenly excited. "It does indeed!"

"They might, if you acquaint them with what is afoot," the colonel asserted. "Rustchuk is barely fifty miles from Silistria overland but Cannon told us that the earliest he could commence his attack would be the night of the seventh. You will have to ride hard and not draw rein until you come up with the gunboats.

That is why I am proposing that you should go, taking Arif, who knows the country well, and perhaps three or four others, with good horses. You can leave the baggage with us. And you may, it goes without saying, rely on me to carry out any commissions on your behalf in Varna." He sighed, with more than a hint of regret. "I must go on, since it is imperative that I talk with Lord Raglan as soon as possible. If he *does* decide to accept the offer of a Bashi-Bazouk brigade, I shall need time to select and train the best men I have available."

"Yes, sir, of course," Alex agreed readily. "Obviously I am the one to go and I'll do so gladly. . . ." A heavy eagerness now possessed him at the realization of what, if it were successfully accomplished, his interception of the two British gunboats might mean.

The town of Guirgevo, on the Wallacian side of the Danube, had been captured during the initial Russian advance and was strongly held. Facing it, across the river, was a Turkish army under Hussein Pasha which was based on Rustchuk and General Cannon, with a number of British and Indian army volunteers from Silistria, had planned an attack on the Russians with a small, picked force, relying on surprise and daring to carry it through. They were aware that, with only rowing boats to ferry them across, very few troops could be brought into action and these only under cover of darkness. But with a bridge across the river, there would be nothing to prevent Hussein Pasha from throwing in his whole army, once a bridgehead had been established on the far bank. In fact, he might well be shamed into doing so and, with Guirgevo restored to Turkish hands, the Russians would be compelled to withdraw from the Danube, the threat of invasion of the Danube provinces considerably lessened and perhaps even averted.

Of more importance to him personally however, Alex thought, was the fact that he might be able to send aid to the gallant Cannon and those other officers of his own service, Lieutenants Arnold, Hinde and Bullard, at a time when they might need it very badly. It had been they who, with Colonel Ogilvy, Cannon's British aide, and Bent and Meynell of the 75th had planned to undertake the hazardous attack. They had received very lukewarm encouragement from the Turks. Hussein Pasha was known to consider it a forlorn hope and the Danube an impassable obstacle to the passage of the main body of his troops. With close on a hundred thousand men under his command, he had made no attempt to do battle with the Russians in Guirgevo and General Cannon had gone to Rustchuk with an avowed intention of forcing the Turkish commander into action. Or, as he himself had put it, of "perishing in the attempt."

Alex smiled grimly to himself, recalling these words. The Turks fought bravely enough but they were, at times, unheroically led. While he had had nothing but admiration for the conduct of Mussa Pasha, who had died in the defense of Silistria, there had been an occasion during the siege when James Butler had actually had to drag a high-ranking Turkish officer from hiding and, at the height of a battle, deliver him to his post by propelling him there with the toe of his boot. Mussa Pasha and his mulatto second in command, Hussein Bey, had fought with great personal heroism. But, had it not been for the courage and inspired leadership of poor young Butler and the support given him by his fellow Indian army volunteers, Nasmyth and Bullard, Silistria must long since have yielded . . . a fact which Omar Pasha had recently acknowledged, when paying public tribute at Butler's graveside.

In the light of this, he found himself wondering what success General Cannon had met with, as he discussed a possible plan of action with Colonel Beatson. The black-browed Arif, acquainted with his new orders, grinned with savage pleasure, and went to choose the men and horses to accompany them on their mission. He returned with four of his compatriots a few minutes later and, still grinning his wolfish grin, announced their readiness for departure.

On the point of taking leave of his commander, Alex wondered whether or not to tell him what Phillip had said concerning Lord Raglan's probable reaction to the offer of a Bashi-Bazouk brigade to augment the British Cavalry Division. He finally decided against it—Phillip, like Lord Cardigan, might conceivably be prejudiced. But, as they shook hands, William Beatson promised to recommend him for a staff appointment when he saw the British commander-in-chief and Alex asked him whether, in addition, he could find time to call at a house in the Street of the Silversmiths in Varna.

"Phillip Dunloy's two sisters are staying there, sir," he explained. "He asked me to see if there were any way in which I could be of service to them. Phillip is anxious on their behalf, because they are in Varna without official sanction."

Once again, he was conscious of the older man's gaze, fixed thoughtfully on his face, as if seeking some clue to his feelings but this time he was prepared for it and at pains to give nothing away. William Beatson appeared satisfied as the result of his scrutiny and, having agreed very willingly to call on Phillip's sisters at the first opportunity, he bade Alex not to delay.

"You have a long ride ahead of you. The best of luck, Alex and . . . take care of yourself. I shall await you at Lord Raglan's headquarters. Inquire for me there when you arrive."

"I will, sir. A pleasant journey and success to your mission." Alex saluted and, with the Bashi-Bazouks jogging at his heels, set off in the direction from which, earlier that morning, they had come.

Reaching a valley with a small stream flowing through it, Arif raised a brown hand and announced that if they followed the valley, it would take them back to the river by a less circuitous route than the one they had previously followed. The rising sun was warm in their faces as they rode back towards the Danube. It sank and the moon rose before their quest was ended. Then Alex heard the rhythmic chug of paddles and the splashings of churned-up water and, looking down from the bridle-path on which he rode, glimpsed the first of the gunboats some distance ahead at a bend in the river.

Thankfully he urged his flagging horse in pursuit.

CHAPTER THREE
⋙ • ⋘

THE LONG, HOT DAY was drawing to a close in Varna but the going down of the sun brought little relief to the inhabitants of the airless Bulgarian town—least of all to those recent arrivals who had not as yet become accustomed to its climate.

Emma O'Shaughnessy, her own *toilette* completed as well as it could be in their present cramped quarters, was aware of a feeling of intense depression as she stood waiting for her stepsister, Charlotte Cassell, to finish dressing. They had both been invited to a *soirée,* given by the French General Canrobert, by a member of his staff who—with true Gallic gallantry—had chosen to ignore their lack of official status and had insisted on their accepting his general's invitation.

"Mais voyez vous, mesdames," he had pleaded, "it is not right
that two such charming ladies should remain closeted like nuns,
simply because the milord Lucan has decreed that they should
not be here. I should be failing in my duty, to France and to my
génèral, were I not to urge you to grace his reception with your
presence. . . ."

Emmy sighed. Tired and oppressed by the heat, she was unable
to view the prospect of attending a crowded reception with anything like enthusiasm at this moment. And, as she surveyed her
image in the small, cracked mirror which was all the room boasted,
her depression grew. Her gown had suffered in transit and looked
decidedly shabby; her face, small and elfin and always inclined to
pallor, was white and over-thin. Her dark eyes, which were her
best feature, seemed far too large for their setting, she thought
unhappily—an effect that was heightened by the smudged shadows beneath them, caused by anxiety and lack of sleep. Yet
Charlotte, who had suffered the same privations as she had and
who was three years older, still contrived to look beautiful and
would, she knew, soon emerge from her bedroom elegantly
gowned and apparently radiant, to attract admiring glances and
extravagant compliments from General Canrobert's susceptible
staff officers.

It was grossly unfair, Emmy told herself, for none of the
Frenchmen who ardently kissed her hand would suspect that
Charlotte had not wanted to come here and that, since her arrival,
she had done nothing but complain and wish that she were still
in Constantinople. . . .

Disconsolately, Emmy crossed to the window and stood with
her face pressed against its steamy glass and gazed at the scene
before her. The Street of the Silversmiths was dirty and uninvit-
ing, scarred by the wheel tracks of the endless procession of

transport wagons which had passed along it since the disembarkation of the British Expeditionary Force. Its centre formed a drain that, as far as she could make out, was never cleaned and from which the stench—even from behind closed windows—was unbelievably nauseating. The street was deserted now, save for a few emaciated mongrel dogs, engaged in the seemingly hopeless search for some means of keeping themselves from starvation, and an ancient peasant woman who squatted, wrapped in a shawl, sleeping close to the doorway, oblivious to the proximity of the snarling dogs.

It was typical, Emmy reflected, of most of the streets in Varna. The little town, so picturesquely situated in a lovely, undulating valley at the mouth of the River Dwina, had presented an enchanting appearance from the packed lower-deck of the troopship in which she and Charlotte, in conditions of indescribable discomfort, had sailed across the Black Sea from Scutari. She had been wild with impatience to go ashore, she remembered, eager to explore the fine castle commanding the heights and to wander, breathing God's pure fresh air once more, among the vineyards and orchards by which the town was surrounded. But, alas . . . on closer inspection, Varna had proved much less enchanting than its distant vista had led her to hope it would be.

It was primitive and insanitary, the town itself consisting of two-story wooden houses and frequently half-hidden by a damp pall of fog, which rose from the steaming ground on which it was built. The people were listless and unfriendly and not at all disposed to welcome the British soldiers as they poured, in their thousands, from the heavily laden ships, demanding food and shelter and transport. They were willing enough to supply the latter, at a price, but food was in short supply and the houses they were prepared to vacate filthy and vermin-infested, so that even the highest ranking officers preferred to live under canvas with their men.

All water had to be carried from wells and, when it arrived was undrinkable and, indeed, scarcely fit even for washing purposes, although it cost almost as much as wine. Such necessities as milk, butter and eggs were jealously hoarded and could only be obtained by means of exorbitant payments, after hours of wearisome bargaining.

Phillip had done his best for them, Emmy thought; it was not his fault that she and Charlotte were wretchedly uncomfortable in the tiny, barely furnished hovel he had rented for them. He had contrived to engage servants also but the two slovenly women and the sullen, unprepossessing man—the husband of one of them—were untrained and spoke no English. Although highly paid for their services, they seemed disinclined to render these, once Phillip had gone and could no longer coax or coerce them into doing so. They simply vanished where there was work to be done, and turned deaf ears and unrepentant faces to pleas and reproaches alike.

Emmy drew a long, exasperated breath, closing her eyes to the glare from outside and the unwelcomed sight of the mangy, half-starved dogs roving the gutters. She wished that Phillip had not had to leave them and then, her conscience pricking her, that he had not been so angry with them, because they had followed him to Varna without permission. His anger was justified, she knew . . . it had been wrong to come, a mistake she was beginning bitterly to regret and one Charlotte had regretted from the moment they had set foot on shore. The mistake had been her own, of course, since the idea had been hers in the first place, and Charlotte had always been opposed to it but she had thought . . . Emmy bit her lower lip fiercely, feeling it quiver. From the room next door, she heard Charlotte's voice, raised in futile reproof, "Oh, no, Maria . . . not like that, please!" and the guttural, unintelligible reply from the younger of the two peasant women pressed, so unwilling, into their service. Maria, she knew from experience, was hopelessly clumsy and she sighed again, hearing the petulant weariness in her stepsister's voice and aware of what it portended.

She had always loved and admired Charlotte, always looked up to her since she had been a small child. but there were times when Charlotte's inability to adapt herself to the inevitable hardships of campaigning became unbearably trying and taxed her patience to its limit. Had Sophie accompanied her, instead of Charlotte, which had been the original plan, she would, Emmy was certain, have been able to bear the discomfort and the misery without a qualm. She and Sophie would happily have followed the example set by Lady Errol and Mrs Duberly and lived, as they were doing, in a tent—but Charlotte had flatly refused this suggestion and Phillip, with unexpected firmness, had also refused to hear of it.

So . . . they were here, virtually prisoners in this dark little house in the Street of the Silversmiths, their presence only tolerated because, officially, it was not recognized. Charlotte's husband was somewhere in the interior, buying horses, and had no idea that she and Emmy had arrived. And even Phillip had been compelled to abandon them, because he had been ordered to accompany Lord Cardigan on a reconnaissance into enemy-held territory, from which the date of his return was uncertain.

Tears came to prick at Emmy's closed eyes but she blinked them back. When, at the beginning of March, she had embarked so gaily in the sailing ship *Henry Wilson* for Malta, it had seemed to her that she was embarking on the adventure of her life.

Military bands had played the troops away in an atmosphere of wild enthusiasm, which had been repeated in London, at Woolwich and in Southampton, as well as in Portsmouth and Devonport. There had been crowds lining the route, to cheer and wave, and thousands had waited all night on the docks in order to wish their loved ones a final Godspeed.

On board the *Henry Wilson* had been two squadrons of the 11th with their horses, Charlotte and her husband, with other members of the quartermaster-general's staff, Phillip and Sophie and eleven soldiers' wives . . . among whom, disguised as a maid-servant, Emmy had smuggled herself aboard. Permission to accompany the army to Turkey had been readily granted to those officers' wives who desired to do so and, as always, many of the other ranks' wives sailed with their menfolk, according to the established custom of the times. Indeed, such was public enthusiasm for the campaign against the Russians that, in the end, a good many ladies and far more than the usual number of soldiers' wives had been allowed to sail, all of them in the highest spirits as they boarded the waiting transports.

The scenes, as their ship weighed anchor, had been deeply moving and Emmy felt a lump rise in her throat as she recalled the forest of waving handkerchiefs on the quayside and the strains of *Rule Britannia* played by a Royal Marines band, floating across the widening gap between ship and shore. Yet despite the tears and the farewells, they had left England more in the atmosphere and spirit of a vast picnic party than that of an army going to war and the picnic party spirit had continued to prevail after their arrival at Scutari from Malta. It had not, Emmy reflected ruefully, prepared them for what they would have to endure in Varna.

In Scutari and in Constantinople, where she, Charlotte and Sophie had been guests of the British Ambassador, Lord Stratford de Redcliffe and his wife, they had enjoyed every sort of social distraction. There had been dinner parties, receptions, wonderful sight-seeing trips across the Bosphorus and into the Sea of Marmora in sailing boats, and splendid military reviews attended by royalty. With young Lady Errol, whose husband was a captain in the Rifle Brigade, and the charming, high-spirited Mrs Duberly, she and Charlotte and her brother's attractive young wife had been in great demand, snowed under by invitations to this or that function, sought after and fêted and never at a loss for entertainment. Charlotte had been in her element, loving every moment of it, with a host of handsome young officers eager for her company whenever Arthur Cassell's duties took him from her side.

Which, Emmy thought, looking back, was why she was so utterly lost and miserable now, so petulant and so ready to complain for here, quite suddenly, the harsh realities of war had caught up with them. Varna was not a healthy place, as they soon discovered. The army was under canvas, the infantry close to the town, the cavalry a few miles outside, with the Light Cavalry Brigade in a delightful park-like valley known as Devna, whence they had moved soon after their disembarkation. But, owing to bad organization in the commissariat and transport departments, the men were short of fresh food, of medicines and water and even, in some cases, of tents and blankets and the sanitation was deplorable. Despite the outward beauty of their surroundings, the camp sites quickly became a breeding ground for disease and many men were ill.

Dysentery had broken out among the soldiers on board ship and since their landing had increased. Without adequate hospital accommodation and on a diet of salt pork and ship's biscuits, the plight of the unfortunate victims was pitiable, for there were too few doctors and, in most cases, only untrained medical orderlies to care for the sick men. There was also a rumor that the still more terrible scourge of cholera had struck the French Zouaves, but this had not been confirmed.

Emmy started to move restlessly about the room. Phillip had forbidden Charlotte and herself to live in camp and she rebelled against having to obey these instructions. But Charlotte was adamant and, in her present mood of fretful boredom, it was becoming increasingly difficult to maintain their normal friendly relationship, when they were cooped up together, day after day, in this small house, seeing no one but their servants. If only Sophie had been here, Emmy thought wistfully, how different it might have been. Sophie and she were of the same age and they had much in common, including the views they held concerning the war and the part they both believed that officers' ladies ought properly to play, if they accompanied the army into battle.

These were serious views, which Charlotte did not share and of which Emmy had long since ceased to speak to her or endeavor to explain, since it was evident that she did not want to understand them. But . . . she passed a hand over her moist, throbbing brow. Because Charlotte did not understand, she lived in almost hourly fear that her stepsister would announce, suddenly and without warning, that she had endured enough and not only demand that she be sent to the ambassador's summer residence at Therapia but would also insist on Emmy's going with her.

It would be quite impossible for her to remain in Varna by herself, of course, and if Charlotte compelled her to leave, this would be the end of everything she had lived for and hoped so desperately to accomplish. She had never been able to forget her childhood dream of caring for the sick—it lingered on, in her heart together with the futile, hopeless dream she had once had about Alex Sheridan. The two were linked together, as such dreams often are and when Alex had failed to send for her to join him in India, as he had promised he would, she had decided that she would not marry at all.

Even when she had sent him a copy of the newspaper in which Charlotte's forthcoming marriage to Arthur Cassell had been announced, he had not replied and so, regretfully, she had come to the conclusion that he wanted no more to do with either of them. Not all the British girls who went to India were unattached . . . he had probably married himself, by this time, and it would be useless for her to go on hoping that he would remember and keep his promise. It had been then that she had resolved to take the veil—a decision reached after much anxious heart-searching and which she had confided to no one but her mother, who had smiled sympathetically but had not taken it seriously.

"Enter a nursing order, Emmy my darling? I think that would be rather unwise. You will change your mind," she had spoken with affectionate tolerance. "When you are older and you meet some young man who takes your fancy . . . you will see."

But Emmy had not changed her mind. She had, it was true, met a number of nice young men but none had taken her fancy, none had succeeded in erasing Alex Sheridan's memory from her heart. *He* was lost to her but her other dream remained, as vivid and as enduring as it had ever been. Accordingly, at eighteen, with her mother's reluctant consent, she had returned to her native Dublin, there to enter the Hospital of the Sisters of Mercy as a postulant to the order. At first she had been content with the cloistered life of self-sacrifice and service and had believed that she had found her vocation but, after a time, doubts had assailed her and a restlessness which she could neither explain nor assuage. After almost three years of arduous training, she had won high praise for her skill as a nurse, but the Mother Superior had gently advised her against taking her final vows as a nun.

"You have a calling, my child, but it is not here, within these walls . . . it is out in the wider world, I believe, where God can best use your talents. Go with a clear conscience, for you have nothing with which to reproach yourself. Yours is an unruly, adventurous spirit which you have tried hard to subdue, and it is not your fault that you have failed to subdue it. I have watched and grieved over the efforts you have made and I do not think that it is right for you to have to continue to struggle so hard against your own nature which, after all, is God-given. You go with my blessing, child, and with my prayers, possessed of knowledge and skill which few young women of your age and class ever acquire. All I ask of you is that, in future, you use them well. . . ."

Emmy's slender dark brows came together in a worried pucker. She wanted, with all her heart, to use her medical knowledge and skill; it had been for this reason that she had come to Turkey, for this express purpose she had followed the army to Varna. But for a young lady of good family, it was impossible; convention decreed very strictly against it and even the soldiers' wives, in whose company she had travelled from Scutari, had laughed at the idea when she had mentioned it to them. They washed and mended their husbands' uniforms and sometimes cooked for them but it was no part of their duty to nurse them when they were sick or wounded. The army provided an ambulance corps of pensioners, it set up hospitals and staffed these with doctors and male orderlies, and women had no place inside the wards. In any event, the women had hinted darkly, the scenes enacted in army hospitals in time of war were too horrible to be witnessed by feminine eyes— least of all by the eyes of a young lady of quality. Emmy would be wasting her breath if she attempted to seek permission to nurse the British army sick, for it would be refused. Indeed, it was unheard of . . . only the French permitted their *vivandières* and *cantinières* any sort of contact with wounded on the field of battle and they, the British women said, with meaning glances at each other, were coarse creatures, of low morals, scarcely deserving the name of women. They . . . hearing a movement from the adjoining room, Emmy turned, forcing a smile.

The door opened and Charlotte came in looking, as Emmy had known she would, fresh and young and, as always, very beautiful in the elaborate gown she had donned and somehow—despite the hazards of travel—had contrived to keep bandbox neat and without a crease. Maria, the dark-faced maidservant, hovering anxiously about her, muttering under her breath in her own language as she attempted, with awkward, untutored hands, to adjust a frill.

Charlotte waved her impatiently away. She said, her voice still querulous, "Oh, you are ready, Emmy. I am sorry if I have kept you waiting but Maria is so slow and she hasn't the remotest idea of how to dress my hair. Do you think you could do it for me?"

"Yes, of course I will," Emmy asserted readily, glad of an opportunity to please her. "And you did not keep me waiting, I assure you . . . I was ready much too soon. Sit down, will you not? That gown becomes you well—you look charming in it."

"Do I?" Charlotte returned indifferently. She seated herself in one of the stiff-backed wooden chairs with which the room was furnished and suffered Emmy to attend to the dressing of her hair. When it was done, she studied her reflection in the mirror from the bedroom which Maria held for her but evidently found little cause for satisfaction in what she saw. The glorious auburn hair was braided neatly enough but she shook her head, pouting. "Loosen it a little, Emmy—you've drawn it much too tightly. Oh, dear, I wish now that we had not to go to this wretched affair. It is such an effort going anywhere here, is it not? So different from Constantinople and it's so hot, one can scarcely breathe!"

"You will enjoy yourself when you are there," Emmy suggested consolingly, although privately she doubted it. "They say that General Canrobert is a delightful person and a splendid host."

"Oh, yes, perhaps I shall," Charlotte conceded. "At least it will be a change of scene and of company, which will be welcome. I am sick to death of being cooped up here in this dreadful little house. Maria, fetch my fan . . . my *fan,* don't you understand?" By means of pantomime, she made her request clear at last and the peasant girl clumped sullenly off in search of the missing fan. When this had been found and delivered to her, Charlotte brusquely dismissed her maid. "All right, you may go, Maria. Go, go, go! Oh, goodness, why doesn't this stupid creature speak English? It is so wearying always having to tell her everything a dozen times."

"I think she is beginning to understand a little, Charlotte," Emmy began, but Charlotte cut her short. "I wish Phillip had not had to go on that patrol—*he* could always make her understand. Besides, it is undignified to attend this reception without his escort."

"Captain and Mrs Duberly have promised to call for us. In fact, they should be here soon . . . it is already past the time when they said they would be here."

"They have probably forgotten," Charlotte said tartly. Emmy sighed and returned to her post by the window, peering out in search of the Duberlys' carriage. "They have probably been delayed," she suggested, "or bogged down on these awful roads."

"Yes, indeed, that's more than likely. Emmy, we cannot stay here, you know . . . we simply cannot! My nerves, my health will not stand it. I wish I had never allowed you to persuade me to come to Varna, truly. I was a fool, I should not have listened to you."

Emmy's heart sank. This was what she had dreaded.

"Oh, but Charlotte!" she exclaimed, shocked and perturbed. "We cannot leave until Arthur and Phillip return, surely? Having come so far and endured so much, we must make sure that they are safe."

"They are in no danger," Charlotte answered scornfully. "Arthur is merely buying horses and he has Captain Nolan with him, who knows the country well—or he should, he has been here since April, I believe."

"But Phillip is on patrol, in enemy-held territory—!"

"Little goose . . . everyone knows that the Russians are in full retreat. In any case"—Charlotte spoke with authority befitting the wife of a cavalry officer—"a reconnaissance patrol is not supposed to engage the enemy. It must observe them only and then report on their movements to headquarters. Those are Lord Raglan's orders; Phillip told me so."

"But with Lord Cardigan in command, one cannot be sure," Emmy objected. "One cannot be free of some anxiety, Charlotte. He has such a reputation for reckless daring and he has only two hundred men with him."

"He is a soldier," Charlotte replied, "and even Lord Cardigan must obey orders when he is on active service." But a shadow crossed her face and she added, in a more reasonable tone, "Very well, if you are so concerned for him, we will wait until Phillip gets back from his patrol."

"And . . . Arthur?" Emmy ventured innocently. "Do you not want to wait until *he* returns?"

A wave of embarrassed colour flooded Charlotte's lovely face.

"Perhaps," she said evasively, "although it is scarcely necessary. If Arthur wishes to see me, he can ask for leave and visit me at Therapia. I fancy he would prefer that to visiting me here." She rose and came to join Emmy at her vantage point by the window, her cheeks still a trifle pink, as if the question had disconcerted her and said, in an obvious attempt to change the subject, "For goodness' sake, Emmy, what do you find of such absorbing interest in the street? You have been gazing out there for the past five minutes!"

"There is nothing of interest," Emmy confessed, "only those dreadful dogs! But I thought the Duberlys' carriage might be coming."

"Oh, those dogs!" Charlotte shivered distastefully and averted her gaze. "They make me quite ill . . . I do not know how you can bring yourself to look at them. And that woman, sleeping in the gutter, with all the dogs around her . . . ugh!"

She returned to her chair and, picking up the fan, started to fan herself vigorously. Emmy abandoned her contemplation of the street outside and studied her stepsister anxiously. She had wondered once or twice during their stay in Constantinople whether Charlotte's relationship with her husband was as happy as she had always imagined it to be. Charlotte's beauty had attracted a number of admirers about her but . . . Emmy caught her breath. Her convent education, allied to a natural innocence, tended to make her unsuspicious in such matters and, until this moment, it had never occurred to her to have any misgivings where her stepsister was concerned. She had been brought up to believe that marriages were made in heaven and that a wife's duty was to be submissive to her husband and to obey him. Yet she was uneasily aware—because on several occasions she had overheard them quarreling—that Charlotte was not always submissive to Arthur Cassell and that, quite frequently, she disobeyed him, with or without his knowledge.

Arthur was a man of forty, titled and immensely rich, but inclined to corpulence and not particularly good-looking. He was proud of his young wife and appeared to be extremely fond of her, solicitous of her comfort and unfailingly courteous to her. But he had resented the attentions paid her by a handsome Guards captain in Scutari and, on one of the occasions when Emmy had overheard them indulging in a heated difference of opinion, he had told Charlotte so, without mincing any words. In spite of which, she recalled uneasily, Charlotte had continued to receive the young Guardsman and to accept his escort when her husband's military duties took him from her. And now, it seemed, she was far from anxious to await Arthur Cassell's return to Varna, the prospect of which, indeed, evidently did not please her as it should in the circumstances, if. . . .

"Emmy," Charlotte asked sharply, "why are you staring at me?"

"I . . . I'm not. That is, I did not mean to stare at you, Charlotte." Emmy glanced once again out of the window and this time, to her relief, she saw the carriage approaching their door. She called this news over her shoulder and Charlotte's smile returned and she rose, impatiently reaching for her shawl. "At last! Is Mrs Duberly riding in the carriage or on horseback?"

"She is in it, I think . . . yes, she is." Emmy helped Charlotte to drape her shawl about her and picked up her own, echoing the older girl's smile almost apologetically, ashamed of her own thoughts. As if she had guessed them, Charlotte said, with brusque affection, "Little nun! That is what you should have been, you know, Emmy, whatever your Mother Superior told you . . . a nun. But you're the strangest mixture—I suppose you always have been, really. You know nothing of love, you do not understand how a woman feels about a man . . . yet you are intelligent. I remember Alex Sheridan once said that your tragedy was that you were too intelligent."

"Alex Sheridan?" Emmy stared at her in bewilderment. "I thought you had forgotten him long ago."

"No. Alex Sheridan is not a man one forgets." There was an odd note in Charlotte's voice, of excitement, almost of anticipation. "He is here, in this country somewhere, in the Turkish service. Phillip met a friend of his in Scutari—a colonel in the Indian army, called Beatson, I believe, who told him so. It is strange to think, is it not, that we may at any time meet Alex again?" Without waiting for Emmy's reply, she led the way to the street door.

Emmy followed her numbly, bereft of words. Phillip had told her nothing, had not mentioned Alex Sheridan's name to her and Charlotte's announcement had taken her completely by surprise. But she had recovered her outward composure when she reached the carriage—in reality a Turkish *araba,* well cushioned but poorly sprung.

The lively and attractive Fanny Duberly, in a blue taffeta gown which became her admirably, was seated inside it. She greeted them both with evident pleasure and made room for Charlotte at her side. Her husband, who was mounted, bowed to them each in turn and, when Emmy had taken her place in the cumbrous equipage, he waved to the driver to proceed. The *araba* lurched down the narrow, rutted street and Captain Duberly cantered ahead of it, scattering the squabbling mongrel dogs with well-aimed flicks of his whip. The dogs made off with shrill yelps, watched sulkily by the old peasant woman, who had at last been roused from her sleep by the commotion they set up. In the carriage, the three ladies exchanged what news they had, Fanny Duberly telling, with a wealth of amusing detail, of a recent visit to the Cavalry Division of the Turkish commander-in-chief, Omar Pasha.

"He was not in the least what I imagined a Turkish general would be like . . . really quite civilized and European-looking. He is a Croat, of course, not a Turk at all, and they say his wife is German. His dress was, to my idea, perfection—a dark grey frock-coat, magnificently embroidered in gold. It was fastened at the waist by a sword belt, the buckle of which, as well as the sword-hilt, was blazing with diamonds, if you can imagine it, Lady Cassell. He did wear a fez but even that was embroidered with diamonds, instead of the usual tassel. And when he had finished his inspection, he insisted on leading the Light Brigade charge . . . which made us smile. He was on a small Turkish horse and had to scramble, with spurs well in, to get out of the way of our long-striding English horses. But the men were delighted and cheered him loudly. And I was delighted, because he evidently noticed me there and asked if he might be introduced to 'the beautiful lady with the flaxen curls who rides so well.'" She laughed, in high good humour. "Or so Lord Raglan told me, after the introductions had been performed. To tell you the truth, I did not understand a great deal of what he said—he speaks a curious mixture of French, German and Italian and *very* rapidly! But he presented me with a souvenir, which I must show you both . . . an autographed copy of one of his despatches, in Turkish. It was all tremendously exciting."

"I am sure it must have been," Charlotte agreed enviously. "I hope that we may also have the pleasure of meeting him while he is here."

"He has gone on to Shumla," Fanny Duberly explained. "And Lord Raglan is to go there also, in the near future, to confer with him and to inspect his troops, I'm told. But I fancy he will come back . . . he enjoyed his visit to us and expressed *great* admiration for our cavalry. In fact, according to one of General Airey's aides, he was heard to say that with *one* such regiment he would grind to dust four regiments of Russian cavalry at least! It is a pity that Lord Cardigan was not present to hear his compliments, is it not? He especially praised the turn-out of the Light Brigade."

"There is no word yet of Lord Cardigan's return, is there, Mrs Duberly?" Emmy asked shyly.

Fanny Duberly smiled at her. "No *definite* word, Miss O'Shaughnessy. But"—she looked from Emmy to Charlotte, her blue eyes dancing—"there is a new arrival in camp who may be able to give you tidings of Lord Dunloy. He, too, is a Turkish general—a brigadier-general in command of a force of Bashi-Bazouk cavalry, with which he helped to relieve Silistria. And he is not only European but British, although of the East India Company's service, I understand. They say, although I cannot vouch for the truth of this, that he is to be at tonight's affair . . . so that you may well have the opportunity of making his acquaintance. He encountered Lord Cardigan's patrol on his way here, a few days ago, and Henry says there is a rumor that he gave Lord Raglan a report of the meeting which upset his lordship a good deal. I know no details . . . but ask Henry"—she gestured to her husband, riding jauntily ahead of them—"he has talked to several people about it, and they are all scandalized. Apparently Cardigan's horses are in an appalling state, lame and with their backs galled, because he has used them too hard. . . ."

Emmy listened, as Mrs Duberly continued to talk with great animation but she took very little of it in.

Was it possible, she wondered, that the new arrival of whom Mrs Duberly spoke could be Alex's friend, Colonel Beatson . . . the man Phillip had met and talked with in Scutari? And, if it were, would he have news of Alex, as well as of Phillip—would he know Alex's whereabouts, what he was doing in the Turkish service? Might he, perhaps, even have seen him?

She glanced covertly at Charlotte and guessed, from her heightened colour and eagerly parted lips that she, too, was asking herself much the same questions. A coldness gripped Emmy's heart. Charlotte was married but . . . she was no longer in love with her husband, if she could flirt as outrageously as she had with the young Guards captain, in spite of her husband's openly expressed disapproval. If she could care so little for his safety and well-being that she was prepared to leave Varna without waiting for his return . . . and what had she said, just before they had left the house to join Captain and Mrs Duberly?

"Alex Sheridan is not a man one forgets. . . ." Despite the oppressive heat of the evening, Emmy shivered. As the *araba* came to a creaking halt outside the French commander's marquee, she found herself praying that the stranger who had encountered Lord Cardigan's patrol should not, after all, be Colonel Beatson.

Captain Duberly handed over his horse to a French orderly and came around to assist his wife and her friends to alight.

"It seems we are a trifle late," he announced, offering Charlotte his arm. "The place is packed already."

From the interior of the brightly lit tent came the hum of voices, as if to bear out his statement and, as they were ushered inside, Emmy saw that the marquee was thronged with brilliant uniforms. The youthful staff officer who had invited them, came hurrying to greet them and then, flushed with importance, led them to be introduced to their host.

Emmy had seen General Canrobert before but this was the first chance she had had of meeting and speaking to him informally.

She quickly took to the small, brisk man with the twinkling brown eyes and neatly trimmed Imperial and, as he talked to her charmingly, remembered with interest the rumor which held that François Canrobert bore a closer relationship to the French emperor than his Imperial Majesty cared publicly to acknowledge. Certainly at close quarters, his resemblance to Louis Napoleon Bonaparte was striking, and the general—unlike his immediate superior, Marshal St Arnaud, the French commander-in-chief—had the impeccable, polished manners of an aristocrat, which suggested that there was a possibility of the rumor being true.

Emmy's French was good and Canrobert seemed pleased by this and kept her by his side for several minutes. Then, when he turned from her with flattering reluctance in order to greet a new arrival, she saw that Charlotte and Mrs Duberly had crossed the room and were engaged in earnest conversation with an immensely tall man, whose uniform of green and gold was unfamiliar to her. He made an impressive figure, standing there, dwarfing the French officers around him, his uniform outstanding in its magnificence, even when contrasted with the brilliance of theirs. But it was not only his uniform that impressed her. He was not young—Emmy estimated his age at about fifty—yet he was of so splendid a physique that he gave the impression of youth and of a strength and vitality few others in the crowded tent could match. His hair was fair and might have been turning grey, although this was not apparent, and he wore a beard, trimmed to a point, which grew luxuriously half way down his gold-laced chest.

As Emmy approached him, his eyes met hers in friendly reassurance, banishing her shyness, and he extended a big, gentle hand to take hers.

"And you, I feel sure, must be the little sister of whom Lady Cassell has been telling me? The one who rides so brilliantly and has no horse to carry her . . . which we must do our best to rectify. My name is William Beatson, Miss O'Shaughnessy."

"I . . . how do you do, General Beatson?" For all she had dreaded his presence here, Emmy found herself instinctively liking and trusting this huge, kindly stranger. Charlotte, having presumably obtained from him the information she wanted, had moved on and she and Mrs Duberly were now surrounded by a crowd of French officers, vying with each other to press wine and refreshments on them. Henry Duberly kept close to his wife, with an air of possessive pride and she had her hand on his arm but Charlotte, smiling radiantly, accepted the homage of the bowing Frenchmen gaily and as her due. She was enjoying herself, Emmy saw, with a pang but at least, if she did, perhaps she would be more reconciled to prolonging their stay in Varna than she had been earlier that evening. Perhaps she would even be willing to wait until Arthur rejoined them. . . .

William Beatson, following the direction of her gaze, said politely, "Your stepsister is a very beautiful woman, is she not?"

"Yes," Emmy acknowledged, her voice, for all her efforts to control it, a trifle strained. "Yes, she is, General Beatson."

"I am only a colonel in the Indian army, Miss O'Shaughnessy," he corrected. "But come . . . let us sit down and I will fetch you some refreshments." He gave her his arm, led her ceremoniously to a chair and brought her a glass of red wine, setting a plate of sweetmeats at her elbow. "Now," he said, "we can talk— if you will allow me that privilege, Miss O'Shaughnessy. You see, I have a commission to perform on behalf of a mutual friend. A friend"—he smiled—"who asked me to call on your sister and yourself, to see if there was any way in which I could be of service to you. I promised him that I would do so as soon as I reached Varna but, for various reasons, I have been delayed. I had, in fact, intended to present myself to you tomorrow morning."

"That is very kind of you, Colonel. And we shall, of course, be delighted to receive you tomorrow morning," Emmy assured him. She started to explain the whereabouts of the house but he cut her short. "I know where the house is—I took the precaution of finding out." He eyed her keenly. "Are you not curious as to the identity of our mutual friend?"

"Oh, no . . . for it is Alex Sheridan, is it not? Indeed, it could be no one else."

"Yes, it is Alex." Colonel Beatson's blue eyes continued to appraise her. "He was with me when we set out from Silistria a week ago, and he renewed his acquaintance with your stepbrother, Lord Dunloy, when we came unexpectedly on a British light cavalry patrol, under the command of the Earl of Cardigan."

"So I had heard," Emmy confessed. She waited, sipping her wine, whilst he told of their meeting with Phillip, feeling a strange sense of unreality creeping over her as she listened. He did not refer to Alex again and finally she said, forcing herself to ask the question with pretended indifference, "Did not Alex come with you to Varna, Colonel Beatson?"

He shook his head. "No, Miss O'Shaughnessy. He undertook a mission of some importance which will delay his arrival. Nevertheless, it is his intention to seek employment under the British command and, if all goes well and his mission is successful, he should reach here within the next day or two."

"So soon? It scarcely seems possible!" Emmy could no longer pretend indifference and she smiled up at him eagerly. "That is wonderful news, I—" From the other side of the marquee, came the gay, uninhibited sound of Charlotte's laughter and her smile abruptly faded. "Did you tell Charlotte—my stepsister—this, Colonel?"

Again Colonel Beatson glanced speculatively in Charlotte's direction. "Yes," he confirmed, "I told her and she expressed herself delighted by the news."

"And so am I," Emmy put in quickly. "I am so pleased to think that Alex is coming here and that we shall see him again. He is a very old friend of the family."

And she *was* pleased at the thought of seeing Alex again, she realized, in spite of her anxiety on Charlotte's account, in spite even of his broken promise to herself. His promise had not been meant seriously . . . how could she ever have imagined that it was? He had made it because she was a child—a foolish child, whom he had not wanted to hurt, whose childish illusions he had been reluctant to damage. But it was Charlotte with whom he had been in love . . . perhaps it was Charlotte still although, for his sake, she hoped that it was not. Emmy set down her glass and essayed one of the sweetmeats. It was conceivable, of course, that all her fears would prove to be groundless. As she had realized earlier, Alex might be married, as Charlotte was . . . it was a long time since they had heard news of him, a long, long time since that day in Windsor, at the Royal Review, when they had last seen and talked to him.

"Alex will be anxious to reach here," Colonel Beatson said. "The more so, I don't doubt, since Lord Dunloy informed him of your and Lady Cassell's presence in Varna, Miss O'Shaughnessy. It will be good for him to meet old friends again. He is a fine soldier and he has served with great distinction, both in India and in Turkey but, like many fine soldiers, he is a lonely man . . . even a solitary one. I fear you may find him greatly changed."

"One expects changes, Colonel, after so many years," Emmy responded gravely. "And *we* have changed, Charlotte and I . . . I, for example, have grown up. I was a child of fourteen the last time that Alex called at our house."

"The change in Alex Sheridan is fundamental. It lies in his attitude to life, Miss O'Shaughnessy," the colonel told her. Emmy sensed something more behind his words, a warning, perhaps, and looked up at him inquiringly.

"You say he is lonely, Colonel Beatson. Has he not married?"

"No, Alex has not married. This is not an unusual state of affairs among the East India Company's officers, you know. We spend so much of our time fighting that few of us marry until comparatively late in life. . . . We're doomed to constant separation if we do." He shrugged. "I myself was nearing forty when I married, Miss O'Shaughnessy, and I've seen little enough of my wife since. But Margaret is a patient and very understanding woman. She waits for me, if I cannot take her with me, and does not complain. She was a soldier's daughter and knew what she might expect, if she married a soldier. Yet all the same, it takes a special kind of love and a great deal of courage for any woman to endure being married to a soldier . . . in India, particularly." He talked on about his wife, with so much admiration and affection that Emmy warmed still more towards him.

"Do you ever regret your choice of a career?" she asked him diffidently, when he was silent.

Colonel Beatson frowned. "No," he answered, after a momentary hesitation, "in all honesty, I must confess that I do not. It is the ideal life for a man who enjoys travel and yearns for adventure, and I have known no other since I was a boy of sixteen. It is a selfish life, perhaps. But fighting is my trade and I am content to practice it."

"And you love India, do you not, Colonel?"

A gleam lit his keen blue eyes. "You are a young woman of remarkable perception, Miss O'Shaughnessy . . . yes, I do. But I will admit that there are certain disadvantages in being a professional soldier—some of which I have learned, for the first time, since coming here for the purpose of offering my sword to my own countrymen. The French, you see"—his gesture took in the officers crowded about them and the spry figure of General Canrobert, moving among his guests—"the French are professional soldiers. But the British are not, they are amateurs."

"But . . ." Emmy stared at him in, astonishment. "I do not understand, Colonel."

"Ah!" The colonel's expression relaxed. "This is rank heresy to you, I fear. But it is true! That is to say, the British army is officered by amateurs, with very few exceptions. Its men, its rank and file, are the finest and best disciplined troops in the world . . ." he started to explain to her and then broke off, flashing her an apologetic smile. "I am boring you, my dear, for which I must humbly apologize. You cannot be expected to understand and, in any case would, I am sure, much prefer the company of some of these good-looking young aides to that of an old man like myself. I have no possible right to monopolize you any longer." He brushed aside Emmy's protests. "*They* will not forgive me, even if you are willing. But, before I let you go, there is just one question I want to ask you and I trust you will pardon its seeming impertinence. Tell me . . ." for a third time, his gaze went to Charlotte who, her lovely face flushed, was still holding court at the other end of the marquee . . . "was Alex Sheridan betrothed to your stepsister at one time?"

The question was unexpected and, for a moment, Emmy felt more than a little put out by it. But she answered it truthfully. "Yes, Colonel Beatson, he was. Their engagement was broken when Alex was compelled to sell his commission in the 11th Hussars. Lord Cardigan . . . that is to say, he—"

"Alex has told me what happened between Lord Cardigan and himself," Colonel Beatson interrupted gently. "I take it that your stepsister subsequently married someone else?"

"She married Lord Cassell," Emmy said. "Arthur Cassell, who is also in the 11th. But he is at present serving on the staff of the quartermaster-general, Lord de Ros."

"Then he is here, in Varna?" the colonel suggested.

"No." Emmy felt herself redden beneath his searching gaze. "He is somewhere in the country, with Captain Nolan, buying horses for the army. I . . . we are not sure when he will be returning to Varna." She felt impelled to defend Charlotte against his unvoiced criticism and added quickly, "Charlotte is naturally very worried, for he does not yet know that she has come here to join him. And we have no means of letting him know."

"I see. In that case . . ." Colonel Beatson did not complete his sentence. There was a stir at the entrance of the marquee. An aide-de-camp went hurrying across, there was a brief conference and then he returned, evidently searching for someone. Catching sight of Colonel Beatson, the young officer thrust a way through the crowd to his side. Bowing, he murmured something unintelligible in heavily accented English and the colonel thanked him and rose to his feet.

"Forgive me, Miss O'Shaughnessy," he apologized, "if I leave you, but Alex Sheridan has this moment arrived and is asking for me urgently. It seems he has news to impart to me which cannot wait—even for long enough for him to remove the stains of travel from his person, so as to present himself at this reception. But permit me to introduce Lieutenant de Colbert"—he drew the young aide-de-camp forward—"who will, I know, be most honored to wait on you. And I shall bring Alex with me tomorrow, if I may, when I call upon you and Lady Cassell, at your house in the Street of the Silversmiths. Good night, Miss O'Shaughnessy. It has been a great pleasure to make your acquaintance."

Emmy thanked him and bade him good night, at pains to conceal her disappointment. She watched his departure with chagrin, wishing that she might have accompanied him, if only in order to catch a glimpse of Alex. The young Lieutenant de Colbert, eager to serve her, insisted on fetching her more wine, assuring her that he would return to her side immediately if she would remain where she was.

She did so and, as she sat waiting for him to come back, observed a tall officer, in a dust-stained uniform, appear briefly in the open flap of the marquee's entrance. He looked white with fatigue, a grave-faced, unsmiling stranger, and yet there was something familiar about him, something about the stiffly upright set of his tall body and the way he moved which told Emmy instantly that he was Alex Sheridan.

Something else told her too, beyond all shadow of doubt. For he was looking across the length of the marquee at Charlotte and there was recognition in his eyes and a kind of pain as his gaze rested on her beautiful, flushed face. Charlotte, suddenly sensing that curiously intent regard, looked up to meet it but her eyes passed over him without acknowledgement and she turned back, smiling, to the French officers grouped about her, apparently without being aware of the identity of the new arrival.

Alex spun round on his heel and, a moment later, was gone.

Colonel Beatson re-entered the marquee a few minutes afterwards. A colonel of Zouaves led him to General Canrobert, to whom he spoke earnestly and then, as Emmy saw Lieutenant de

Colbert struggling through the press towards her, all three officers unobtrusively left the tent.

There was a good deal of coming and going after that but
General Canrobert was soon back, once more, with his guests,
and it was not until nearly an hour later that Emmy heard a hint
of the momentous news which Alex had brought. Mrs Duberly,
coming to warn her that it was time they took their leave, whispered excitedly that she had heard rumors of a great Turkish
victory at Guirgevo.

"It may be only a rumour but everybody is talking of it," she
said. "And if it is true the war may well be over, without our having fired a shot! Colonel Thibault, of the Chasseurs de Vincennes,
insists that Prince Gortchakoff's army is in retreat to Bucharest
and that only a few stragglers are left in the Dobruja . . . and
Henry thinks it's more than probable." She sighed. "I wonder
where they will send us now? To Sebastopol, perhaps, or even
Odessa. There is talk of Vienna, too. I shall be content . . . so
long as they do not send us home. That will be *too* inglorious!"

Emmy was silent during the slow, uncomfortable drive back
to the Street of the Silversmiths, while Charlotte and Fanny
Duberly indulged in eager speculation and conjecture as to the
future conduct of the war. Alex, she thought, would tell them
what was happening or likely to happen, when he called with
Colonel Beatson next day. He had brought the news of the Turkish victory and would, therefore, be in a position to separate fact
from rumor.

She did not mention his arrival in Varna to Charlotte, salving
her conscience with the thought that he would announce this in
person very soon. In any event, Charlotte did not ask . . . she was
too full of her conquest of a handsome French captain of Chasseurs to wish to speak of anything else.

Emmy was glad, next day, that she had said nothing, for neither Alex nor Colonel Beatson made their expected appearance. A messenger came, however, from the colonel—a Greek youth, leading two sturdy little half-bred Arab horses which, he explained in excellent English, the colonel hoped they would find useful. His own services, the messenger explained, were to be theirs also, if they wished, as groom and general factotum, for as long as they remained in Varna. And Colonel Beatson had thoughtfully arranged stabling and a supply of fodder for the two animals, so that their acceptance of his offer need involve them in neither trouble nor expense. Emmy was overjoyed and even Charlotte expressed unbounded pleasure at this generous gift. Free at last of the hateful confines of their dark little house, the two girls set off on horseback to call on Captain and Mrs Duberly at Devna.

They were there, with Fanny Duberly, when Lord Cardigan's patrol returned to the Light Brigade lines. In stunned dismay, they watched as men on foot, dropping with exhaustion, led in their stumbling horses, followed by an *araba,* drawn by bullocks, filled with others who had collapsed on the march and could no longer either walk or ride.

All day, in groups, sometimes in twos and threes, carrying their saddlery on their backs, the men straggled into camp. They had marched through the night and, during the seventeen days of their patrol, had eaten nothing but salt pork. Seventy-five of their best horses were either dead or dying; all had saddle-sores, few but were lame, and the men themselves were little better off, although not a single casualty had been inflicted on them by the enemy. Lord Cardigan led them in; he spoke to no one and, without offering either explanation or apology, sought the privacy of his own tent immediately.

It was just before sunset that Phillip limped in, with half a dozen troopers of the 11th, all of them leading their chargers, some of which had to be goaded into completing the last few yards of their disastrous journey. He recognized his sisters but was too tired to do more than smile at them wanly before staggering to his tent, as his commander had done, in silence.

Wisely, they made no attempt to follow him and as they rode back to Varna, even Charlotte could find nothing to say.

CHAPTER FOUR
➤➤➤ • ≼≼≼

"HIS LORDSHIP is at liberty to see you now, Captain Sheridan," Lord Raglan's aide-de-camp said politely. "If you will be so good as to come this way."

He was a pleasant young man, a nephew of the British commander-in-chief, and had done his best to while away the tedium of waiting by an entertaining flow of anecdotes and gossip. In spite of this, Alex could not help contrasting his reception here with that accorded him the previous evening, when he had sought out William Beatson at General Canrobert's *soirée*. On hearing the news he had brought, the general had conducted him in person to Marshal St Arnaud, before returning to his guests and his interrupted *soirée*. The French commander-in-chief, roused from sleep and suffering from a chill, had nonetheless sent for Colonel Trochu, his principal aide, and had kept them both with him for over two hours, poring over maps and discussing every detail of the Turkish capture of Guirgevo and its probable consequences. . . . Alex sighed. Lord Raglan, on the other hand, having summoned him at nine o'clock, had let him cool his heels until midday, whilst a procession of staff officers came and went . . . presumably on business considered of greater importance than his own.

He followed the A.D.C., his mouth compressed but his expression carefully blank. "Captain Sheridan, my lord," the aide announced, "of the East India Company's service." Alex saluted and stepped past him, with a brief word of thanks.

Lord Raglan was seated at a desk piled high with papers. He had aged a great deal since the last time Alex had seen him and he looked pale and careworn, as if the responsibilities of command sat heavily on his shoulders and the hours of work demanded of him were a constant drain on his reserves of strength. But his smile had all its old warmth and charm and his tone was as courteous as ever when he invited his caller to sit down.

"I apologize for keeping you waiting, Captain Sheridan," he said. "I had some urgent despatches to deal with, before I could be free to give you my undivided attention." He turned to the waiting A.D.C. "When Brigadier-General Scarlett comes, you may show him in immediately. Otherwise do not disturb us, if you please, Nigel."

"Very good, my lord." The young man withdrew and Lord Raglan pushed back his chair, again smiling in Alex's direction. "We have met before, have we not, Captain Sheridan?"

Alex returned his gaze steadily. "On the termination of my service with the 11th Hussars, your lordship had occasion to summon me to wait you at the Horse Guards."

"Yes . . . I recall the occasion. You are now, I understand—like your immediate superior, Colonel Beatson—an officer of the East India Company's cavalry, attached as a volunteer to the Turkish army?" When Alex nodded, he asked with interest, "What rank do you hold under the Ottoman command?"

"That of *Kaimakan,* your lordship, with the title of Demir Bey. I have recently been promoted, on General Cannon's recommendation."

"Ah yes . . . that is the equivalent of lieutenant-colonel, is it not? You have done well in the Turkish service, Captain Sheridan. Colonel Beatson speaks highly of your conduct during the recent siege of Silistria and has asked me if there might not be a possibility of an attachment for you under my command. Let us hope that something can be arranged." He spoke non-committally, Alex thought, but at least had not rejected his request and, realizing this, his flagging spirits rose and he murmured his thanks. Lord Raglan shrugged his thin shoulders, as if to dismiss the subject and was questioning Alex about his service with the Turkish army when an aide announced General Scarlett.

The Heavy Brigade commander was a stout, red-faced man in his middle fifties, whose bushy white brows and straggling moustache gave him a curiously unmilitary air, which was enhanced by the fact that his uniform was ill-fitting and devoid of decorations. He acknowledged Alex's introduction with a hearty, "Good day to you, Captain Sheridan," and then seated himself in response to Lord Raglan's invitation and added expectantly, "I understand you've brought us a report of a Turkish success at Guirgevo?"

"Yes, sir." Alex commenced his report and both generals heard him without interruption. Lord Raglan did not refer to his maps, but listened attentively, nodding his approval when Alex mentioned the decisive part the two British gunboats had played, with their volunteer crews. He offered no comment until the report was almost concluded. Then he said, with a hint of disparagement in his quiet, cultured voice, "It is as I suspected . . . the Turkish High Command is not anxious to do battle and only does so when spurred on by the example of a few valiant English offi-cers. Yet, when battle is joined, the French retreat—even when numerically superior."

"The *French,* my lord?" Alex echoed, puzzled, and met General Scarlett's warning glance. "

"Lord Raglan is referring to the Russians, of course, Captain Sheridan. That was a slip of the tongue."

The British commander-in-chief forced a weary smile. "It is a slip I am prone to make rather too frequently," he confessed. "But it is not easy, when one is a veteran of the Peninsular War, to accustom oneself to the fact that the French are now our allies. However, pray continue, Captain Sheridan. You said, I think, that General Cannon's attack was launched on the seventh of July, with only a few hundred men?"

Alex inclined his head. "With three hundred, I was informed, my lord, under the command of General Cannon and Captain Bent. They made a landing on the small island of Mokan, which is nine hundred yards from the fortress of Rustchuk, on the south bank of the Danube. It is separated from Guirgevo by a narrow channel, of considerable depth at its centre but fordable on either side. A second small force, under Colonel Ogilvy and five other British officers, made the crossing in rowing boats further down-stream, intending to wade through the ford on their right flank. They were driven back and had to fight their way across the island to join up with General Cannon. I did not reach Rustchuk until twenty-four hours after the attack had been launched, by which time some five thousand reinforcements had been landed on the island . . . all of them Turkish volunteers, my lord, who fought with great courage. They had established a bridgehead but were under heavy attack by elements of Prince Gortchakoff's army, from the Wallacian side of the river and suffered severe casualties. . . ."

Young Burke, of the Royal Engineers, Meynell of the 75th and Arnold of his own service had all been killed that day, Alex recalled, with a tightening of the throat.

Prince Gortchakoff's unexpected arrival had come as a bitter blow to them. The prince, hearing of the impudent attack on Guirgevo, which he had imagined safely in Russian hands, had made a forced march with sixty thousand men to come to its defense. Cannon's hard-pressed volunteers had been cut off on their narrow, two-mile-long island, under a withering fire which made it impossible for further reinforcements to reach them in daylight. And none would have been sent when darkness fell, had it not been for the providential arrival of the gunboats, with their bridging equipment, for Hussein Pasha had refused to commit any more men to the hazardous crossing in small boats. . . .

"Well, Captain Sheridan?" Lord Raglan prompted. "What action did you take when you reached Rustchuk? You have told us nothing of that but presumably you rode on, ahead of the gunboats?"

"Yes, my lord. My orders from Colonel Beatson were to acquaint General Cannon with news of the arrival of the gunboats, as soon as I had intercepted them and directed them to his support. It had been our hope that I might deliver this news to him before he launched his attack but, as I told your lordship, I was twenty-four hours too late." Alex spoke with controlled calm but his voice held regret. He had ridden hard, with Arif and the Bashi-Bazouks; they had neither eaten nor slept and had paused only when it became essential to rest their exhausted horses, but they had been too late.

His mouth tightened, as he remembered the carnage on the tiny island, the dead and dying, the piteous cries of the wounded and he went on, keeping a tight rein on his emotions, "I found

General Cannon in Rustchuk, my lord. He had returned there, at great risk, to plead with Hussein Pasha to send him reinforcements. We went together to the Turkish commander and informed him of the presence of the gunboats, and General Cannon urged him to prepare to cross with his main body as soon as a pontoon bridge could be constructed. To his credit, my lord, Hussein Pasha showed no reluctance but promised to be ready whenever the bridge was prepared. He kept his word and he had men waiting to assist with the bridge-building, when Captain Page, of the Royal Engineers, landed with his detachment and their equipment. They worked through the night and had the bridge in place by dawn. The two gunboats then engaged the enemy with great effect, placing themselves in the deep channel immediately to General Cannon's front and providing covering fire, which afforded his force on the island an opportunity to re-form."

"It was a well executed manœuvre," Lord Raglan approved. "I must inform Admiral Dundas officially of the success of his enterprise. Can you tell me the names of the officers responsible?"

"Yes, my lord. They were Lieutenant Glyn of H.M.S. *Britannia* and Lieutenant Prince Leningen—a young German officer, attached to the Royal Navy and presently serving in the *Britannia*."

The British commander-in-chief noted these names. He asked a number of other questions regarding the manner and direction of the Russian withdrawal, which Alex answered briefly. He added, "As soon as the main body of the Turkish army began their advance across the bridge, my lord, the Russians withdrew, leaving a screen of Cossacks to cover their retreat. There were none left, save wounded, when Hussein Pasha's advance troops entered Guirgevo. They told us that Prince Gortchakoff and General Bubatoff had both been wounded and that the prince was carried out on a litter."

Lord Raglan and General Scarlett exchanged significant glances.

"It would seem to me, my lord," the Heavy Brigade commander observed, "that great credit must go to all concerned in this highly successful affair. Not least"—he gestured to Alex, his eyes twinkling good humoredly from behind the bushy white screen of his brows—"to this young officer, who has borne himself well and given us an admirably clear picture of everything that took place."

"Indeed yes, General," Lord Raglan agreed. "It remains to be seen, of course, whether Lord Cardigan is able, as the result of his reconnaissance, to confirm that the enemy has withdrawn all his forces from the Bulgarian side of the Danube. However, your report, Captain Sheridan, gives us reason for optimism, I think. You will please accept my thanks for having, as General Scarlett says, given it with such clarity. And my congratulations on your praiseworthy devotion to duty and personal courage."

It was his dismissal and Alex rose. He saluted and was about to take his leave when General Scarlett called to him to wait. He turned obediently and the general laid a hand on his arm. "Attend me outside, if you please, Captain Sheridan. I will be with you in ten minutes."

"Very good, sir."

It was a little over ten minutes later when he emerged from Lord Raglan's headquarters, his rubicund face wearing a pensive expression. A trooper of the Scots Greys waited with his horse; the general swung himself heavily into his saddle and signed to Alex to join him. "Ride back with me to my tent, Sheridan," he invited, "and we'll take a glass of wine together. I should like to talk to you."

Alex, who was mounted on a Bashi-Bazouk horse, since his own was suffering from the after-effects of his hurried journey from Rustchuk, saw the Greys trooper grin as he reined in beside Scarlett's seventeen-hand weight-carrier, and he grinned back, aware of the odd contrast they made. The general eyed his horse with unconcealed disfavour and said gruffly, "You've been serving with Colonel Beatson's cut-throat Bashi-Bazouks, I understand. How did you find them?"

"My experience of them has been limited, sir," Alex qualified. "But I have found those under Colonel Beatson's command undeserving of the bad reputation they have acquired in British eyes."

"Really? But Beatson is an exceptional man," General Scarlett stated, with conviction, "particularly where the handling of Oriental troops is concerned. If anyone can discipline the Bashi-Bazouks, it is he. All the same, I do not believe they can be disciplined. You know he's made an offer of a brigade of them to Lord Raglan, I imagine?"

"Yes, sir." Alex hesitated. This big, unsoldierly man inspired confidence; he would tell the truth, without fear or favour and was evidently well disposed towards William Beatson, judging by his last words. "Is his lordship going to accept the offer, sir?" he asked.

Scarlett shook his head emphatically. "No, Sheridan, he is not. You can take my word for that . . . and tell Beatson so, if you feel inclined, just in case he's still cherishing any illusions. Lord Lucan is violently opposed to the suggestion and Lord Cardigan is likely to be even more so, when he returns. Even if the commander-in-chief were willing to listen to it—which, between ourselves, Sheridan, he is not—he would be bound to be influenced by the opinion of his two senior cavalry commanders."

It was as Phillip had prophesied, Alex thought—and as William Beatson himself had half expected. He would be disappointed, no doubt, although hardly surprised. "I will tell Colonel Beatson, sir," he promised. "But I do not imagine that he cherishes any illusions."

"What will he do," Scarlett asked bluntly, "when his offer is officially turned down . . . continue in the Turkish service?"

"I think not from choice, sir," Alex said.

"You mean he would like to find employment with us?"

"Yes, sir. Colonel Beatson is hoping that his services—with or without the Bashi-Bazouk levies—may be considered of sufficient value to the British command to ensure his being given a staff appointment of some kind."

"Ah! That's very interesting, Sheridan." General Scarlett turned in his saddle to eye Alex keenly. "Do you happen to know whether or not he's been offered such an appointment?"

Alex was compelled to deny it. "As far as I am aware he has not . . . but I've scarcely had more than a few minutes' private conversation with him since my arrival here, sir. I know only that he has approached Lord Lucan—"

"Lucan!" the general exploded, his face redder than ever. "Good God . . ." but he controlled himself and went on, more mildly, "Lord Raglan told me just now that *you* were looking for employment also, Captain."

"That was my intention, sir. But . . ." Wondering how much Lord Raglan had told the Heavy Brigade commander concerning his previous record in the British army, Alex again hesitated. He was tempted to ask straight out if there were any chance of a vacancy on Scarlett's own staff but, after a moment's thought, he decided against it. If the general had any desire for his services, he would ask for them; to volunteer them prematurely might, in view of his record, place them both in an embarrassing position, with Scarlett being forced to refuse his request.

And, besides, there was Charlotte. A knife twisted agonizingly in Alex's heart as he conjured up a vision of her, as she had been the previous evening, when he had glimpsed her at General Canrobert's reception. She had not changed, he thought—she was still as beautiful as he had remembered her, still as gay and charming and desirable . . . and still tantalizingly beyond his reach. Now more than ever, since she was Arthur Cassell's wife. . . . He felt the blood in his veins take fire, as he sought vainly to drive Charlotte's image from his mind. But the image would not be banished; it was imprinted on his memory, a torment from which, if he remained in Varna, there could be no escape.

Would he not be wiser, he asked himself, to return after all to the Turkish service? To ride within the next day or two to Omar Pasha in Shumla, where his new rank would entitle him to a cavalry command? Or, better still, to rejoin General Cannon, who had assured him, on the blood-soaked sands of Mokan Island, that there would always be a place for him among his officers? If he stayed here, if he succeeded in finding employment under the British command, Charlotte would be there to haunt his dreams and rouse once again his old longings—even if he exercised iron control and refrained from seeing her, even if he deliberately avoided a meeting and failed to seek her out. She . . .

"I imagine," General Scarlett said, breaking into his troubled thoughts, "that in view of Prince Gortchakoff's retreat, we shall not be kept rotting here in Varna for very much longer. There have always been rumors that we'll be sent to take Sebastopol, and others that our eventual destination will be Odessa. With the present uncertainty as to the role Austria is to play, it may even be Vienna. But my own belief is that they'll ship the whole force, with the French, to the Crimea within the next few weeks." He frowned. "We've no means of knowing what troops the Russians have in the Crimea . . . although Lord Raglan may have some information. What is your view, Sheridan?"

Alex considered. "The same as yours, sir . . . that Sebastopol will be our final objective. Turkish opinion is that its capture will be the only effective means of deciding the war and bringing Russia to reason. I think it may well be correct." If it were, then the problem of Charlotte's presence would no longer arise, he realized, conscious of relief. She and Emmy might have contrived to smuggle themselves to Varna but it was unlikely that either would be permitted to follow the army if it were sent to invade the Crimea and take Sebastopol. Phillip would forbid it, even if Lord Raglan did not. In which case . . . he drew a quick, uneven breath. Could he not call on them, after all, at their house in the Street of the Silversmiths? Emmy would be hurt, if he did not, Phillip offended by his seeming discourtesy, and to see and speak to Charlotte, just once more, would be a bitter-sweet pleasure which surely, after so long, he might permit himself without courting disaster or straining his self-control beyond its limit?

General Scarlett continued to talk about the likelihood of a landing somewhere in Crim-Tartary until they reached his tent, which was pleasantly situated on a rising spur of ground, over-looking the narrow river which joined the two Devna lakes. His groom took their horses and he led the way inside, pouring wine with a lavish hand and hospitably urging his guest to take the only available chair.

He lived austerely, Alex observed, with few of the comforts with which others of his rank surrounded themselves. A truckle bed, a table and a single chair comprised the tent's furnishings and trunks and portmanteaux were neatly stacked at one end. But he kept a good wine and an ample supply of excellent cigars and the meal which was served to them, if simple, was appetizing.

Over luncheon, Scarlett confined himself to general topics but when they had finished and his servant brought in a tray of Turkish coffee and passed round the cigars, he started to question Alex about his service in the 11th Hussars.

"I understand, from Lord Raglan, that you sold out in order to avoid a court martial, Captain Sheridan? That's so, is it not?"

"Yes, General Scarlett, it is, although"—Alex could feel every muscle in his body stiffening into rigidity. He had dreaded the question, even though it was not unexpected, and he was aware that it might be fatal to reply to it completely truthfully. He said cautiously—"I was not anxious to avoid a trial by court martial. Rather I would have welcomed it, if I am to be honest, sir. But I was ordered to sell out . . . by Lord Raglan, as he may have told you."

The general took him up swiftly. "If you're to be honest . . . I urge you to be, my young friend." He gestured to the barely furnished tent. "We are alone, that is why I invited you here . . . and you may rely on my discretion. I shall not divulge anything you tell me but I should like to hear your side of the affair, frankly and without prejudice. I have my reasons for wishing to know. When you hear them, I hope you will consider that they justify my curiosity concerning you."

Alex set down his coffee cup. "I will gladly tell you anything you want to know, sir, as frankly as I can."

"Thank you." General Scarlett leaned back, inhaling the smoke from his cigar. He had unbuttoned his frock coat, revealing the homely flannel shirt he wore beneath it and he looked, just then, more like a country squire, relaxing after his Sunday dinner, than a general in the aristocratic British army. He asked, his tone gruff, "Lord Cardigan was your commanding officer in the 11th, was he not? For how long did you serve under him?"

"For eight years, sir. Including one year in India, when his lordship assumed command of the regiment."

"And it was he who applied for your court martial on charges of insubordination? Were you guilty of insubordination to his lordship?"

Alex nodded grimly. "Had I been tried, sir, I should have been found guilty, and cashiered. But—"

"Yet you say you would have *welcomed* the trial by court martial?" The general's heavy white brows rose in perplexity. "You surprise me, Sheridan, indeed you do. Although—" He sat up suddenly, thumping one large hand into the palm of the other and a gleam of comprehension lit his eyes. "Good Gad, I remember now! You were the one who called Cardigan out . . . there was a couplet about you, published in the *Globe*. As I recall it, the poet's sentiments were as deplorable as his muse."

"The couplet was a gross exaggeration, sir," Alex asserted. "I fired no shot."

"But you were prepared to, if I remember rightly . . . as well as to stand your trial." General Scarlett smiled faintly. "You were either an exceptionally foolhardy young man or you had great faith in the justice of your cause. Which was it, Captain?" Before Alex could reply, he shook his head. "No, don't tell me. Having met you and having listened to the report you made to Lord Raglan, I'm prepared to decide which for myself. And to back my own judgement by offering you an appointment on my staff."

"Thank you, sir." Alex's relief and pleasure were such that his voice shook. "I am most grateful."

"I intend to make a similar offer to your friend Colonel Beatson. You and he are the type of officers I need to advise me. I've had no experience of fighting, Sheridan. I have never taken part in a battle and my knowledge of cavalry tactics is limited to field days and reviews, in peacetime conditions." The general sighed. "My present staff are in a similar state . . . willing and, I am sure, able young men, but not of the slightest use to me when it comes to mounting an attack. As a brigade commander, I shall have the responsibility for men's lives . . . and their deaths on my conscience if, through inexperience, I employ faulty tactics. One cannot take such a responsibility lightly, Sheridan . . . or I cannot." He held out his hand. "I shall, of course, have to confirm your appointment, subject to Lord Raglan's approval. I do not imagine that he will raise any objections to it, since it was he who invited me to be present when he received your recent report on the action at Guirgevo."

Alex could scarcely believe the evidence of his own ears.

"*Lord Raglan* invited you to be present, sir?"

"Indeed he did. His lordship, as you may know, does not like to force his opinion on his subordinates. But he has heard me bewailing the fact that I've no one on my staff with battle experience and he hinted that I might find you useful . . . as I'm sure I shall. Evidently he had not forgotten you, Sheridan."

"No, sir, I . . . evidently not. I am deeply beholden to him." Had Lord Raglan's memory also gone back to that strangely contradictory interview at the Horse Guards, of which his own recollections were so fraught with bitterness, Alex wondered. Was this his way of making amends for what, against his personal inclination, he had been compelled to do? It seemed that it must be . . . he took his new commanding officer's hand and shook it warmly. "I shall do my utmost to justify your confidence in me, General Scarlett. But . . ." He hesitated. "There is just one thing, sir, that I ought to mention."

"And that is, Captain Sheridan?"

"Sir, it is possible that Lord Cardigan may raise objections to my being appointed to your staff. In view of which, sir—"

"*I* am in command of the Heavy Brigade," General Scarlett stated, with emphasis. "Lord Cardigan has his own command, with both of us subordinate to Lord Lucan, as divisional commander. I can assure you, Captain Sheridan, that the only objections to which I should pay the slightest heed are those of Lord Raglan. And he isn't likely to express any, as I've just told you. So . . ." he smiled. "You may beg, borrow or steal a cocked hat for yourself and report to me here tomorrow evening. And, whilst you're about it, steal one for Beatson too, if you can prevail upon him to join us. *Au revoir,* Sheridan."

Alex rode out of camp, his emotions somewhat mixed. The new appointment pleased him; he liked General Scarlett but . . . there was still the question of Charlotte and whether or not he should try to postpone their almost inevitable meeting, now that he was to remain in Varna.

He was cantering towards the Turkish camp, some four miles beyond the British tents, where both he and William Beatson were at present quartered, when he saw coming in his direction a straggling troop of Hussars on foot, leading their horses. He recognized them as men of the 8th and watched their limping progress in horrified disbelief, taking in the dusty, disorderly state of the men's uniforms and the fact that at least half the horses looked ready to drop in their tracks from exhaustion. He drew rein when he reached them, thinking to offer what assistance he could but the men shuffled past him like sleepwalkers and the officer at their head appeared oblivious to his surroundings. From the sergeant who, unlike the rest, had maintained some measure of alertness, Alex was able to ascertain that this was part of Lord Cardigan's patrol returning from reconnaissance, and that Phillip

Dunloy was safe, although some distance behind. The patrol had not been in action, the sergeant told him; its casualties were the result of the pace their commander had insisted upon and the distance they had covered.

Alex waited to hear no more. Putting his sturdy little Kurdish horse to a canter, he hurried on to the Turkish encampment. He found Colonel Beatson in his tent, seated cross-legged on the carpeted floor and drinking coffee with three Turkish officers.

"Join us, Alex," the colonel invited cordially, and introduced his companions, one of whom leaned forward to pour him a cup of the sweet black brew from its burnished copper container. The Turks stayed for about an hour, conversing in friendly fashion, and then took their leave. William Beatson rose and stretched his cramped limbs before crossing to his camp bed and flinging himself down on it wearily. "You look as if you have news, my friend," he said. "But before you tell me what it is, I have some to give you."

"I hope it is good news, sir."

"It is not, Alex. First—Lord de Ros has sent me an official intimation that Lord Raglan has refused my offer of a Bashi-Bazouk brigade. I was thanked very courteously but the refusal was quite uncompromising. So I am leaving tomorrow for Shumla, with the men I had gathered, and I shall hand them over to Omar Pasha. One of the three officers you met just now, Nasiri Bey, will take command of the whole force, including those in Shumla and he'll continue their training, with Arif as his lieutenant. Arif deserves promotion, don't you agree?"

"I do indeed, sir," Alex confirmed. He waited and the colonel went on, "Earlier today, whilst you were waiting on Lord Raglan, I received a summons from General Canrobert. And—this is confidential, Alex—he told me that nothing would satisfy Marshal St

Arnaud but a sally, in force into the Dobruja to harass the retreating Russians!" He shrugged expressively. "I have the greatest
respect for Canrobert but St Arnaud is a very different type,
an opportunist, who seeks easy military glory. He has learnt from
some source of his own that there are ten thousand Russian stragglers cut off, without support, south of the river—and he intends
to destroy them. For which purpose, he is about to mobilize thirty
thousand Zouaves and lead them on a forced march into that
plague-ridden swamp!"

Alex pursed his lips into a silent whistle of dismay. He knew
the low-lying, marshy plains of the Dobruja—called by the Russians the Dobrudscha—and was aware of the evil reputation it
possessed. "But surely, sir, the marshal hasn't decided on this plan?"

"He has—and nothing will dissuade him," Beatson returned,
frowning. "Although, at Canrobert's request, I did all in my power
to turn him from it. Turkish intelligence reports the Dobruja
empty of Russians and I told him this, but he simply said he had
no faith in Turkish intelligence. There is feverish activity in the
French camp now, as the Zouaves make ready, and my guess is
that they will be gone by tonight." He paused significantly. "Without consulting either Lord Raglan or Omar Pasha."

Alex stirred uneasily. "I trust that my report to him last night
did not inspire such madness? For madness it is, sir."

"No, I fancy he's been considering the idea for some time,
encouraged by Trochu. When you informed him that Gortchakoff's main army was withdrawing to Bucharest, he decided that
the moment had come for him to attack these mythical stragglers
with impunity. Perhaps it would be . . . if they existed. Turkish
intelligence apart—and I concede that it is sometimes wildly inac-
curate—Luders is too experienced a general to abandon ten
thousand of his troops. Or allow them to be cut off, when he's

had plenty of time to get them across the river." Colonel Beat-son shrugged. "He's had no one but Cardigan to harass him, since he retired from Silistria!"

"Lord Cardigan's patrol has just returned, sir," Alex said. "I met some of his men on my way here. His lordship appears to have knocked up a great many of his horses and the men are in little better shape. But he must surely have brought back much useful information, he's covered a lot of ground. A sergeant informed me that they reconnoitered the edge of the Dobruja. Do you suppose the marshal would listen to *his* report?"

"St Arnaud places reliance only on reports from his own patrols. And"—the colonel's tone was dry—"he has no very high opinion of Cardigan." He lay back on his cot, arms folded behind his head, and gave vent to a tired yawn. "I fear there's nothing to be done, Alex. But . . . on a happier note. I made the acquaintance of the Lady Charlotte Cassell and Miss Emma O'Shaughnessy at General Canrobert's *soirée* . . . two exception-ally charming young ladies, if I may say so." He avoided Alex's gaze, staring thoughtfully up at the roof of his tent. "I had made a promise to call on them this morning but, as I've told you, I had a more urgent call to make at the French camp. So I had to postpone the pleasure. However, I sent them two good little horses, as a gift—hearing that they had none and were, in con-sequence, confined to their quarters. I sent also a young Greek, by the name of Constantin Nitulas, who had been recommended to me as honest and reliable, to act as their dragoman. He deliv-ered this letter to me, a short while ago." William Beatson took the letter from his pocket. "Perhaps you would care to read it. They are pleased with the horses, evidently."

Alex read the letter. It had been penned by Emmy expressing her gratitude and Charlotte's very gracefully. The horses, she said, would be a joy—they were about to set off on them, to pay a visit to Mrs Duberly. And to have a servant who spoke English and was both pleasant and willing was, in Emmy's own words, "a luxury beyond belief." Alex smiled as he read the brief little note and returned it to its owner. "That was good of you, sir . . . and as Emmy O'Shaughnessy says, extremely generous also."

"A pleasure, my dear Alex. I was much taken with the little Miss Emmy and talked to her for a while last evening. She has wit and intelligence and rare spirit." The colonel's eyes were on him now and Alex returned the look, his expression carefully blank. "She has not her sister's striking beauty, perhaps, but nevertheless I found her enchanting. I imagine that you will be calling on them, now that you're here. . . ." It was as much a statement as a question. "When you do so, be so kind as to express my regret at my inability to pay my own promised call on them and explain the reason for my absence in Shumla."

"Yes, of course I will, sir," Alex agreed. He was uncomfortably aware of the older man's continued scrutiny. "I last saw Emmy when she was a child of fourteen. And Charlotte—"

"When you were engaged to be married to her?" William Beatson suggested. Alex inclined his head reluctantly.

"Yes, Colonel. On that occasion I was compelled to break my engagement to her and I have not seen her since."

A kindly hand was laid on his shoulder. "I can appreciate, now that I have met her, what your loss has been, Alex my friend . . . and how keenly you must have felt it."

"She has since married someone else, sir."

"So I understand. Her husband, as I learnt from Miss Emmy, is at present up-country buying horses with Edward Nolan, the date of his return here uncertain."

"Phillip Dunloy informed me of it," Alex managed. "He asked

me to look after them until he returned from his patrol. But presumably he's back now . . . I heard he was on his way."

"Which should lighten your task, Alex . . . and absolve you from sole responsibility for their care."

"Yes, sir, it should." Alex did not pretend to misunderstand him and reddened. Then, recalling the message he had been charged to deliver from General Scarlett, he broke the little silence that had fallen between them. "My news is better than yours, sir. I lunched today with General Scarlett who commands the Heavy Cavalry Brigade and he's offered me an appointment to his staff. He is anxious to make a similar offer to you as soon as you are free of your Turkish commitments and asked me particularly to tell you so. He has the highest opinion of you, sir, and told me that he had great need of an officer of your experience to serve him as adviser."

A look of almost ludicrous astonishment on William Beatson's face was succeeded, an instant later, by one of pleasure.

"Upon my word, Alex," he exclaimed, "I did not imagine that any of the British generals would go so far as to *offer* me employment! I went, cap in hand, to Lord Raglan, who turned me down as courteously but just as uncompromisingly as he turned down my Bashi-Bazouks. Lord Lucan's refusal was not even courteous. He is a strangely embittered man and I fear I struck him in an evil mood. He told me he had no division to command and therefore needed no more staff than he was burdened with at present and added that, if he did, he would not recruit them from the Indian army! This is indeed good news you have brought me." He rose. "I'm dining with Nasiri Bey but I shall pay a call on General Scarlett this evening."

"In order to accept his offer, sir?"

"My dear fellow, do you take me for a fool? Of course I'll accept it, with the deepest gratitude."

"I'm glad," Alex told him, with sincerity. He met the older man's shrewd and searching blue eyes without flinching. "And I, sir," he said, "shall call on Lady Cassell and Miss O'Shaughnessy this evening, in order to pay my respects and deliver your message."

CHAPTER FIVE

⇛ • ⇚

EMMY WAS ALONE in the small living-room of the house in the Street of the Silversmiths, endeavoring to effect some repairs to her riding habit, when Constantin, their newly acquired Greek dragoman, came in to announce a visitor.

She had been alone since the ride out to the Light Brigade Camp at Devna for Charlotte, complaining that this had fatigued her beyond bearing, had retired early to bed. She was only a passable horsewoman and did not enjoy riding, but it had been the sight of Lord Cardigan's returning patrol which, Emmy guessed, had been the real cause of her decision to retire so early. The sight had not been pleasant . . . the pitiful, jaded horses, limping and plagued by flies and the plodding, weary men in their dust-caked uniforms had brought tears to her own eyes, as she had watched them straggling in. Even now, she found it hard to forget them and Fanny Duberly's agonized cries, "Oh, those wretched, wretched horses!" lingered still in her memory, the echo of her own distress.

In consequence, the prospect of a caller was one to be welcomed and she jumped up eagerly. "Who is it, Constantin?" she asked, wondering whether to awaken Charlotte or to leave her—as she had petulantly demanded to be left—to seek forgetfulness in sleep. "Is it Colonel Beatson?"

The Greek boy shook his dark head. "No, Madame, it is not the colonel. Another officer, very tall . . . his friend, I think."

Alex . . . Emmy's heart leapt in joyful anticipation.

Alex had come at last, for surely it could be no one else? But . . . she caught her breath. If he had come, it was to see Charlotte.

"Show him in, if you please, Constantin. And then go and knock on Lady Cassell's door and tell her ladyship that we have a visitor." She hesitated, uncertain of how to word the message and then said, with finality, "One whom I am sure she will wish to receive."

"Certainly, Madame," Constantin promised. "At once. First I will show in the gentleman and then I will knock on the door of the Lady Charlotte's chamber and convey to her this message. Afterwards, I will bring wine."

Alex was announced with due ceremony. He looked, Emmy saw with relief, much less wan and tired than he had the previous evening, much more like his old self. Although, as Colonel Beatson had warned her, it was evident that he had changed a great deal. But he greeted her with affectionate warmth and without the smallest constraint, taking both her hands in his and retaining them in his clasp, as he stood looking down at her as if she were a vision from another world.

"Why, Emmy . . . this is unbelievable! You've grown up."

"What did you expect, Alex?" She smiled back at him. "I could not stay a child forever."

"No," he conceded. "But this was how I'd remembered you—as a high-spirited, precocious little girl, with her hair down her back and the strangest notions filling her head. As a little madcap, with more nerve on the bunting field than I ever had and . . . goodness, you had some impossible idea of studying medicine, had you not, and becoming the first lady physician in England?"

"I believe I had," Emmy admitted, her cheeks scarlet. He had remembered so much about her, she thought—but had he remembered that this same child, whose strange notions he was now recalling had once offered to marry him? That, because she had so deeply deplored her elder sister's refusal to wait for him, she had promised, quite solemnly, to wait for him herself, until he should send for her?

"And now," Alex observed, "you are a young lady. A very charming young lady if, as the privilege of an old friend, I may be permitted to say so, Emmy my dear."

She studied him critically, taking in the faded uniform, with its patched sabre cut and tarnished braid, the worn leather of his boots. "And you, Alex?" she asked. "Are you not a distinguished soldier, who has covered himself in glory both here and in India?"

His smile vanished. "No, I am just what I seem, child. A simple and most undistinguished soldier, for whom the word glory has now something of a hollow ring, I fear."

A lonely, even a solitary man, Colonel Beatson had told her, Emmy thought, with compassion. But the colonel had omitted to add that the intervening years had made Alex Sheridan steel-hard—a man's man, not a woman's, whose eyes held disillusionment, even when he smiled, and whose memories were bitter and engraved in harsh, revealing lines about his mouth and in the stern contours of his face. A man who had suffered and whose battles with a tangible, flesh and blood enemy had been no fiercer than those he had been compelled to wage, against himself and the devil of doubt which rode him. A man whose victory over these had cost him more than mere physical agony. . . .

There was an oddly tense little silence, as they stood looking into each other's eyes. Then Alex released her hands. "Is Charlotte at home?" he asked evenly. "I had hoped to see her also."

Emmy felt tears come welling up into her eyes. Of course, he had hoped to see Charlotte. That was why he had come . . . not to see her, whom he remembered only as a child. She bit back the tears and answered, lowering her gaze, "Charlotte was very tired. You see, we rode to Devna today on the horses your friend, Colonel Beatson, so kindly provided for us, and that wearied her. But I have sent Constantin to tell her that you are here."

"If she is sleeping," Alex put in quickly, "do not disturb her, Emmy, please. Not on my account."

"But you'd like to see her and she will want to see you—"

"Not if it means rousing her from sleep. That's the last thing I should want to do, when I can call again at a time which is more convenient." His smile returned and now, Emmy observed, it touched his eyes, melting their cynical coldness. "I shall be in Varna for as long as the British Expeditionary Force remains here, God willing. So there is no urgency about my call."

"Oh, Alex!" The implication of his words sank in and Emmy echoed his smile. "Does that mean that you have ended your service with the Turks? Are you to rejoin the British army?"

He shook his head. "No, not that. But the next best thing to it, let us say . . . I'm to be appointed to General Scarlett's staff, as one of his aides. Or I hope to be by this time tomorrow, subject to Lord Raglan's approval. And Colonel Beatson also—he's to act as Scarlett's military adviser, as soon as he is free of his obligations to Omar Pasha and can hand over his Bashi-Bazouk command. He goes to Shumla tomorrow, for that purpose."

"That is wonderful," Emmy said happily. "General Scarlett is an extremely good commander and all his officers and men are devoted to him. I am so pleased for you, Alex . . . and Charlotte will be overjoyed when you tell her of your appointment."

"I scarcely flatter myself that it will matter to Charlotte very much if I go or stay, Emmy." Alex's tone was harsh.

"But of course it will! Did you imagine that any of us—Charlotte or Phillip or I—had ceased to care about you because you went out of our lives?"

Alex expelled his breath in a deep sigh. "I feared you had, I . . . well, I should have had more faith perhaps. But when I heard of Charlotte's marriage to Arthur Cassell, it seemed to me the end of everything that had been between us."

"The end of friendship?" Emmy chided gently. She laid a hand on his arm. "Charlotte had to marry, Alex—she's the eldest of three daughters. Of four, if you include me. It was expected of her."

"Yes," he conceded. "I know. And I expected her to marry . . . it would be untrue to pretend that I did not, when I had made it plain that she was under no obligation to me." His momentary bitterness was gone. "Arthur Cassell is one of the best, as I recall. I hope they are happy together?"

"Oh, yes," Emmy assured him, with more conviction than she felt. "Arthur is devoted to Charlotte and most indulgent to her." To her relief, Constantin returned with a tray of coffee, which he set down at her side, and she broke off to thank him.

"There is no wine, Madame," Constantin told her, in a whisper. "So I am bringing coffee. And I am to say to you that her ladyship is now dressing and will be with you very soon."

Emmy smiled at him, thinking how indispensable he had already made himself. Even the sullen Bulgarian servants, who had hitherto been so difficult to manage, had responded to his charm and, with Constantin to act as interpreter, it was now quite simple to make them understand what was required of them. She told Alex this, as she poured coffee for him, apologizing for the lack of wine.

He offered quickly, "I'll get you wine, Emmy, and anything else you need. You have only to tell me what it is . . ."

"That is kind of you. But Phillip is back, I'm sure that he will attend to it . . . or Constantin will. It isn't that we are short of money, only that it has been difficult to buy what we required because our other servants do not speak English."

Alex accepted the coffee. "Have you seen Phillip yet?"

She nodded. "Briefly, that was all. He was quite exhausted after Lord Cardigan's patrol. I saw them coming back to camp. . . ." Emmy shivered. "Their state does not bear description."

"I also witnessed their return," Alex said, with grim emphasis. "It scarcely even bears thinking about. In any event, the subject of Lord Cardigan is one I prefer to avoid. Let's talk of something else."

"Of what? Charlotte is coming down, you know . . . she is dressing and says she will not be long."

"You should have let her rest. But since she is coming down, you had better bring me up to date with your family's affairs. Tell me about yours, to begin with." He looked down at her ringless left hand. "You have not married. Why . . . was it not expected of you?"

"No. That is, I did not choose to marry." The swift, betraying colour leapt unbidden to Emmy's cheeks. "The others are married, Alex. Lucy to Michael Ward of the 20th and Melanie to—"

"It was you about whom I asked, Emmy," Alex reminded her, with mock severity. "Why did you not choose to marry and what are you doing here?"

Her colour deepened. "I entered a convent . . . for almost three years I was a postulant to the Order of the Sisters of Mercy in Dublin. But I . . . on the advice of the Mother Superior, I did not take my final vows. She said that I had the wrong temperament."

"And I think that she was right, child." Alex's expression softened into tenderness as he looked into her small, shamed face. But he offered no other comment and Emmy, realizing that in the uncannily perceptive way he had always had, he understood both her motives and the sense of failure she still felt concerning this part of her life, went on to tell him about it. He listened gravely and asked, when she had done, "Is this why you have followed the army to war, Emmy—in the hope, perhaps, that you may exercise your medical skills by caring for the wounded?"

"That was my idea," Emmy confessed. "But I have since learned how foolish and impractical it was to imagine that I might be needed. It was one of my . . . strange notions, I am afraid." She added, with sudden bitterness, "I travelled with some of the army women below decks in a transport. It was from them I learned the truth. They laughed at me." She changed the subject abruptly and was giving him news of her mother when she sensed that his attention had strayed.

Charlotte had descended the uncarpeted wooden stairs almost without a sound but as if he were aware, even then, of her presence, Alex was on his feet a moment or so before the door opened to reveal it. And Charlotte had taken some pains with her appearance, Emmy saw. The short sleep she had enjoyed had rested and refreshed her, so that she looked lovelier than ever when she entered the lamp-lit room and glanced about it expectantly. For an instant, she regarded Alex in some bewilderment and then recognition dawned in her eyes and she went towards him with a cry of pleasure.

"Constantin said that an officer had called but never, in my wildest dreams, did I imagine it could be *you!* Oh, Alex, Alex . . . to see you again, after all these years. I can hardly believe it. You should have warned me, Emmy—you should have told me it was Alex. How could you be so cruel as not to tell me who it was?"

Emmy did not answer her reproachful question. It was doubtful if either of them would have heard her if she had attempted to, she thought miserably. Alex had neither eyes nor ears for anyone but Charlotte; he was like a man bemused as he bore the hand she gave him to his lips. And she, radiant with happiness, was gazing up into his face with shining eyes, as if he were the only man she wanted, or ever had wanted to see.

"You have not changed, Alex. You are a little older but otherwise you're just the same and yet it is . . . how long? Nearly eight years since you went away. But I'd have known you anywhere."

"As I would have known you, Charlotte," he asserted.

"But I am eight years older. . . ."

"My dear, you are more beautiful—if that's possible—than you used to be. Like a young girl. . . ." His voice was choked with emotion, grating harshly, as if the sight of her had hurt him deeply. But he did not move, simply stood there facing her as though turned to stone, a tall, stiff figure, deprived of the power of movement yet not, Emmy realized, of the power to feel. The pain he felt was in his eyes, in every tense muscle of his body, as well as in the stammered words, and she sensed that for him in that moment, it was well nigh unendurable.

She slipped silently from the room, leaving them together. Neither noticed her going for neither had been conscious of her presence since Charlotte had entered the room. If she had stayed, she told herself wretchedly, it would have made no difference. She could not assuage Alex's pain or warn Charlotte that his love for her was not to be trifled with, because it went too deep and had never changed. She could not tell her sister that it would be cruel to treat him, as she treated the young French officers or the Guardsman with whom she had flirted in Constantinople, as merely another conquest. Perhaps Charlotte was aware of this; she did not know. Perhaps Alex meant more to her than any of the others—more, even, than her husband had ever done—perhaps she was still in love with him.

In her helpless misery, Emmy could not have said which she hoped it would be; her own emotions were confused, her pity for Alex so intense that, when she reached the sanctuary of her own room, she flung herself on her bed and wept.

From the room below came the low hum of voices and the sound continued for a long time, Charlotte's higher pitched than his, Alex's deeper, more level and controlled. At times, Emmy imagined that she could hear sobs, as though Charlotte were weeping; at others, she laughed, and later her voice sounded angry, as if raised in argument, but the pitch of Alex's voice did not alter. She could not hear what passed between them, could only imagine what it was and pray, her eyes closed and her hands tightly clasped in front of her, that God, in His infinite mercy and wisdom, might guide and protect them and that, having led them to the right decision, He might grant them the strength and courage to adhere to it.

And then suddenly the voices ceased and there was silence. The street door creaked shut on its rusty hinges and, after a while,

Charlotte's light footsteps echoed faintly on the bare wood of the narrow staircase as she ascended to the upper floor. Emmy sat up, half hoping—yet half dreading—that her stepsister might come in, might want to talk, to tell her what had transpired or even ask for comfort or advice. But Charlotte did not come, did not even pause by her door. The footsteps went past and the door of Charlotte's own bedroom slammed. She did not call for Maria, as she usually did, to help her to undress. It was late, of course, past midnight, but Charlotte did not, as a rule, worry very much what hour it was, if she were in need of Maria's services.

Emmy rose from her bed, feeling achingly chilled now, and herself began to undress. Wrapped in her voluminous flannel night-gown and pulling the bedclothes up to her chin, she felt warmer and a trifle less worried but, in spite of this, it was dawn before, at last, she fell into an uneasy sleep.

Next morning Charlotte was wretchedly depressed. She complained of a *migraine* and made no mention of Alex and when Emmy, deeply concerned for them both, attempted to bring the conversation round to the subject of his visit, her diffident questions were met with a blank, uncomprehending stare. The suggestion of a ride to Devna, for the purpose of inquiring for Phillip, elicited no more encouraging response. After luncheon, which was eaten in glum and uncomfortable silence, Charlotte retired once more to her bed.

Phillip called towards evening but his call did little to restore Emmy's spirits, for he was weary and out of sorts, bitterly critical of Lord Cardigan's ill-managed patrol and the probable results of it. They had lost a great many horses which they could never replace, he told her, the morale of all who had taken part had suffered considerably and the patrol itself had achieved nothing of practical value—certainly insufficient to justify the loss of the horses, all of which had been brought with them from England.

"Cardigan is conferring with Lord Raglan now," he told his stepsister wryly. "After driving his staff nearly mad, writing out half a dozen different versions of his report. And, to cap it all, there is a rumor which appears to be well-founded, that he's to be given a brevet promotion to major-general!"

"But surely that can't be true, Phillip," Emmy objected.

"I've reason to believe that it is," Phillip asserted. He shrugged. "To add to our troubles, Lord Lucan has chosen this moment to order a field day for the whole Cavalry Division and we've less than forty-eight hours to prepare for it. So do not expect to see much of me until it's over, Emmy. I'm sorry but I shall have my work cut out getting even one troop mounted, in the circumstances."

He was so worried and upset that Emmy made only casual mention of the fact that Alex had paid them a visit—not having the heart to add to his anxieties by suggesting that this might lead to complications where Charlotte was concerned. But he seemed genuinely pleased when she told him of Alex's appointment to General Scarlett's staff and, when he took his leave, promised to make contact with his onetime friend as soon as he could.

Charlotte appeared for supper, pale and listless and without appetite. But she recovered a little when two of the French Chasseur officers, whom she had met at General Canrobert's reception, paid a brief call at the house, in order to deliver a welcome present of some game they had shot. They could not stay long, they explained regretfully. Marshall St Arnaud's sudden mobilization of the Zouaves and his departure for the Dobruja the previous night—of which the two girls learned, with some amazement, for the first time—had caused a considerable stir in the French camp and both officers were required to be on duty. When they had gone, Charlotte talked quite animatedly for a time of the news they had been given but, as the minutes ticked by and there were no other callers, she lost interest in talking to Emmy and went back to her own room.

The following day was almost a repetition, except that Phillip did not make an appearance and only one of the Chasseurs was able to obtain release from his military duties for an hour. He seemed anxious and distrait and eventually admitted, as he was about to return to camp, that a number of Marshall St Arnoud's Zouaves had had to be sent back to Varna by bullock cart, all of them suffering from a sickness which, it was feared, might be cholera.

Emmy heard this with dismay and her apprehension grew when, next morning, Mrs Duberly rode in and told her that cholera had been confirmed, quite definitely, among the Zouaves who had fallen out on the march into the Dobruja, and that a fresh batch of them had arrived in camp during the night.

"So far it has not hit *us,*" Fanny Duberly said, but she sighed. "I wish we could get away from here, don't you? The rumor that we were to go to Vienna has, of course, turned out to be false, but I hear that Sir George Brown is to go, within a day or so, by ship to the Crimea, for the purpose . . ." She paused, to let the full significance of her announcement sink in. "For the purpose of discovering the best place to land troops! If this is so, we can hardly doubt that we shall be following him before long, can we? And I confess that it will be a relief, for Varna is not the salubrious place we were led to hope it would be, by any stretch of the imagination."

Charlotte, who had listened in unresponsive silence to what Mrs Duberly had to tell them, asked with a note of bitter envy in her voice, "Why do you say that we shall be following Sir

George Brown? Have you permission to accompany your husband, if the army embarks for the Crimea then?"

"No, not as yet," Fanny Duberly replied. "But Lady Errol and I are both equally determined to accompany our husbands, wherever they are sent, Lady Cassell. For my part, even if I have to do as you and Miss O'Shaughnessy did and smuggle myself on board one of the transports with the soldiers' women, I intend to go with Henry. Although I am hopeful that it may not come to that." She smiled and added cheerfully, "If necessary, I shall seek Lord Cardigan's aid and protection and I believe he will give it, for he has already assured me that he has the greatest admiration for my pluck. He is a detestable man, of course, and like everybody else, I abhor him but, if I am compelled to, I shall invite his assistance . . . and keep on plaguing him until I get it!"

"You are indeed determined, Mrs Duberly," Charlotte said, eyeing her with barely concealed misgiving. But she allowed herself to be persuaded to accompany their visitor back to Devna, to Emmy's heartfelt relief, in order that they might all witness the field day and Lord Lucan's inspection of the Cavalry Division, due to take place there that afternoon.

They rode over in pleasant sunshine and the inspection, contrary to Phillip's gloomy foreboding, went off without mishap. The full division did not parade—part of the Heavy Brigade and the 4th Light Dragoons were quartered elsewhere—but nevertheless the cavalry gave a brilliant display, the men's uniforms blazing in the afternoon sun, the horses groomed to perfection, as squadron after squadron wheeled and circled with impeccable precision in obedience to the shouted commands.

Emmy thrilled to the sound of galloping hoofs and her heart beat faster when an imperious trumpet call brought the Light Brigade charging in extended line across the flat, open country, led by their brigadier. And Lord Cardigan, she was forced to concede, played his part with breathtaking skill. Whatever else he might be, he was a superb horseman, with a well-deserved reputation for spectacular daring. Mounted on his great chestnut, with sabre drawn and fur-trimmed pelisse flying behind him in the wind of his passing, he commanded admiration for the manner in which he rode and the unforgettably splendid figure he cut, as he headed the charge at breakneck speed, aiming straight as a die for his objective.

His brother-in-law, Lord Lucan, enjoyed less success when he assumed command of the assembled regiments towards the end of the afternoon's proceedings. He was, to begin with, a very much less impressive-looking man than Lord Cardigan and, by comparison, he was nowhere near as accomplished a rider. In addition—although, until Mrs Duberly whispered the information in her ear, Emma had not been aware of it—he had held no active command for seventeen years and in the interim, cavalry drill had been considerably altered and many of the words of command changed. Lord Lucan's orders were misunderstood; in an alarmingly short space of time, the well-ordered precision of regiment after regiment dissolved into something approaching chaos and the earl, red of face and furiously angry, made matters worse by losing his temper.

"He's clubbed the Green Horse!" Fanny Duberly exclaimed disgustedly. "And now he is blaming them for it . . . as if they could possibly help what happened, when his orders were so utterly confusing."

The review came to an abrupt and inglorious conclusion with the regimental commanders having to extricate their men from each other's ranks and the divisional commander, accompanied by his embarrassed staff, riding off in a towering rage, without waiting to take the salute.

Lord Cardigan watched him go, a smile of satisfaction which he did not try to hide, curving his lips as, in the absence of his superior officer, he dismissed the parade. It was then that Emmy noticed General Scarlett, who had taken no part in the review, save that of a spectator, wheel his horse round and canter over to the colonel of the 5th Dragoons, evidently to commiserate with him, for the way they had been treated. Alex, she saw, was with him together with three others of his staff. He recognized her, smiled and, a little later, came in search of her.

"Well," he said ruefully, when greetings had been exchanged, "I trust you will not have to witness a spectacle like that again! It was almost unbelievable, was it not?"

"It was a great pity," Emmy agreed, "because up till the moment when Lord Lucan took command, everything had been going so well."

"Indeed it had, child!" There was a gleam in Alex's eyes, of pride, mingled with nostalgia. "They are magnificent regiments . . . I had forgotten, until today, how truly magnificent they were. As you say . . . it was a pity." He looked about him. "Is not Charlotte with you?"

"She came with me," Emmy assured him. "We both rode over before lunch with Mrs Duberly and—"

"She is over there," Alex interrupted, "talking to Lord Cardigan." He was frowning, Emmy saw. Following the direction of his gaze, she observed that Charlotte was, indeed, talking to Lord Cardigan. She and Mrs Duberly were the centre of a group of officers, now dismissed from the parade, but it was to Charlotte that the brigade commander was giving his flattering and undivided attention, bending gallantly over her hand and smiling into her lovely face with every appearance of pleasure and admiration.

Mrs Duberly looked a trifle put out but recovered herself when her husband joined the little group and, after a while, Charlotte excused herself and rode across to where Emmy and Alex were waiting. Her greeting to Alex was cool and somewhat offhand and turning to Emmy, she said abruptly, "I suppose you are wanting to leave now?"

"Well . . . " Emmy hesitated. "We have a long ride and it will be dark before we reach the town, unless we make a start now. It is rather unwise for us to be out after dark, with so much drunkenness among the troops, I think."

Charlotte shrugged. "Lord Cardigan has invited me to take refreshments in his marquee with himself and his staff. As an added inducement, he has offered to send an escort to see me safely home afterwards. But I refused, on your account, Emmy. I was not sure whether you would manage to persuade Alex to give you his escort."

Faced with so direct and disconcerting a question, Emmy reddened unhappily, having not the least idea how to answer it. It had never occurred to her that Charlotte who was, as a rule, very careful to observe the proprieties, should even consider deserting her in such a situation. Alex, seeing her discomfiture, put in quickly, his voice low and devoid of expression, "It will, of course, be my pleasure to ride back with Emmy—or with you both, if you will permit me to do so, Charlotte. General Scarlett is dining here, with the officers of his old regiment, so he will not require me until later on. If you wish to change your mind and accept Lord Cardigan's offer of hospitality, I pray you to do so. Emmy, as you know, will be quite safe with me and I will gladly look after her. In fact, I would have suggested it, had I realized that the opportunity to escort her might arise."

For an instant, Charlotte appeared undecided, her eyes searching his face. She was smiling but, in spite of this, Emmy sensed that she was angry, as if for some reason she considered that Alex had offered her a slight.

"Well, I should like to see Phillip," she said at last. "I was feeling unwell and in my bed the last time he called, so that I have had no opportunity to talk to him since his return. I will stay, then . . . if you are sure that it is not too much trouble for you, Alex, to ride back with Emmy?"

"I am quite sure," Alex returned crisply. "As I told you, it will be my pleasure." He bowed politely and, when Charlotte bade him a distant good night, echoed it with one as cool. Then, urging his horse forward, he set off in the direction of Varna, with Emmy at his side.

The ride back in the fading sunlight and with a cool, refreshing breeze in their faces, was pleasant enough. Emmy would have enjoyed it—as she had always enjoyed a ride in Alex Sheridan's company in the old Dublin days—had she felt less concern for Charlotte and been less bewildered by her stepsister's attitude towards him, which she found impossible either to explain or to understand. She was tempted several times to question him about it, to ask him point-blank whether his avoidance of Charlotte was deliberate, but Alex's manner did not encourage questions. He talked quite freely about the review, about General Scarlett and his satisfaction with his appointment to the Heavy Brigade commander's staff and he even mentioned his new commander's strained relationship with Lord Lucan . . . but he did not utter Charlotte's name.

Since he did not, Emmy was unable to do so, yet she sensed, as he led her on to tell him of their life in the small house in the Street of the Silversmiths, that he wanted to talk of Charlotte. It was in Charlotte's daily doings that he was interested, not in hers, yet with stubborn obstinacy, he would not admit that he was and would not speak of her. Even when the possibility of the army's move to the Crimea cropped up in the course of their conversation, Alex asked only whether she intended to seek permission to accompany it and, when she told him that she was undecided, he advised her firmly against doing anything of the kind.

"Mrs Duberly is determined to go," Emmy said. "And Lady Errol also, I believe."

"They do not wish to be parted from their husbands," Alex suggested. "You have no such reason."

"No. But . . ." greatly daring, she turned in her saddle to face him, "Charlotte has and I want to stay with her, Alex."

"You would both be better off in Therapia," Alex returned shortly. "In any event, I think it extremely unlikely that permission will be granted for Lady Errol or Mrs Duberly. We do not know what forces the Russians have in Crim-Tartary and our landing there—if it takes place—may be met with strong resistance. You can have no conception of how terrible a sight a battlefield can be, Emmy. It is no place for a lady of gentle birth."

"I worked in the Hospital of the Sisters of Mercy in Dublin," Emmy reminded him. "For almost three years, Alex. I have seen death and disease before. I nursed some of the victims of the Irish famine."

His voice softened. "Yes," he conceded, "I know you did, child, and I am conscious of how much courage it must have taken for you to endure such an experience. Nevertheless the aftermath of a battle is worse than anything you could ever have seen or imagined . . . I know, I have witnessed many battles. I beg you to believe me when I tell you that, even with your brave spirit, you would be unable to bear the sight of the ghastly carnage that is wrought in battle. And you would be helpless, Emmy, for all your nursing skill. That is almost the worst part of it, I think—one is powerless to help the dying, to make their passing easier, to alleviate the agony of the wounded. The most one can do, even for one's dearest friend, is to offer him a sip of water. The surgeons are skilled and they do their best but . . . they lose more lives than they can save and often, in order to save a man's life, they must add to his suffering and inflict horrible mutilations on his body. An army hospital is a nightmare place, even for a man. For a woman it would be quite unendurable."

"I see." She knew that he was telling her the truth, minimizing rather than exaggerating the horrors at which he had hinted. "Have you been wounded, Alex?" she asked gently.

"Yes," he answered, "several times. But I have been fortunate, I have never suffered a severe wound. And I will make a confession to you, Emmy—a confession of cowardice, which I have never before made to a living soul. Each time that I ride into battle, each time I hear the sound of the trumpet sounding the charge, I am afraid. Not of death—that is a hazard all soldiers must accept—but of being wounded. And"—in the dim light, Emmy saw that his face was pale and his expression very grave— "I pray that, if it is to be my fate, I may die cleanly and quickly, with a sword-thrust through the heart."

"I can understand your feelings," she assured him, and added shyly, "If it will help, I . . . will add my prayers to yours."

"The same prayer?" Alex asked.

"Not quite the same prayer, perhaps. Mine would be that you should survive the battle unscathed."

"And live, to fight another day?" he quoted cynically. "I think I am tired of fighting, Emmy . . . weary of war, and of life sometimes. I told you that to me the word glory has a hollow sound now, did I not?"

"Because you are alone?" Emmy ventured. "Because you have no one but yourself to fight for . . . to live for?"

He shrugged. "No wife, you mean—no home and children? Ah, but in India, in the Company's service, one sees little of one's wife and less of one's home if one is a junior officer, Emmy. Besides I—" he broke off, frowning.

Emmy drew a deep breath. Summoning all her courage, she said, avoiding his gaze, "You are still in love with Charlotte, are you not?"

For an instant, resentment flared in his eyes. Then it faded and he answered, without attempting to prevaricate, "Emmy, I do not think I have ever loved anyone else. That has been the trouble. I compare every woman I meet with her—compare and find each one of them wanting. But now . . ." Again he was silent and Emmy, anxiously studying his face, could find in it no clue to his feelings.

The lights of Varna came into sight, flickering here and there in the gathering twilight. Alex kneed his horse on, as if, Emmy thought sadly, he were impatient to reach there, impatient to deliver her safely to her door and then, free of his responsibility on her account, to make his escape from her. They rode in silence, neither anxious to break it, yet neither at ease in its isolation.

At the door of the little house in the Street of the Silversmiths, Constantin was waiting. He ran to assist Emmy from her horse but Alex was before him, holding up his arms to her as, she recalled, he had been wont to do when she had been a child, mounted on a horse that was too big for her. She went into his arms, shyly, half fearful, yet half eager, and he held her for a moment, looking down into her eyes, the expression in his own strangely tender and questioning. "You are a sweet child, Emmy," he told her and then asked unexpectedly, "Do you ever regret not having become a nun?"

Surprised, she shook her head. "Oh, no, not any more. I had not the vocation for such a calling. The Mother Superior was right, I have realized that now, so I cannot regret it."

"Then you will marry, I suppose?"

"Marry?" She felt confused and flushed under his scrutiny. "I do not know, I suppose I may one day, I . . ." and then Constantin was beside them, taking the horses' reins, and Alex released her.

"May I come in for a few minutes?" he requested.

Emmy stared at him, puzzled and then remembered her manners. "Why, of course, if you would like to, I should enjoy it if you would. And we have some wine now, we—"

"I am not in need of your wine, Emmy my dear. It is just that I have something further to say to you."

"But you will drink a glass of wine while you are saying it," she insisted. Perhaps he wanted an excuse to enable him to wait until Charlotte returned, she thought, and added quickly, "If you would like a meal, I am sure that Constantin—"

Again he cut her short, his tone a trifle brusque. "No, I have not time to wait for a meal, thank you, Emmy. I must return to camp." He followed her into the living-room. The wine, with a tray of glasses, had been set in readiness by the attentive Constantin and, having invited Alex to take a seat, she poured a glass of it for him. But he remained standing, looking too tall for the tiny, low-ceilinged room and, for no reason that Emmy could have explained, out of place there as if, instead of being the old friend he was, he had suddenly become a stranger.

"Emmy," he said, and his voice, too, sounded like that of a stranger, "do you remember once, years ago, you promised to marry me?"

"Oh, but I . . ." Tears burned in Emmy's eyes, tears of shame and humiliation and she felt the distressing waves of colour rising to flood her cheeks at the memory of that foolish promise, made so long ago. But she had made it, she could not deny that now. "Yes, I remember only—"

"Only you were a child," he finished for her, "and neither of us took it seriously."

"No." Her smile was shaky and it was one of relief. "Of course not. I believe I told you that you were the only man I should ever want to marry, did I not?"

"You said something of the kind," Alex agreed. He came towards her, putting out a hand to take hers and holding it gently in his own. "You were sorry for me."

"Yes, I . . . yes, I was."

"Take pity on me now, Emmy," he pleaded.

"I do not understand, Alex . . ." she was frightened now, as much of herself as of him. "Please . . . don't make a joke of it, you—"

"I am not joking, Emmy," he assured her gravely. "Upon my honor, I am absolutely serious. Perhaps I have not the right to speak of this to you yet. To be strictly correct, I should address myself to your brother Phillip first, I am fully aware. But we're at war and, in war-time, one is permitted to relax the conventions a little, because there is not much time and we may, at any moment, be separated."

"Yes," Emmy agreed, "I know. But . . ." She was still very much at a loss, still vaguely apprehensive and uncertain of what he was trying to tell her. "Why do you wish to speak to Phillip?"

He smiled. "Why? Emmy dear, you told me a little while ago that I had no one to live or to fight for and it's true, I have no one. Unless it is you . . . I should like it to be you, Emmy. I should like to have the privilege of caring for you and protecting you. More than anything in the world, I should like to have you to come home to, as my wife, when the war is over."

"Do you mean . . ." Emmy drew back, looking up at him in startled incredulity, unable to believe that she could have heard him correctly. This was a dream, of course, she told herself, a dream from which, all too soon, she would awaken. "Alex, are you asking me to . . . *to marry you?*"

"Yes," Alex confirmed quietly, "I am asking you to marry me, Emmy. If you will do me that honor."

"But Charlotte . . ." Emmy managed, her mouth stiff. "You said that you were still in love with Charlotte! That you compared every woman you met with her and . . . and found each one wanting—"

"Except you," Alex amended. "I realized as we rode over here this evening, Emmy, that you are the only woman I could compare with Charlotte and find wanting in nothing. Believe me, my dearest child, it is the truth. I would not lie to you."

"No, I . . . do not think you would," Emmy whispered. She was trembling. His proposal had come as such a shock to her that she could find no words with which to answer him. That he should want to marry her had been the last thing she had expected—yet, after subjecting him to an uneasy scrutiny, she was forced to the conclusion that he appeared to be in earnest. His eyes met hers frankly and unashamedly and, although he was smiling, it was in reassurance, not in mockery or amusement. "Why?" she asked at last. "Why, Alex? Why do you want to marry me?"

"We are both alone, in a sense," he told her gently. "And we are both lonely, I fancy . . . you, as well as myself. And we've known each other for a long time, have we not? If you became my wife, Emmy, I should do everything in my power to ensure your happiness and I should give you my complete devotion, now and always." He patted the hand he held, drawing her closer to him. "There would be no one else, in my heart or in my thoughts, I give you my word."

The touch of his hand and his nearness set Emmy's heart beating wildly. He went on, still in the same quiet, level tones, "I don't have to go back to India, if you felt the smallest reluctance to accompany me there. I have some money now—it is not a fortune but would be sufficient for our needs. And there are other occupations I could follow, besides soldiering, once this war is finished. We could go back to England together, Emmy, if you wished." She was silent and he said apologetically, "I am confusing you, I fear. We can discuss these matters later on, if you would prefer it."

"Yes, I . . . I think I should prefer that, Alex. If I, if we. . . ." Emmy could not go on. She gave him a pleading glance. "I do not know what to say. You see—"

Alex relinquished his clasp of her hand. "Do not upset yourself, child. You will require time to consider my proposal, I know, and I will give you time . . . all the time you need. But with your permission, I should like to speak to Phillip and obtain his formal consent to my courtship. May I do so, at the first opportunity?"

He had not said that he loved her, Emmy thought. He had said many things but not that, which was the one thing she longed to hear—although, perhaps, he had intended to imply it. She drew in her breath sharply. Even if he were still in love with

Charlotte, what difference could it make? Charlotte was Arthur Cassell's wife and, because of that—no matter what he felt for her—she was lost to him. He could not, in honor, pay his court to Charlotte. . . .

"If you wish to speak to Phillip," she heard herself saying, "please do so, Alex." Her voice sounded odd, even to herself, and so tense and strained that she could hardly recognize it as her own. "You have been very kind and . . . and considerate and I am grateful. I should like a little time, as you suggest, to think over what you have said, before giving you my answer. But I will try not to keep you waiting too long, I . . ."

"Thank you, Emmy my dear." Alex bent and brushed her cheek with his lips. His kiss was without passion, almost formal, yet it stirred her deeply. "Bless you," he said softly and then, with a swift change of mood, reached for his cloak, as if now impatient to be gone. "I will leave you now. It is late and I ought not to be here. Take care of yourself, child. I shall hope to see you again very soon."

He would not allow her to accompany him to the door. When the sound of his horse's hoofs had receded into the distance, Emmy returned to her chair. She sat there for a long time, dreaming again the bright dream she had cherished as a child; not eating, although Constantin hovered anxiously in the background, trying to tempt her to partake of something. She was happier than she had been for many years, although still a little frightened, still more than a little confused and uncertain, even now, of what her answer to Alex's proposal ought to be.

She felt the need for advice, for counsel from older and wiser heads than her own and wished that her mother might have been there or, at least, near at hand, so that a letter might reach her, to which the reply could be obtained within a few days.

But her mother was in Dublin and letters home took weeks and sometimes months to reach their destination; Emmy wrote to her but, as she sealed the letter, was aware that in this decision her mother could not help her, however much she might wish to.

The decision must be hers and hers alone. She could not ask Charlotte's advice, in the circumstances—that would be out of the question. But there was Phillip. He was only her stepbrother, it was true, and therefore not as close to her as he was to his own sisters, and to Charlotte in particular, but she knew that he was fond of her and had always had her well-being at heart. Besides, in the old days, he had been Alex's friend, when they had both been in the 11th Hussars . . . and Alex had said, before leaving her, that he intended to tell Phillip of his proposal at the first opportunity. In which case, Phillip would undoubtedly speak to her about it very soon, Emmy thought, with a lifting of the heart as she rose from her chair at last and went upstairs to prepare for bed. When he did so, she would ask for his guidance. . . .

Phillip called, the following evening. Emmy and Charlotte were together in the living-room when he arrived and he made his announcement—to them both—with obvious pleasure the moment he entered the room.

"Alex Sheridan is asking for your hand, Emmy my dear," he said, smiling at her. "He tells me that he has mentioned the matter to you already and that you've promised to consider his proposal and give him your answer, when you've had time to think about it. This is so, I take it?"

Emmy agreed in a small voice that it was. She was watching Charlotte as she said it and saw, from the expression on her stepsister's lovely face, that the news had both shocked and displeased her. But Charlotte said nothing, only turned to look at Phillip with raised brows when he observed that, while the proposal had been made in a somewhat unorthodox manner, the circumstances were themselves somewhat unorthodox.

"Your position here, for one thing," he added reproachfully, "but I see no reason, on that account, to refuse Alex's request. He is the best of fellows, as we all know, and personally I should welcome him as a brother-in-law if you decide to accept him, Emmy." He glanced at her questioningly, his eyes bright with expectation. "Have you decided?"

Emmy hesitated and Charlotte said, her tone derisive, "But of course she has! She has always worshipped Alex, even when he was betrothed to me and she was only a child . . . that is true, is it not, Emmy? You wanted him even then. You were jealous of me and you hated me—yes, hated me—for years because I refused him, after he was involved in that *cause célèbre* with Lord Cardigan and had to sell out of the 11th."

"I never hated you, Charlotte," Emmy denied, shocked.

"Did you not? Well, never mind, you've no cause to hate me now. He has asked for your hand, so why do you hesitate? Let him make you his wife . . . you are no longer a postulant to the Sisters of Mercy, you do not have to behave as if you were still incarcerated in that convent of yours, surely? Phillip, persuade her . . . it is time she was married. Her position here, as you say, is unorthodox."

"Well," Phillip evaded, "I do not think that it is for me to attempt persuasion. Emmy must make up her own mind. But I assure you, my dear little sister, that if you do accept Alex's offer of marriage, you will have my blessing—and I have told Alex as much. So it rests with you, Emmy child."

Emmy lowered her gaze. She was very conscious of Charlotte's hostility but she said evenly, "I understand, Phillip, thank you. But Alex promised me a little time and—"

"There is not much time left to us," Phillip reminded her. He put a hand beneath her chin and lifted her downcast face to his, looking into it intently, and his tone was kindly as he went on, "It is your life, Emmy... your future. But we are about to embark upon the serious business of war and, while I am not seeking to evade my responsibilities toward you, I am compelled to tell you that the fact that you are unmarried renders them the more oner-ous. I should feel them less keenly if I could share them with Alex, as your husband."

"You mean that we should be married, here? In Varna, Phillip?" Emmy was startled.

"That, I think, is Alex's wish. It could be arranged. There are army chaplains here, Emmy." Phillip spread his hands. "When we leave here—and rumor has it that it will not be long before we do—you will be unable to come with us. I shall have to send you to Therapia and depend on Lady Stratford de Redcliffe's good-will to care for you." He sighed. "I should have sent you before, had it not been for that infernal reconnaissance of Cardigan's."

Emmy glanced instinctively at Charlotte, who replied to her unvoiced question with a shrug. "My plans depend on my hus-band's wishes, Emmy. But if Lady Errol and Mrs Duberly are granted permission to sail with the army, then I intend to seek the same privilege." She silenced Phillip's objection with an impe-riously raised hand. "We shall see, shall we not, whether Lord Raglan decides to allow any of us to sail? Do not concern your-self, Phillip dear . . . in any event, I am not your responsibility, am I? So you have really no say in the matter."

They wrangled, a trifle heatedly, and Emmy listened, only half hearing what they said but thankful that Charlotte's hostility appeared no longer to be directed exclusively against herself.

The argument was interrupted by Constantin's announcing

dinner. Phillip dined with them and, mellowed by the excellence of the meal, was in his usual good spirits when he rose to take his leave.

He said, as Emmy lifted her cheek for his farewell kiss, "Good night, Emmy my sweet. Sleep well . . . and do not keep Alex waiting too long for his answer, will you? Because there is really not much time for any of us now, you know."

"I know, Phillip," she responded, "I know. . . ." And suddenly the dream was there again, in all its nostalgic beauty, filling her heart and her mind. But now, she thought, it could become more than just a dream, treasured through childhood—now it could be translated into reality. She was no longer a child, with her head full of strange notions; no longer, as Charlotte had so acidly pointed out, a postulant to the Order of the Sisters of Mercy. She had grown up, she was on the verge of womanhood and its fulfillment, and Alex Sheridan had asked for her hand in marriage . . . shyly she looked up into Phillip's face.

"Well, child?" he encouraged.

Emmy sighed. "Tell Alex that I will give him his answer tomorrow," she whispered. "And . . . it is yes, Phillip. I want to marry him, whenever he wishes. He is the one man, above all others, whom I should be proud to have as my husband."

"I am glad," Phillip told her. "Sincerely glad, Emmy dear, for I am certain that you have reached the right decision and will not regret it." He held her to him, smiling down at her with warm affection. "Although I must warn you . . . Alex will not hear of your attempting to follow *him* to war. He has said so and he has very strong views on the subject."

"He made them plain to me also," Emmy assured him.

"Then you and Charlotte would be well advised to prepare to go to Therapia," Phillip said. "I shall write to Lady Stratford and to the ambassador and see if I can arrange transport for you before we leave for the Crimea." He kissed her again and Emmy went with him to his horse and stood in the open doorway, waving, until he had disappeared into the darkness. She felt happy and secure, now that her decision had been made, and was filled with a sense of eager anticipation.

It fell to Charlotte to shatter her short-lived complacency and prick the bright bubble of her happy dream. When she returned to the living-room, her stepsister glanced at her sharply, taking in her flushed cheeks and air of excitement, and said coldly, "So you have made up your mind to accept Alex's offer of marriage then?"

"Yes, I . . ." Emmy faced her defiantly. "Yes, I have."

"You told Phillip, I suppose?"

"Yes, I told him. He was very pleased."

"Naturally he was—because he does not understand." There was a wealth of scorn in Charlotte's voice. "Phillip does not know why Alex has asked you to marry him. And nor, I fancy, do you. You are very naïve, Emmy."

"Am I?" Emmy's smile flickered and dissolved but she held her ground, returning Charlotte's gaze steadily. "Why should you say that, Charlotte?"

Charlotte laughed. "Oh, you little fool . . . you surely do not imagine that he is in love with you, do you? Alex is in love with me. I should have thought that it was obvious, even to you."

Perhaps it was, Emmy thought bitterly. She felt her lower lip quiver and bit into it fiercely, determined not to betray her uncertainty to Charlotte. "Then why," she asked, "should he ask me to be his wife? Do you know why?"

"Of course I do. Because Alex is a man who has scruples. He is still in love with me but, because I am the wife of a friend of his, he seeks to put barriers between us to strengthen his own resolve. What more effective barrier than marriage to you, Emmy dear? Certainly I can think of none. But"—there was an edge on Charlotte's voice—"even so, I have only to crook my finger and Alex will come running, for all his scruples and in spite of his desire to behave honorably towards me."

"That isn't true!" Emmy protested. "It cannot possibly be true. You are making it up, you are attributing motives to him which he would not entertain. Alex is a man of honor, you have just said so yourself. You are simply trying to hurt me."

"Do you want proof?" Charlotte asked, her smile malicious. "If you do, it will be very easy for me to supply it, I assure you."

Emmy stared at her in numb misery and then, unable to overcome the terrible conviction that what her stepsister had said was true, bade her a subdued good night and went wretchedly up to bed.

In the days which followed, the conviction grew until it became virtually a certainty. Alex—although when he was alone with her, he was all that she could wish for in a betrothed husband—seemed, in Charlotte's presence to take on a different personality. When Charlotte was there, he was only half aware of anyone else. Like a man bewitched, he responded to her overtures, sought her company and obeyed her smallest, most unreasonable wish with every appearance of pleasure and devotion.

Emmy watched them together, her heart close to breaking, her mind beset with doubts. Plans for the wedding were afoot but she left these to Phillip as if, by so doing, she could absolve herself from the necessity to make a final and irrevocable decision to marry Alex. She did not revoke her promise to him, partly because she cared too much for him to want to and partly because, on the few occasions when Charlotte permitted them to be alone, he was obviously so anxious that she should not. She knew that he was torturing himself, sensed the bitter inner conflict he was enduring but, although it was matched and sometimes exceeded by her own, she would not bring herself to leave him to wage his battle alone.

Her relationship with Charlotte became almost unbearably strained beneath the surface, yet above it, they both went to considerable pains to conceal their differences. Neither was happy, neither felt secure and Charlotte, whilst ready enough to demonstrate her power over her stepsister's betrothed by flirting with him, never overstepped the bounds of propriety. She held him by the slenderest of threads but she held him inexorably, refusing to let him go and the tension between them increased to a point when, Emmy was unhappily aware, one or other of them would be compelled to take drastic and perhaps fatal action.

In the end, it was she who was driven to take it . . . but not before all three of them had suffered a great deal of mental anguish. She broke her engagement to Alex and, within a few hours of having done so, returned to the small house in the Street of Silversmiths to find Charlotte in his arms.

Neither of them heard her come in. As on the first occasion when Alex had called on them, she left them together, and went wearily up to her own room alone. This time she did not weep; the grief which racked her went too deep for the relief of tears. But, as it had before, the sound of their voices came to her, distorted and indistinct, and she lay sleepless and fully clothed on her bed, listening to the voices, waiting until they should cease.

A loud, impatient knocking on the street door finally silenced them. Emmy ran to the window and, looking out, recognized Phillip, with a companion, who was muffled in a cloak, so that at first she did not realize who he was. Then he looked up and she saw, with a gasp of dismay, that it was Arthur Cassell.

Charlotte was in the hall. When she reached it, Alex standing in the shadows at her back.

"Who in the world can be calling at such an hour?" Charlotte asked sulkily but every vestige of colour drained from her cheeks when Emmy told her who it was.

"*Arthur* is here? You mean that he has returned?"

"Yes," Emmy answered, from between stiff lips. "You had best let him in, had you not?" She turned to Alex, holding out her hand to him. "And you and I," she said, endeavoring to speak without bitterness, "had best go into the drawing-room, I think, and endeavor to look as if we have been there together all evening."

He followed her without a word as Charlotte went reluctantly to admit her husband and Phillip.

To Arthur Cassell, as Emmy had known she would, she introduced Alex as her stepsister's fiancé, and Arthur, greeting him as an old friend, was loud and enthusiastic in his congratulations.

The awkward moment passed, the crisis was averted, but for Emmy the real torment had only just begun. . . .

CHAPTER SIX

⇉ • ⇇

THE LAST WEEK of July and the beginning of August was a period fraught with terrible anxiety for everyone in Varna. The lurking cholera germs, always present in unhealthy, over-crowded camps, were suddenly released in their full, hideous virulence.

At first the French suffered more acutely than the British. Marshal St Arnaud's expedition to the Dobruja came to a disastrous conclusion, with the loss of over three thousand of his Zouaves from the disease—and without the sight of a single Russian. By the time he returned with his stricken force to Varna, cholera had begun to take heavy toll of his British allies as well.

In a single day—Sunday, 23 July—nineteen men died in the Light Division encampment, all men of the Rifle Brigade. The only precautionary measure the medical officers could suggest was the changing of the camp sites and this, although put swiftly into effect, did not prevent or even slow down the rapid spread of infection.

The Cavalry Division—initially the least affected—was moved to Jeni-Bazaar and then to Issytype, where it was cut off from the rest of the army, 28 miles beyond Devna. But the unhappy infantry, shift about as they might, could find no escape from the dreaded sickness. The Guards Brigade were hardest hit, with over three hundred cases of cholera, dysentery and typhoid in their new camp. When ordered to move yet again to a fresh site at Galata, on the south side of Varna Bay, their packs had to be transported for them by bullock wagon, since the men who managed to march there had not the strength to carry them.

Every day came news of more outbreaks, more cases of cholera, more deaths . . . including one in the Horse Artillery at Issytype, and every day the fear grew.

Emmy heard the rumors and the frightened whispers, despite the fact that such social life as there had been in Varna was abruptly curtailed and, for a time, she and Charlotte had no contact with either Lady Errol or Mrs Duberly—or indeed with anyone else, save for an occasional hurried visit from Phillip.

But they witnessed the dreadful spectacle of the ambulance wagons, passing in slow procession through the streets, bringing the sick to the inadequate and soon overcrowded barracks on the far side of the town, which had been brought into use as a general hospital. Few survived incarceration in its filthy wards and rat-run corridors, and the poor old pensioners, whose duty it was to drive the wagons, died like flies, having little stamina to resist the ravages of cholera and dysentery.

At sea and in harbour, the British and French fleets also suffered. Many ships put to sea, in the hope of leaving the infection behind . . . only to learn that they had brought the disease with them. In the space of sixty hours, the French Admiral Bruat lost 153 of his crew and Admiral Dundas, in H.M.S. *Britannia,* had 100 deaths, with three times this number of unfortunate seamen lying helplessly below decks, all victims of cholera or typhoid. The *Britannia* was forced to return, worked by a skeleton crew.

The fresh drafts of healthy young soldiers from England, sent out to bring the army up to strength, caught the infection almost as soon as they set foot ashore and officers, as well as the rank and file, died in a few short, agonized hours. Men were buried in shallow, hastily dug mass graves, with weary chaplains mumbling the funeral service many times each day.

Lord de Ros, the quartermaster-general and Arthur Cassell's immediate superior, was taken ill—so too, was General Buller of the Rifle Brigade. Both, Emmy heard later, had recovered, although Lord de Ros was much weakened by the ordeal he had undergone. Several other senior officers succumbed to illness but few of them fatally. It was the common soldiers who died, they who were stricken in their thousands by the disease, due to lack of medical attention, the appalling disregard for proper sanitation in the camps, heat and overcrowding. And the unhygienic manner in which their food was stored and cooked did little to aid the recovery of the invalids.

Emmy, deeply distressed by what she had heard of conditions prevailing in the hospital, made numerous abortive attempts to offer her services in almost any capacity but each time her offer was rejected, with pitying condescension, by those to whom she appealed. Once she tried to take gruel to the men in the wards but was sternly ordered to keep away by a horrified army surgeon, who intercepted her at the hospital gates.

"It is bad enough that men must die," he told her reproachfully, "I want no woman's death on my conscience, Miss O'Shaughnessy—least of all that of a lady of quality, like yourself. You would be well advised to leave this town . . . and leave at once, whilst you still can!"

Phillip, on the infrequent occasions when she saw him, also urged Charlotte and herself to leave Varna. But there had been no reply as yet from Lady Stratford, and travelling—with cholera rife in all the available ships—seemed likely to present as great a risk of infection as if they remained where they were. So Phillip did not insist and Arthur Cassell, reunited with his wife and, by special permission, allowed to live with her in the house in the Street of the Silversmiths, seemed relieved when Charlotte stated that, all things considered, she preferred for the time being to stay there.

She made no secret of the fact that she was terrified of catching the infection but, as this was mainly prevalent in the camps and on board the ships, her decision to remain in Varna was probably a wise one, Emmy thought. Apart from those in the hospital, there had been no cases of cholera among the townsfolk—or none had been officially reported—from which Charlotte evidently took comfort.

Her attitude towards her husband had undergone a noticeable change, which Emmy found difficult to understand, in view of what it had been in the past. Arthur had returned with a severe chill and for days, Charlotte had been the model of a devoted wife, cosseting him and fussing about him and seldom leaving his side. She made no mention of Alex, unless it were in Arthur's hearing, when she talked of him to Emmy and went to extraordinary pains to create the impression that their marriage was still about to take place. Emmy, who had at first thought of denying this indignantly, decided in the end that it was useless. Alex did not call; he was with General Scarlett, at the Heavy Brigade's new camp nearly thirty miles away and this—so far as both Charlotte and her husband were concerned—appeared to offer sufficient excuse for his absence.

Arthur, at any rate, did not question it . . . and did not welcome visitors. He was tired and ill, far from his normal hearty, good-natured self and for long hours on end wanted no more than to be allowed to doze fitfully, with his wife seated at his bedside, her hand clasped in his. When he recovered sufficiently to dress and come downstairs, it was to sit in a chair in the tiny living-room, a rug wrapped about him, and allow himself to be waited on by Charlotte and Constantin.

Matters continued like this until well into August, with Charlotte seemingly well content to go on playing the role she had chosen. Then Arthur returned to part-time duty and brought them news of the return of Sir George Brown who, with General Canrobert, had gone by ship to make a survey of the Crimean coast in order to select a suitable landing place for the British and French armies.

"And he has brought back a favourable report, it would seem," Arthur said excitedly. "Of course, we have not yet heard any details but judging by Lord Raglan's increased cheerfulness since receiving it, I begin to hope that we may soon be on the move. There is to be a conference between the British and French High Commands in a day or so, for the purpose of deciding the date for our embarkation and in order to settle upon a plan of campaign for the two armies. It's generally understood, however, that our objective will be Sebastopol." He rubbed his pale, invalid's hands in eager anticipation and then, looking down at them, expressed the plaintive hope that he would completely have shaken off his malaise when the time came to embark on the invasion of Crim-Tartary.

Listening to him, Emmy found herself hoping that the rest of the invasion force might also recover in time. But deaths from cholera continued unabated and more and more soldiers fell victims to other mysterious, undiagnosed fevers, supposedly caused by the climate. Rumors concerning the number of French dead were officially denied, yet these persisted, suggesting that French losses ran into many thousands, chiefly among the unfortunate Algerian troops.

Then at last the weather changed and became cooler, giving rise to optimistic forecasts from the medical authorities that this would aid the sufferers and halt the ghastly spread of infection . . . but it did not. A furious fire broke out in the port of Varna on the night of 13 August—said to have been started by the Greeks for the purpose of delaying the invasion of the Crimea. Thousands of pounds' worth of much needed stores were destroyed before it could be brought under control. . . . Emmy watched the glow in the sky and saw the leaping flames from her window and waited, fearful that it would spread and destroy the whole town. News that it had been put out was followed by the gloomy tidings that the Coldstream Guards had lost eighty of their number from cholera and that the cavalry had also become infected. There had been eleven deaths in the 5th Dragoon Guards—the famous "Green Horse," General Scarlett's old regiment, which formed part of the Heavy Brigade. Then came a note from Fanny Duberly, addressed to Charlotte, to say that officers and men of the 8th Hussars had also fallen sick, including the commanding officer, Colonel Shelwell, to whom she was much attached.

"It is not supposed to be the cholera," Mrs Duberly wrote, *"yet, in spite of this, we have had to have a marquee erected to receive the sick and they seem to be very ill. . . ."*

Emmy, for all her resolve to put the thought and memory of Alex out of her mind, started to worry about him and to wait impatiently for more news. At last, unable to bear the suspense any longer, she told Charlotte, who seemed indifferent to her concern, that she was going out for a breath of air. Constantin brought her horse for her and she set forth in the hope that she might encounter someone who could tell her how the Cavalry Division was faring. But she met no one, save a few staff officers, whose pale, preoccupied faces and general air of lethargy discouraged conversation. She was on her way back to the house, feeling more depressed than when she had started out, when she heard a deep voice calling her name and turned, with a cry of mingled pleasure and relief, to see Colonel Beatson trotting towards her.

"Miss Emmy O'Shaughnessy, is it not?" he said, smiling. "I thought I recognized you. And"—he regarded her with anxious eyes—"I am glad to see you looking so well. In these unhappy times, it is a miracle."

"Oh, I've kept to the house, Colonel," she told him, feeling ashamed that she should have to make such a confession but he nodded approvingly and applauded her good sense. "I, too, have avoided the infection—I have been in Shumla all this time, at Omar Pasha's behest. But he has given me leave of absence at last and now I'm on my way to report to General Scarlett who, I trust, has not forgotten his promise to give me employment on his staff."

"Then"—Emmy could not hide her eagerness—"you will be seeing Alex Sheridan, perhaps?"

"I hope to, my dear young lady. He is on General Scarlett's staff also, as far as I know—although I have had no news of him recently. I had thought that *you* might know more about his present whereabouts and his doings than I do."

"No, I . . ." Emmy lowered her gaze, flushing uncomfortably. "It is a long time since I have seen him, Colonel Beatson."

He did not question her statement but she was aware of his eyes on her bent head and, looking up to meet them, caught the hint of bewilderment in their keen blue depths. "We . . . were to have been married," she told him wretchedly, feeling that some explanation was called for, in spite of her reluctance to offer one.

"So I had heard," Colonel Beatson admitted, when she was uneasily silent. "Alex told me so in the only letter I received from him since we parted. He seemed, in that letter, to be overjoyed at the prospect, Miss O'Shaughnessy, and anxious that the ceremony should take place as soon as it could be arranged." He hesitated, still watching her with puzzled eyes. "I do not wish to press for your confidence, of course but . . . has something occurred to cause you to alter your plans? This cholera epidemic, perhaps? I have heard that it has been very severe."

"No, it was not that," Emmy denied. "There was another reason, I am afraid. No doubt Alex will tell you about it himself."

"No doubt, if he sees fit, he will," the colonel agreed dryly. He sighed. "I cannot deny that, for his sake particularly, I'm extremely sorry."

"I am sorry too," Emmy assured him.

"Is there any message you would like me to convey to him?" the colonel asked.

She caught her breath. Suppose Alex were ill, as he might well be, suppose he had caught cholera or become infected by the fever which had beset others in the cavalry? Suppose—her heart sank—suppose he were dying and, on this account, unable to write, either to her or to Colonel Beatson? This was no time to remember grievances or to bear ill-will, to anyone . . . and her feelings for him had not changed. They had always been the same.

"Please. . . ." She looked pleadingly up into William Beatson's bearded face, "I should be most grateful if you would tell him that I send my love. And . . . and say that I hope he is well."

"I will do that gladly, Miss O'Shaughnessy," the colonel promised. He asked politely for Charlotte and seemed pleased when Emmy told him of Arthur Cassell's return. But, when she invited him to call at the house, he excused himself. "I was, as it happens, intending to drop in for a few minutes, in order to see you and your sister, before riding on. But since I have been so fortunate as to meet you, I think if you will forgive me, I will press on. I have some distance yet to cover and I am anxious to reach my destination as soon as possible. However, if you will be kind enough to renew your invitation for some later date. . . ." He held out his hand to her. "I will take advantage of it with much pleasure."

"Please come at any time, when you are free, Colonel." Emmy accepted the hand he offered. "We shall always be glad to welcome you."

"And Alex?" he asked softly.

"Yes, if . . . if he wishes to come."

"I cannot imagine why he should *not* wish to come, my dear!"

"Unhappily, I can," Emmy told him, with a flash of bitterness. But it was momentary and she added quickly, "Nevertheless he is welcome, so far as I am concerned, Colonel Beatson. We are no longer betrothed but . . . we have been friends for a very long time. It is on this account that I . . . that we should be glad to see him."

"I shall tell him what you have said. *Au revoir*, Miss O'Shaughnessy and take good care of yourself."

"*Au revoir*, Colonel Beatson and . . . thank you."

Emmy felt a great deal happier as she rode back into the town. She had offered an olive branch to Alex, she thought, and now it was for him to decide whether or not to accept it.

He did so, with an alacrity for which she had scarcely dared to hope, two days later, arriving at the door of the house, with Colonel Beatson, at a little before four o'clock in the afternoon. Constantin, pleased to be able once again to announce visitors, came in beaming, to acquaint Emmy with news of their presence. His English had improved in the time he had been with them; now, with the dignity of an English butler, he announced the callers by name, so that Emmy was prepared when Alex entered the room at the colonel's heels. Charlotte was, as usual, resting. It was her habit to come downstairs for tea at five, so Emmy did not send to summon her.

She shook hands with the visitors, noticing with concern how thin and pale Alex looked. But he shook his head to her inquiry. "I suffered some fever and was a trifle off-colour for a week or so. It is nothing, Emmy. I am perfectly recovered now. And you?"

She avoided his gaze. "As you see, I am well, thank you."

Colonel Beatson rose to his feet. "If you will forgive me, Miss O'Shaughnessy, I will leave you and Alex for a time. I have a friend to see—a Captain Lane Fox, late of the Grenadier Guards, who was with my Bashi-Bazouks in Shumla when we first went there. I'm told that he is in Varna and I should like to renew our acquaintance. There is also"—he shrugged his massive shoulders resignedly—"a matter I must take up with Lord Raglan, if I can manage to see him. Lord Lucan, it seems, is raising objections to my appointment as one of General Scarlett's aides."

"Objections, Colonel? But—?" Emmy turned to him in surprise. "Why should Lord Lucan object to your appointment, if it is General Scarlett's wish that you serve him?"

"For the same reason," Alex put in cynically, "that his lordship objects to mine, Emmy . . . we are officers of the Indian army, you see."

When Colonel Beatson had gone, he enlarged on this theme—choosing it, Emmy decided, in preference to anything more personal—and added the information that Lord Cardigan had, for once, agreed with his brother-in-law. "Neither of their noble lordships is anxious to have *me* on the staff of the Cavalry Division, I am afraid. Lord Cardigan has remembered who I am and the circumstances under which we parted, and he's brought considerable pressure to bear on poor old General Scarlett to send me packing."

"And . . . will he do so?" Emmy asked. "Will he yield to Lord Cardigan, do you suppose?"

Alex sighed. "So far he has insisted on my remaining with him. We get on well and he has expressed satisfaction with my work. But it has caused a certain amount of unpleasantness and I am thinking, for his sake, that it might be wiser if I were to seek employment elsewhere."

"But, Alex, with whom?"

His expression relaxed. "Sir Colin Campbell is willing to make use of me, temporarily at any rate. I served with him in India and he does not share Lord Lucan's opinion of Indian officers. The matter is not settled yet, Emmy, but as a means of placating Lucan and Cardigan, I may yet have to resort to it. And," he finished smiling, "there are many worse fates which could befall me. There is no man in the British army that I respect and admire more highly than Sir Colin Campbell."

They were both silent, the topic exhausted, eyeing each other with the uncertain wariness of strangers. Finally Alex said, two bright spots of colour burning in his pale cheeks, "Emmy, I am sorry, you know . . . truly and deeply sorry. I have been wanting to tell you so for weeks."

"It is not your fault, Alex. How can you help it, if you do not love me?"

"But I *do* love you, Emmy—"

"No," Emmy pleaded, feeling suddenly close to tears. "We are friends, Alex—there is no need to pretend to me, to lie to me. I would rather you did not, I . . . it has always been Charlotte, so far as you are concerned, hasn't it?"

He shook his head vehemently. "I can only ask you to believe this, Emmy, for I can prove nothing. But I have had time to think since we last met . . . while I was ill, I had nothing to do except go over it, again and again, in my mind. My feelings for Charlotte have existed only in my imagination for years. They amounted to an infatuation, perhaps, a sort of madness over which I had no control. Yet I do not love her. I do not think I ever really knew her, even in the days when she was engaged to be married to me. The Charlotte I believed I loved isn't real Emmy . . . she must always have been a creature I created for myself, in my thoughts and memories. An image to which I clung, because I had no other and because I was alone. I beg you to try to understand. Emmy child, the reality isn't Charlotte—it is *you*."

"I find it hard to understand," Emmy told him.

"Of course you do. It has taken me years to understand it—how could you hope to, in a few minutes? Yet"—Alex held out his hand to her—"it is the truth."

"Charlotte was . . ." Emmy could not look at him. "When I came in, she was in your arms, Alex."

"That was when I learned the truth," Alex said. His voice was flat but somehow it carried conviction, even to Emmy. "What I held in my arms was an empty dream. Charlotte knew it and so did I."

"*Charlotte* knew it?"

"Of course she knew it. Did she not tell you?"

"No." Emmy bit back a sigh. Charlotte had not told her, in so many words but, in a hundred other ways, she had surely made it plain enough. She had not returned to her husband simply because she had been afraid that she might lose him, as the result of her *affaire* with Alex—or, at least, that had been only part of the reason. She had gone back to Arthur Cassell because Alex no longer had any allure for her; indeed, perhaps the only allure he had ever possessed had been that of the unattainable. His scruples, the fact that he had been about to marry her younger sister, had been a challenge which, being Charlotte, she had found hard to resist. But Alex, it was certainly evident now, meant no more to her than this . . . he probably never had. She had let him go, when he had been compelled to end his career in the British army and she had not loved him enough to wait for him, even then. She had scarcely spared him a thought, during the intervening years. . . . Emmy's hands clenched fiercely. She looked up to find Alex's gaze on her face. He looked so tired and ill, so contrite that her heart went out to him in pity. As it always had, she thought despairingly. As, no doubt, it always would, although it was no longer only pity she felt for him. As a child she had loved and trusted him and that had not changed. She was a woman and she loved him still. . . .

He read her answer in her eyes and taking both her hands in his, drew her to him. "I have been so miserable, not seeing you, Emmy. Yet I thought—I was afraid that you would never consent to receive me again. Or believe me, if I attempted to explain to you. William Beatson told me I was a fool. He said that if I told you the truth, you would know it for what it was . . . and you do, do you not?"

"I think I do, Alex."

He laid his cheek on hers. "It is you I love, Emmy—you and only you, for the rest of time. For all the time God gives me, my sweet love, I shall do everything humanly possible to make you believe it."

He had said at last the words she had longed to hear, Emmy thought, and she knew that he meant them, knew that they were the truth and wondered, even as she let him take her into the safe haven of his embrace, how much time would be left to either of them now, in which this love of theirs could grow and come to fulfillment. . . .

When Charlotte came in, a little later, followed by the faithful Constantin with a laden tea tray, she greeted Alex without enthusiasm, seeming as if she scarcely knew or cared who he was. She was nervy and ill at ease, complaining that she had been unable to rest, that the tea was cold and that Arthur—about whom she worried constantly these days—was late.

"He is not usually so late, Emmy," she remarked petulantly. "And he isn't yet fully recovered. They should not keep him working so hard, when he is still a sick man."

"Lord de Ros is also sick," Emmy reminded her. "I imagine

that his absence from duty must put an extra strain on the members of his staff."

"Arthur says he will be sent home," Charlotte said. "He is fortunate to be able to go. I wish that Arthur could go also . . . he has never got over the effects of that dreadful journey all over the country. Captain Nolan should have stayed with him, when he was first taken ill, instead of leaving him to manage as best he could, and dashing back here so as to ingratiate himself with Lord Raglan." She looked at Alex then, with resentful, lacklustre eyes. "You have heard, I imagine, that Captain Nolan has got himself appointed as one of the commander-in-chief's aides-de-camp?"

"I had heard that," Alex admitted cautiously. "Most of the cavalry staff are of the opinion that it is a very wise and farseeing appointment. Edward Nolan may be young but he is one of the greatest living authorities on cavalry tactics. He has published two textbooks on the subject, which he has studied in Italy, France and Germany and, in addition to holding a commission in the 15th Hussars, he has held one in the Austrian cavalry."

"Have you met him?" Charlotte challenged. "In my view—and it is also that of my husband who knows him well—he is of far too volatile a temperament for any reliance to be placed in him. Lord Raglan will regret the appointment, you will see."

She was not to know how prophetic her chance remark was to be. But Alex, who could not know it either, came to the defense of the young Irish-Italian officer, whose whole hearted enthusiasm for his profession had impressed him deeply, and whose personality had also appealed to him, from the first moment of their meeting.

Arthur Cassell returned while they were still discussing this controversial subject and his appearance instantly silenced them.

For, Emmy realized, he was very ill, and it was no longer

from the after-effects of scouring the Bulgarian countryside in Captain Nolan's company. This was more serious and, with a little half-stifled cry of alarm, she went to him and taking his hand, gently led him to a chair. He sat there mute, smiling at her weakly, his face the colour of dark parchment, his hands clutching the arms of his chair in convulsive agony. Alex came to stand behind her, looking down at the sick man with narrowed, anxious eyes.

"I will get him to bed," he offered and bent to pick him up. "If you will show me where his room is, Emmy, please."

She obeyed him without question and Charlotte, the colour draining from her cheeks, followed them up the narrow, curving staircase, to halt by the door, watching them, reluctant now to venture inside the room that had also been her own.

"What is it?" she whispered. "Emmy . . . Emmy, tell me the truth, for mercy's sake! Is it . . . has he got cholera?"

It was Alex who answered her, with a single, brusque affirmative. But Emmy had known, before he confirmed her fears and they looked at each other, Alex's eyes with a question in them.

"We could move him to the hospital," he said.

"No. Oh, no, not there!" Emmy shuddered. "He would die in terrible agony. I will look after him. I am trained, I know what to do. He must stay here, if he is to have even a chance of recovery, Alex."

"But you will be running a terrible risk, my love," Alex protested. "I cannot let you do that. Besides—"

"I shall be running no greater risk than many others," Emmy put in quietly. "And I shall be doing what I came here to do. Oh, Alex, don't you see . . ." she turned to him eagerly. "They would not permit me to help them at the hospital, although I wanted to do so and offered my help many times. But I can care for Arthur . . . with God's help, perhaps I may save him."

"And Charlotte?" Alex asked. "Is he not her husband?"

But Charlotte was sobbing as, with feverish haste, she started to fling as many of her clothes as she could into a valise. She heard Alex say her name and glanced round at him with frightened, tear-filled eyes. "I cannot stay with him . . . not if he has cholera. I cannot possibly stay in this house, I . . . I am afraid. Emmy, you know how terribly afraid I am. You know!"

Emmy, indeed, knew only too well. She said gently, "Don't worry, I will look after him. But where will you go?"

"I don't know, I don't care!" Charlotte answered wildly. She snapped the valise shut, her hands shaking.

"There isn't anywhere for you to go here," Emmy said.

"Then I will leave this hateful, plague-infested town. I can go back to Constantinople . . . to Therapia. Lady Stratford will offer me hospitality. I cannot stay, Emmy, don't you understand?" She appealed to Alex in her desperation. "Are there no ships in which I could obtain passage? Because I shall go mad with fear if I am forced to stay here."

Alex hesitated, eyeing her in shocked silence. But he saw that she was in earnest and said doubtfully, "Taking passage by ship would present as great a hazard as if you were to remain with your husband, Charlotte. Greater, perhaps if—"

"No," Charlotte interrupted hysterically. "That is impossible. If I stay with Arthur, he will expect me to sit with him, to touch him, to . . . share his bed. And I cannot, I am afraid. He would not let Emmy nurse him if I were there—and she is trained, she isn't afraid, she has worked in a hospital." She covered her face with her hands, her whole body trembling. "For pity's sake, help me! I *have* to get away." She was, Emmy saw, on the point of collapse, so terrified that it would be impossible to attempt to reason with her. People in such a mental state were, she was aware, more vulnerable to physical disease than those who did not fear the infection . . . and it would help none of them if Charlotte got cholera.

She met Alex's concerned eyes. "Are there no ships, Alex?" she asked.

He shrugged. "There is a mail ship, the *Beaver,* due to sail for Scutari on the tide. I delivered despatches to her purser before I came here. He told me that they had been lucky—they had had some cases of the disease but no deaths. If Charlotte were to go down to the harbour at once, she might catch her before she sails." He caught at Emmy's hand. "Do you wish me to take her to the *Beaver* and see if it can be arranged?"

"Yes," she said, decisively, "I think it is the best thing. Charlotte will make herself ill, if she stays."

"But you will be left here alone, Emmy my love. Will you not go with her?" Alex glanced pityingly at Arthur Cassell's grey, pain-racked face and twitching limbs and lowered his voice. "He has it badly, you know. He may not live for more than a few hours."

"I want to do what I can for him," Emmy answered, her tone calm and certain. "For as long as he lives. And I am not afraid to be left here alone. Constantin will be here . . . and the other servants. Truly, Alex, you need suffer no anxiety on my account."

Alex did not argue. He picked up Charlotte's valise and, an arm about her, led her sobbing from the room, as gently and impersonally as if she had been a frightened child placed in his care. He no longer attempted to reason with her or reproach her, for he, too, saw now that she was beyond reason and that reproaches would have no effect upon her. Charlotte did not look back, did not bid farewell either to Emmy or to her husband and he, writhing in pain, did not appear to notice that she had gone.

"Help me," he begged hoarsely. "Dear heaven, help me. . . ."

Emmy bent over him and loosened the constricting cravat from about his neck. Constantin could help her to undress him later on, she thought. Now it was essential that she keep him warm, with hot flannels applied to his back and abdomen. She had some tincture of camphor in a bottle in her room and, if she could get him to take a few sips of that, it might ease his pain. "Lie still, Arthur," she bade him softly but he did not hear as another violent convulsion seized him.

Emmy called out to Constantin to bring her what she would need and, gritting her teeth, set to work, with all the skill at her command, to fight for his life. She knew, as she commenced the battle, that it would take everything she had to give, for already the pain he was enduring was sapping the frail remnants of his strength. Alex had been right when he said Arthur had the disease badly. The rapid onset of its symptoms characterized the virulence of the infection and she had seen too many twisted, blackened faces and writhing bodies, amongst the pathetic cargoes borne by the ambulance wagons, to have any illusions as to the type which Charlotte's husband had contracted. . . .

In a little over two hours, Alex was back. He told her briefly that he had arranged for Charlotte's passage to Scutari in the mail ship and that the captain had placed a single cabin at her disposal. In addition, he had encountered, quite by chance, a British sergeant's wife, who was anxious to leave Varna. "She seemed a respectable woman and she was there, by the dock with her husband—hoping to prevail on the captain of the *Beaver* to take her without paying her fare. I offered her the chance to sail with Charlotte, as her maid, and she accepted at once, with tears of gratitude, poor soul." Alex smiled briefly. "I ascertained that Charlotte had sufficient money for her immediate needs, so I do not think you need worry about her any more, Emmy dear. And indeed, nor need I. . . ." Once again his gaze went to Arthur's face and he expelled his breath in a long sigh. "How is he, poor fellow?"

"He is alive," Emmy told him, feeling that this, in itself, was no small triumph. "But he is still suffering a great deal. I think perhaps you should leave me with him, Alex."

"He is not the first case of cholera I have seen, Emmy. Or the first I've helped to cleanse, either. Come. . . ." He was already taking off his stable-jacket and rolling up his sleeves. "This is not work for a woman, whatever you say. Leave him to me for half an hour, while you go and try to eat something."

Afterwards, they sat together at the bedside in silence, as Emmy managed to spoon a few sips of brandy between the sick man's clenched teeth.

"I shall have to ride back to camp," Alex told her regretfully. "But before I go, Emmy my darling, there is just one suggestion I should like to make to you."

She looked up to him. "And that is?"

"We'll be leaving here very soon—rumor has it that orders for the army to embark are about to be issued. I do not want to leave you alone and unprotected."

"How can you do otherwise?" Emmy asked.

He reddened a little but met her inquiring gaze steadily.

"Constantin told me, when I came in, that you had sent for a chaplain—"

"A priest," Emmy amended, "for Arthur. He promised he would come as soon as he could." She stifled a sigh. "All the chaplains are kept busy, night and day. But he will come."

"When he does," Alex said gravely, "will you allow me to ask him to marry us? I should like to give you at least the protection of my name, Emmy. It is all I can give you now but—"

"It is enough," Emmy told him and suddenly she was weeping in his arms. He held her tenderly to him. "My sweet love, why do you weep?"

"Because . . . oh, because in spite of everything, I am happy."

"Yet you shed tears!"

"They are tears of joy, Alex. I know that you love me now. I believe it."

He lifted her face to his and kissed her. "Whatever happens to either of us," he told her huskily, "go on believing that, it is the truth. You will be my wife, Emmy, and I shall come back to you, God willing. Because this is what I have prayed for, my darling. You are all I love. . . ."

A little later an exhausted chaplain, having administered the Last Rites to Arthur Cassell, turned and murmured the few words necessary to make Emmy the wife of Alex Sheridan. The two men left together—Alex to ride the thirty miles back to the Cavalry Division's camp at Issytype, the chaplain to stumble wearily among the dying in the over-crowded hospital, offering what comfort he could.

Emmy was left to her vigil and, by morning, Arthur was conscious and able to speak her name. That day orders came for the British and French armies to embark for the Crimea and she saw her husband only once again, when he rode through Varna in the wake of the Highland Brigade, later to board the steam-transport *Emeu* with Sir Colin Campbell's staff.

CHAPTER SEVEN
❯❯❯ • ❮❮❮

ALEX WROTE to Emmy, from the *Emeu,* managing to pen a few lines to her each day. He wrote admiringly of Sir Colin Campbell, to whose staff he was now attached.

"Sir Colin received me kindly and I do not regret my temporary change of service. It is a privilege to serve under a general of his caliber . . . yet seems a grave reflection on the system of promotion now obtaining in the British army that he should merit command only of a brigade when others, of far less ability and certainly less experience, are given divisions. He is 62 years old and has had 46 of those years in the army . . . he was with Sir John Moore at Corunna, in every battle of the Peninsular War and, as a colonel, Lord Gough gave him a division at Chillianwalla, the same he commanded, with equal distinction, at Gujerat. He fought on the Indian frontier under Sir Charles Napier . . . in fact, I do not think there is a major battle, during his lifetime, in which he has not taken part. Yet here he is ranked second to General Bentinck, who commands the Guards Brigade, and the brevets go to Lucan and Cardigan! But he does not complain and, indeed, sets an example of generosity of heart and true greatness of spirit, which I myself would do well to follow. . . ."

The letter broke off at this point, to be continued:

"It is now 2 September and we are all embarked on board the transport *Emeu.* We have the 42nd with us—the other two regiments of the Brigade, the 79th and the 93rd, are divided among other ships. A vast armada of ships is gathering at Baldchik Bay, under the command of Admiral Lyons, as embarkation proceeds. It is said that there are over six hundred ships in all, including 37 British line-of-battle sail and a hundred frigates, to serve as our escorts. Admiral Dundas, we are told, is patrolling the Crimean coast, with a smaller force, in expectation of a Russian sortie from Sebastopol. The French and Turks have been accommodated—in conditions of some discomfort, I imagine—on board ships of the line. They have completed their embarkation and grow impatient . . . for we have not. But it is the horses which are causing us so much delay—the French have no cavalry and are taking only seventy guns, with four horses to each. We, on the other hand, have to load the Light Cavalry Brigade—a thousand horses—and a further four hundred and fifty is the minimum requirement for our Horse Artillery's guns and limbers.

"An order has been issued, restricting officers' chargers to one apiece and we have heard that the six thousand pack horses—so labouriously collected in Bulgaria by Lord Cassell and Edward Nolan—are to be left behind. So, too, to my sorrow, is the Heavy Cavalry Brigade . . . they are to follow us, as soon as transports can be sent back for them, together with the siege train and the men's tents.

"I have not seen Phillip but am told he is aboard the *Himalaya* with Cardigan and his headquarters . . . and that your friend, Mrs Duberly, has contrived, with his lordship's consent, to smuggle herself aboard also. Lady Errol also is rumored to be with the Rifles, but I cannot vouch for the truth of this. Rumors are legion. Marshal St Arnaud sailed this evening in the *Ville de Paris,* which flies the flag of Admiral Hamlin, together with the rest of the French ships . . . evidently our rate of loading is too slow for him. Men continue to die of cholera but the medical officers assure us that, once we are at sea, the infection will lose its virulence and we shall be freed of it at last. I pray that this may be so and my thoughts are constantly with you, my courageous wife, and the cholera victim for whose life you are fighting.

"We, who are leaving Varna, may escape but you, my darling, for whose safety I would a thousand times gladly sacrifice my own, must remain. Go as soon as you can to join your sister in Therapia, Emmy my love, and take no more needless risks. I have asked William Beatson to do what he can for you in the matter of a passage to Scutari and I beg you, if you love me, listen to his advice and permit him to serve you. . . ."

The letter continued, on a more optimistic note, under the date of Thursday, 7 September.

"Last night, driven back it is believed by bad weather, the French fleet returned. And, in the early hours of this morning, while it was still moonlight, Admiral Lyons' signal to weigh anchor was received, with great thankfulness, by our fleet. It was obeyed as dawn broke and never was there so splendid a sight as when our ships started to put to sea. The day promised fair and as the sun rose it shone down on a veritable forest of masts and spars. Sails were hoisted and unfurled; on deck, the bands played and the men cheered. Steamers took the transports in tow, a pair to each, and the whole manœuvre smartly executed, each wheeling into line with her next ahead. We leaned on the rail and tried to count them but the task was beyond us, as more and more ships appeared from nowhere to join us.

"We have received our orders for landing although, as yet, no hint has been given as to where our landing will be made. Most of us are of the opinion that it will be as near as possible to Sebastopol itself since this, it is now known, is to be our objective. The Infantry is to land by divisions; the Light, then the 1st, which is ours, followed by the 2nd, 3rd, and 4th. Each man is to carry ashore with him nothing save his ammunition and three days' rations and from this, Colonel Cameron of the 42nd, has deduced that we may expect our landing to be opposed. But Sir Colin disagrees with him; in his view, Lord Raglan will endeavor to put the army ashore at some point where the Russians are least expecting it."

On Tuesday, 12 September, Alex wrote:

"Last Sunday, leaving the fleet at anchor off Cape Tarkan, Lord Raglan's ship, the *Caradoc,* detached herself and departed for an unknown destination. His lordship was accompanied by General Canrobert, Admiral Lyons, Sir George Brown and Sir John Burgoyne and we have since learned that they made a reconnaissance of Sebastopol, approaching within range of the guns. As a precaution, the *Caradoc* hoisted a Russian flag but she was unmolested and, indeed, appears to have conducted her survey without arousing the smallest interest in those on shore!

"And now we have weighed anchor and are making for Calamita Bay where we are to make our landing at the place chosen by Lord Raglan, which is some ten miles north of the Bulgnak River, and not far from the ancient Ottoman town of Eupatoria. This town surrendered to us today, without a shot being fired."

The final paragraphs of the letter bore the date of 15 September.

"I landed yesterday, with Sir Colin and his staff and, as he had predicted, our landing was unopposed. We were watched by a few Cossacks but that was all. No horses could be landed and no tents . . . after trudging five miles inland on foot, the sunshine turned to heavy rain. Colonel Sterling, the brigade major, had provided himself with a portable bivouac shelter, purchased in London but this, alas was too small to take us all. He and Sir Colin kept reasonably dry but I, in common with the rest of the British army, was soon soaked to the skin. The French were better off, each man carrying a dog-tent in his pack and the Turks, who landed fully equipped with tents, had an encampment set up before the downpour commenced, thus putting us to shame. Our poor fellows had no protection save their greatcoats and sodden blankets and could light no bivouac fires, so that they were hungry, as well as damp and cold. Many, hardly yet recovered from the effects of cholera and dysentery, suffered a relapse and had to be carried back to the ships—some, I fear, dying.

"Today bright sunshine has succeeded the rain but we have made the unhappy discovery that the countryside is almost waterless. Men who have exhausted the contents of their water-canteens, are drinking from muddy pools, despite orders to the contrary, and this too, has led to many falling sick. Sir Colin Campbell's Highlanders are the least affected—they are accustomed to sleeping in the open, wrapped in their plaids, and the kilt is a wonderful protection for those who wear it, against cold and damp. In addition, they obey orders and bear their thirst stoically, good fellows that they are.

"I am writing these last lines to you, seated on a sand dune, watching the unloading of the Light Brigade's horses. As their disembarkation threatened to cause as much delay as did their loading, they are being lowered over the ship's side and left to swim ashore by themselves. It is an unpleasant spectacle but the majority have landed safely. A few, too frightened to see where the shore was, set their faces out to sea and were drowned. Our own horses, including my grey Arab, Shahraz, were put ashore more humanely for which I, at least, am thankful.

"I now await an opportunity to approach the purser of the *Himalaya* to whom I intend to entrust delivery of my letter to you. I hope you will receive it although, in my heart, I confess to the contradictory wish that you may not be in Varna when the ship returns there . . . rather is it my hope that you are even now on your way to join Charlotte in Constantinople or Therapia, and Lord Cassell with you. Wherever you are, my dearest Emmy, my thoughts and my prayers are constantly of you and for you. God bless and keep you, my love."

There was a postscript, scrawled across the back of the envelope, to say that Alex had seen and passed the time of day with Mrs Duberly who, parted from her husband, had been on her way to take passage in the *Shooting Star.*

Emmy received the letter from one of the *Himalaya*'s officers but it did not allay her anxiety on Alex's account for, even as she read it, there were rumours of a terrible battle being fought at the Alma. But Arthur Cassell, still weak though convalescent now, offered her comfort and William Beatson, calling to bid her farewell before sailing for the Crimea with the Heavy Brigade, urged them both to return to Scutari.

"It is said," he told her, "that a certain Miss Nightingale is coming out under the auspices of the British government, to organize a band of nurses to care for our sick in the hospital at Scutari. I am certain that, with your experience and training, Mrs Sheridan, your assistance would be welcome."

Emmy inclined her head. "When Arthur is fit to travel," she agreed, "I'll take your advice, Colonel Beatson. In the meantime"—she put a letter in his hand, smiling up at him—"would you be so kind as to give this to Alex when you see him?"

He took it and, having placed it carefully in his wallet, lifted her hand to his lips. "*Au revoir,* my dear . . . may God have you in His keeping. We shall meet again, I hope."

Emmy echoed his wish, with tears in her eyes.

The British and French armies had marched to the banks of the Alma, crossing the Bulgnak on the afternoon of 19 September. Apart from a skirmish, in which the Light Cavalry Brigade had been somewhat ingloriously involved, they had met with no opposition although, as the march progressed and the heat increased, more and more men fell out.

They had made a brave and memorable spectacle when they set out, in their ordered ranks and brilliant uniforms, with bands playing and the men singing, the French with drums rolling on the right of the line, marching in their traditional diamond formation. But after a while, the singing ceased and the bands were silent. Men collapsed, writhing in the agony of a cholera attack; others started to discard the heavier items of their equipment—greatcoats, shakos, bearskins, mess-tins, crossbelts—as the sun rose higher and the pangs of thirst grew more acute. They plodded grimly on, leaving a trail of dead and dying comrades behind them, to be given whatever attention the small, desperately overtaxed band of stretcher bearers in the rear could provide. With the merciful coming of darkness, they halted and lit bivouac fires and the exhausted men gathered round them to cook their evening meal. A number, too tired to eat, flung themselves down and slept where they fell; some died during the night, unheard by those who lay stretched out beside them.

Contact was made with the fleet at the river mouth and the sick were transferred to the ships. From the fleet came also the news that the main Russian army from Sebastopol, under the command of Prince Menschikoff, was established on the Heights above the Alma, prepared to dispute the invaders' march south. A major battle was now, it seemed, inevitable and it remained only to decide upon a plan of action. Lord Raglan, in the deserted posthouse he had taken over as his headquarters, conferred with some of his senior generals and, toward evening, received a visit from Marshal St Arnaud. The French commander-in-chief had drawn up a plan for the coming battle, which he urged Lord Raglan to accept.

Details of the plan were not made known, even to the British divisional commanders but they, as well as the brigade commanders, were soon in possession of as much information concerning the Russian troop depositions as the observers on board the Allied warships were able to supply. Sir Colin Campbell's subordinate command precluded his presence at Lord Raglan's council of war but he kept his small staff busy gathering reports from French as well as British sources until, working far into the night, he had finally satisfied himself that he had learnt all he could of the situation.

Alex, working under his direction, compiled a sketch map, which showed clearly that the Allies' task was likely to be a formidable one, if they were to dislodge Prince Menschikoff from the line he had elected to defend—and whose defense he had apparently been preparing since news of the landing at Calamita Bay had reached him. Based on naval observations, it appeared that the Russian commander-in-chief had positioned his army along a line of hills which, starting as a sheer cliff at the mouth of the Alma, ran precipitously to a high point known, from an unfinished telegraph station at its summit, as Telegraph Hill. From here, the Heights curved into a ravine-indented natural amphitheatre, about a mile across and half a mile in depth, with the post-road from Eupatoria to Sebastopol running through it.

On the other side stood Kourgane Hill, marked on the map as being four hundred and fifty feet high and rising from the river in a series of steep plateau, which afforded excellent concealment for heavy gun batteries. Sir Colin Campbell, studying the map with furrowed brows, expressed no opinion as to grand strategy to his staff. As a mere brigadier-general this was not his concern and, with the good sense which characterized him, he confined himself to his own immediate responsibilities, only issuing such orders as he deemed necessary for the direction of his brigade. But it was evident, even to the weary Alex, that he was thinking deeply. He said, before retiring for the few hours that remained of the night, "If I were Prince Menschikoff, I should station no troops at all on these cliffs within a mile or so of the shore, where they would be at the mercy of our naval guns. The cliffs themselves may be depended upon to keep his line inviolable and a few trenches, dug above the coast road, well-manned, could hold them . . . with covering fire from the artillery on the Heights. To my mind, Kourgane Hill is the key to the whole position, for it is there that he will almost certainly concentrate his artillery where it will command, from above, the low ground south of the river, which we must cross in order to commence our attack. But I wonder . . ."

He sighed and was silent, as if reluctant to express his thoughts and fears aloud, even to the members of his own staff.

The next morning, without bugle or trumpet call, the British army was roused to a hot, sultry day. As the divisions were wheeled into line and the ammunition train was brought up, details of Marshal St Arnaud's plan were rumored and talked about.

This was, it seemed, for the French to cross the river at the Almatamak and attack from the right, striking the Russians on their left flank and rolling it up toward the centre. While this operation was in progress, the British were to attack the centre and the right flank—mounting their attack from the village of Bourliouk, where they would cross the river, with Kourgane Hill as their objective—and catch the Russians in a pincer movement.

General Bosquet's division of Zouaves and the Turks were to begin the battle by attacking the sparsely held cliffs close to the shore, supported—as Sir Colin Campbell had suggested—by the guns of the fleet. When Bosquet had attained his objectives, the French, in line with the British, would cross the Alma. . . .

Marshal St Arnaud paid a visit to the British lines, where he received an ovation which obviously moved him very deeply. Alex, attending an unusually grim and uncommunicative Sir Colin Campbell, witnessed the marshal's departure and, soon after ten o'clock, the order to advance was given. The British army marched in square formation, the Light Division leading, with the 1st in support on the left and the 2nd on the right, in line with the French division commanded by Prince Jerome Napoleon. It was very hot and frequent halts had to be made, but by noon the Heights of the Alma came into sight and, two miles ahead, down a gentle slope, the river ran between lines of poplar trees to the sea. Another halt was called, in a sunny cornfield where the troops ate their midday meal and Lord Raglan rode forward with his headquarters, to reconnoiter the enemy position.

From below, this looked impregnable. On the opposite side of the river rose a double line of heights. The first were steep green hillocks, upon which masses of Russian infantry could be seen, the sunlight glinting on their bayonets. Behind and above rose a series of rocky plateau on which gun batteries had been placed, to command the whole of the flat, low-lying ground on the south bank of the Alma. Highest of all, steeper and more rugged, the crest of the hills held reserves of infantry and still more gun emplacements, whilst a dark mass of cavalry could just be discerned, over to the left, where they waited in support of the infantry, on the lower slopes.

The advance proceeded until, at about two o'clock, the first Russian guns opened fire. The order was given to deploy into line and at this point, it was found that the British and French armies had drawn too close to each other. The 2nd Division of the British army, commanded by Sir George de Lacy Evans, was jostled by Prince Jerome Napoleon's and, in turn, crowded into Sir George Brown's Light Division on its left. Sir George ordered his men to take ground to the left in fours but the Russian fire had now become heavy and the order was not complied with in sufficient depth to relieve the congestion. The men of the two leading British divisions were left without room in which to maneuver and the flank regiments were soon inextricably muddled and marching on each other's heels.

Sir Colin Campbell, watching the imperfect deployment of the Light Division with some dismay, exclaimed to his brigade major, in Alex's hearing, "By God, those regiments are not moving like English soldiers!"

But when the 1st Division's turn came to deploy, his own divisional commander, the Duke of Cambridge—anxious not to make the same mistake as Sir George Brown—spread his line on so wide a front that it stretched far beyond the Light Division's left. To make matters infinitely worse, the right encroached on the ground which Sir Richard England's 3rd Division would need for its own deployment and in consequence, the 3rd had to be pulled out and placed in support. Then the order came for the two leading divisions to halt their advance and lie down. In their rear, the supporting divisions, still out of effective range of the

Russian batteries firing from the lower slopes of Kourgane Hill, were halted and stood at ease.

Now began a time of nerve-wracking strain for the waiting men of the 1st and Light Divisions, few of whom had been in action before. They were compelled to lie inert for over an hour, under heavy fire, without the means to retaliate. Lord Raglan, whose personal courage was never more admirably demonstrated, seeking to share his men's ordeal, rode up and down in full view of the enemy, the plumed hats of his staff drawing upon them and himself a fierce but apparently disregarded fire. He was waiting—although they did not know this or realize that it was the cause of the delay—for news of General Bosquet's assault on the cliffs behind Almatamak, the essential prelude to the main British and French attack. Until this came, they could do nothing but wait. Bosquet's Zouaves and the Turkish infantry had accomplished the first part of their mission with speed and dash, finding the cliffs—as Sir Colin had said they would be—virtually unmanned, but they were now held up by the almost insuperable difficulty of getting their artillery up the steep cliff path. Finally, however, word reached Marshall St Arnaud that Bosquet had succeeded in establishing himself firmly on the Heights by the river mouth but had neither enough guns nor enough men to continue his advance.

The marshal, waving his arm toward the river, ordered General Canrobert and Prince Jerome Napoleon to go to Bosquet's support and attack the left of the Russian centre. They began their attack but, just before three o'clock, an urgent request for help reached Lord Raglan. Prince Napoleon's division was being massacred, the message stated, Canrobert's had crossed the river but was pinned down and driven to seek shelter beneath the overhanging rocks they were endeavoring to ascend. Bosquet was now under heavy pressure and would be compelled to retreat, unless the British launched an immediate counter-attack on the Russian right.

Lord Raglan ordered the British line to advance and not to halt until the Alma was crossed. The men in the leading divisions sprang to their feet, eager, after the long wait they had endured, for action. Under continuous fire, they were meticulously dressed into line, two deep and thus, in splendid alignment, two miles in width, the Light and 2nd Divisions began their advance, preceded by men of the Rifle Brigade in extended order. As they did so, the Russians set fire to the village of Bourliouk, which stood in the path of the 2nd Division. Partly due to the dense pall of smoke which rose from its blazing houses, partly due to the uneven nature of the ground—which was broken by walls and fences, enclosing vineyards—the line of advance was broken and swiftly became disorderly. De Lacy Evans's leading brigades were compelled to separate and pass on either side of the blazing village. The general himself led the troops on the left, his brigadier, Pennefather, wheeling to the right, and both reached and forded the river to begin the ascent to the lower slopes under a withering fire from the Russian guns above them.

The men of the Light Division crossed the river as best they could, further to the left, some wading up to their necks in water, their rifles and ammunition pouches held above their heads, others finding a sandbank and wading across, little more than ankle deep. A murderous fire of grape and cannister, directed on them from above, took heavy toll, and, in places where the river was deep and swift-flowing, many were swept off their feet and drowned. By the time they reached the steep bank on the opposite side and started to draw themselves up on to a narrow ledge of dried mud immediately beneath it, they had become completely disorganized. Regiments were mixed, officers had lost touch with their men and small groups, cut off from the sight of others to the right and left by bends in the river, found themselves isolated and without any clear idea of what they should do.

Here and there an officer appeared who took command of any groups, irrespective of formation, that he could rally round him. General Codrington ordered the remnants of his brigade to fix bayonets and advance to the attack and they did as he bade them, with splendid gallantry. Colonel Lacy Yea, of the 7th Royal Fusiliers, and Colonel Blake, of the 33rd Duke of Wellington's Regiment, led another spirited up-hill bayonet charge against a column of Russian infantry, descending the hill to meet them. General Buller, with two regiments of his brigade, the 77th and the 88th, halted on the far side of the river, apparently expecting a cavalry attack, but the rest went on. On his left, the 19th Regiment joined with Codrington's Brigade, together with some of the 95th from the 2nd Division. The 23rd Royal Welsh Fusiliers had contrived somehow to keep together under their own officers and, with the 7th, under Yea, they drove back the first wave of Russian infantry.

The British line, ragged and nowhere more than two deep, followed them, now pausing to fire into the grey mass of Russians, reloading to fire a second volley, then continuing the advance. The Russians, unnerved by their dauntless, purposeful steadiness, wavered and took flight, seeking the protection of the well-entrenched battery of twelve brass guns in the Great Redoubt to their rear and confident of their gunners' ability to break and drive back the straggling, irregular line of British soldiers. The guns were unable to fire until their own men were out of range, but once they were the Russian gunners opened up with deadly precision. For several minutes, the advancing line was halted, then, backed up by more men scrambling up to the top of the river bank, it came on again. Great gaps were torn in its ranks but they were filled; whole groups of men fell under the hail of exploding shells and were mown down by grape and cannister and round shot . . . yet always there were others to take their places.

The line was too thin, too elastic to break; those who composed it were too courageous and too well-disciplined to fall back when their orders had been to advance. They came on, spent and breathless, straight into the mouths of the guns—men of the 33rd, the 95th and the Rifle Brigade, under officers who were strangers to them, in many cases, and N.C.O.s whom some of them had never seen before. Colonel Yea's Fusiliers were in the van, close on their colonel's heels, cheering as they ran. Then suddenly, to their stunned astonishment, the Russian gunners started to remove their guns, hitching them to cavalry horses and galloping off at full speed. An ensign of the 23rd, first to reach the Great Redoubt, died as he planted the Queen's Colour of his regiment on the parapet, but his men swarmed in to take possession of it, yelling in triumph, only to find themselves under heavy fire from other gun emplacements higher up the hill. Despite support from two British batteries, which had come up from behind the burning village of Bourliouk to open accurate fire, their position became desperate when strong reserves of Russian infantry started to pour in volleys of musketry from above, preparatory to counter-attacking. Sir George Brown, despairing of support for his shattered division, ordered them to retire.

Support was, at that moment, on its way to them from the 1st Division but had been delayed by undue caution on the part of the Duke of Cambridge. He had advanced to the vineyards on the south bank of the Alma but here halted his men and ordered them to lie down and take cover. Able to see little of what was going on through the smoke of battle, he hesitated to risk the lives of his men in what appeared to be the rout of the Light Division. But he risked his own in going forward to seek the advice of General Buller, who confessed to being himself in no little confusion and somewhat uncertainly advised an advance. This suggestion the duke, in spite of the fact that he had asked for it, neglected to take, until General Airey sought him out and repeated it.

Alex, with Sir Colin Campbell on the left of the line, sensed a growing restlessness both in his commander and the Highlanders of his brigade, borne of inaction and a common reluctance to take cover when other men were engaged in battle. But this vanished when one of the duke's aides came galloping up to inform them that they were now to advance across the river in support of the Light Division.

Sir Colin addressed his men briefly before leading them off.

"Now, men, you are going into action. Remember this: whoever is wounded, I don't care what his rank is, must lie down where he falls till the bandsmen come to attend to him. No soldier must go off carrying wounded men. Be in no hurry to fire. Your officers will tell you when to do so and then—aim low. Be steady. Keep silent." And then he concluded gruffly, "The army will be watching you—make me proud of the Highland Brigade!"

The brigade moved off in echelon, the 42nd (the Black Watch) slightly ahead on the right; the 93rd (Sutherland Highlanders) in the centre and the 79th (the Camerons) somewhat withdrawn on the left.

To their right, Alex could see the Guards Brigade advancing with parade ground steadiness, the Scots Fusilier Guards in the centre, leading the advance. Ordered to break ranks on reaching the river, the Scots were over first and were starting to align themselves when General Codrington's A.D.C. reached General Bentinck pleading for instant support. Bentinck, without waiting for the arrival of the Grenadiers and Coldstream, spurred his horse to their head, shouting above the roar of the guns and the crackle of musketry for them to follow him. They did so, into so fierce a hail of fire that, still in imperfect formation and without support on either side, they lost over a hundred men in a matter of minutes. To add to their confusion, the Russians had now brought strong reserves to the Great Redoubt and these, firing a shattering volley at point-blank range into the gallant remnants of the Royal Welch, sent them hurtling downwards into the ranks of the advancing Fusilier Guards.

This would have been damaging to the morale of the finest troops, for it broke the already straggling line and added immeasurably to the Scots Fusiliers' difficulties, but worse was to follow. A shout was heard, which was taken up and repeated on all sides: "Fusiliers retire! The Fusiliers must retire!"

Intended, undoubtedly, for Yea's 7th Royal Fusiliers, who were isolated on the right of the Great Redoubt, it was heard in the heat and confusion of the battle by the Scots and they obeyed it. A number formed about their Colours, borne by Ensign Robert Lindsay, and held their ground, unable to believe that they had been ordered to retreat; the rest broke and fell back, as the order was repeated by their own adjutant, to whom Bentinck, hoping to save his men from massacre, had now given it. The Russian reserves leapt from the epaulement of the Great Redoubt, with bayonets fixed, and charged after them.

The Grenadiers and Coldstream, five minutes behind them in crossing the Alma, were held by their regimental commanders until they were property aligned. Then, in the order which Bentinck's haste had not permitted the Scots, they advanced up the Kourgane Hill with magnificent steadiness—but with a great gap in their centre where the Scots should have been—to be met by the main body of the Russian infantry reserves. The Guards greeted them with volley after volley of withering and accurate fire and, as the Russians fell back, they continued their advance. With great gallantry, the Scots Fusilier Guards reformed and came toiling back up the hill to fill the gap which their precipitate retreat had left in the line.

The whole brigade vanished into the smoke of the Russian guns.

The Highland Brigade, last of the division to cross the Alma, did so in perfect order. The point at which they crossed, to the left of the Guards, was one at which a bend in the river took them to the north-east.

Alex, two days later, wrote an account of the action to Emmy.

"I had been despatched to deliver Sir Colin Campbell's orders for the advance to Colonel Douglas of the 79th and was on my way back to my post when, to my astonishment, I observed our divisional commander, His Royal Highness the Duke of Cambridge, gallop over to Sir Colin. He was in a state of visible distress and agitation and I heard him announce that the Scots Fusilier Guards had met with a terrible reverse and were falling back.

"He said, 'There must be a disaster, Sir Colin, unless the division is withdrawn . . . a disaster!'

"Sir Colin's reply was characteristic of him and I heard it with pride. 'There must be a disaster if they are withdrawn, your Royal Highness. Permit me, if you please, to continue to their support with the Highland Brigade!'

"The duke gave permission with evident reluctance. He said, in a voice so low I could barely make out the words, 'We shall be tried for this, Sir Colin . . . the Guards will be destroyed.'

"To which Sir Colin answered firmly, 'Sir, it were better that every man of Her Majesty's Guards should lie dead on the field of battle than that they should turn their backs upon the enemy.' Then he saluted and placing himself at the head of the 42nd, ordered them forward.

"They are magnificent soldiers, these Highlanders, and they fell in behind him as if they had been on the parade ground. Sir Colin's orders were to maintain our echelon formation, the same as that in which we had crossed the river, with the 42nd leading, on the right, the 93rd in the centre and the 79th behind and to the left. Our line thus extended for more than a mile and, only two ranks deep, deceived the Russians as to our strength, as well as presenting a much smaller target for their fire.

"On our left, we brushed by the 77th, in line facing east, and the 88th on the right, who were halted in a square, under the command of General Buller, and Sir Colin, angry for the first time I had seen him that day, told them to get into line and follow us. They did not and I heard an Irish voice shout after us, in bitterness, 'Let the Scotchmen go on . . . they'll do the work!' It was plain that such doughty fighters felt great distaste for the orders their own commander had given them, but had no choice save to obey them.

"Sir Colin led us in a wide sweep round the back of the Great Redoubt which, through the haze of smoke, we could see the Guards approaching. He gave the order to advance firing, which is something only the most highly disciplined troops can do, and I was filled with admiration for the way in which the Highlanders carried out his orders. They advanced at a rapid pace, alternately firing and cheering, and never halting. The gunners of a sixteen—or eighteen—gun battery to the left of the Great

Redoubt, seeing our advance as a threat to their guns, started to withdraw them, without actually coming under our fire.

"Some reserves of Russian infantry, seeking to cover the withdrawal of the guns, massed to attack the 42nd and Sir Colin sent me back to order up the 93rd so as to outflank them. But after I had gone to deliver this order to Colonel Ainslie, Sir Colin was apparently not satisfied with the dressing of the 93rd, for the men were over-eager and pressing forward, and he came cantering back to attend to it himself. The regiment was under heavy fire and his horse was shot in the heart and fell dead, throwing him, I feared, heavily. But I gave him my horse and he remounted and calmly held the 93rd until their dressing was to his approval. Then, warning them against overhastiness, he returned to the 42nd and later sent my horse back to me, having obtained his chestnut from his groom.

"The 93rd, very much steadier after his admonition, took the Russians by surprise, for they made their appearance suddenly, from the concealment of a ridge, and a cavalry attack, launched against them, was met and beaten off by the 79th, employing the same tactic. They poured several volleys into the exposed flank of the Cossacks, who retired in great disorder . . . the value of our brigades echelon formation being again splendidly demonstrated.

"Following up behind the 79th were two excellently commanded batteries of the Horse Artillery, which completed the rout of the Russians by directing a deadly enfilading fire against them. Our men were now ordered to fix bayonets and charge, which they did with great cheering, gaining the summit of Kourgane Hill with the Russians running before them. We entered from the flank of the battery named by our troops the Great Redoubt, the Guards disputing for the honor with us, but Sir Colin called out in a great roar, 'We'll hae nane but Hieland bonnets here!' Our men, in an excess of pride and excitement, raised their bonnets on the points of their bayonets and, as long as I live, I shall not forget the cheer they gave him.

"It was taken up by the Guards, who had fought magnificently, and by those gallant survivors of General Codrington's brigade, passing down right through the 2nd and 3rd Divisions to the 4th in the rear. We had gained Kourgane Hill, the Russians were in full retreat and, to our right, the French divisions were in possession of their objectives, with their artillery firing down now, from the Heights, upon the defeated enemy. They, closing in to get through the gorge through which runs the post-road to Sebastopol, presented a perfect target.

"As we waited on the summit of Kourgane for the 3rd Division to pass through us in pursuit, Lord Lucan and Lord Cardigan rode up with the cavalry. Both seemed to be in an evil temper and Edward Nolan, who was with them, told me that they had endured a day of extreme frustration, being held on the extreme left flank, with orders to remain there. Their role was, it seems, to guard against attack from that quarter—an attack which never materialized, though no doubt prevented from doing so by their presence.

"Nevertheless all felt conscious of humiliation and were eager to set off in pursuit of the retreating Russians and attempt to capture some guns. But scarcely had they come up with us than an order came from Lord Raglan, forbidding the cavalry to attack. There was much complaint and dissatisfaction when this order was repeated; Lucan despatched an aide to question it, but he had gone only a few yards on his way when a second order arrived. The Light Brigade was to divide, Lucan on the left and Cardigan on the right, and escort the artillery to a forward position. The instruction that the cavalry was, in no circumstances, to attack was once more emphasized.

"They obeyed it, with such reluctance that my heart bled for them, and later I heard from Phillip—who has come through unscathed—that a third order was sent, commanding the return of the brigade the instant it had completed its escort duty. Most of them were well nigh speechless with indignation and it is said that it was as much as a man's life was worth to approach Lord Lucan after the third order had reached him. I have no doubt that the cavalry's hour will yet come but I confess, my dearest Emmy, that after this day, I have no regrets for my temporary change of service. It has been a rare privilege to fight with these splendid Highland Regiments and the greatest honour to have served, even for a little while, under Sir Colin Campbell.

"A somewhat touching and most appropriate ceremony marked the end of the day. Lord Raglan sent for Sir Colin and thanked him, with tears in his eyes and his emotion so great that he could hardly speak, for his zeal and bravery. He then asked whether there was anything he could do to gratify him and mark the occasion. Sir Colin's reply touched us all deeply, and the hearts of his gallant Highlanders deepest of all. 'My lord, if you seek to gratify me,' said he, without hesitation, 'then will your lordship grant me permission henceforth to wear a Highland bonnet, in place of my general's cocked hat!'

"Permission being duly granted, with a smile of pleasure and surprise, by Lord Raglan, Lieutenant Drysdale, working through the night, delivered to him next morning a bonnet, in which the hackles of the three regiments were combined. Sir Colin has worn no other since its presentation, thus endearing himself more warmly than ever to his men.

"Our casualties, in the brigade, are remarkably light thanks be to God . . . fifteen killed and 83 wounded. I myself sustained a minor bruise or two and a sword cut on my left arm, but I feel little discomfort from either and it does not keep me from work. In all, they say we have lost between three and four hundred killed and some sixteen hundred wounded, but the French losses are held on good authority to be greater and the Russians' greatest of all, although no one can yet come near to estimating a figure. The surgeons and the burial parties are still at work on the battlefield, and every day a mournful procession of wounded is on its way to the ships, which leave for Scutari as they are filled.

"The rest of us wait in bivouac, wondering when the order will come for us to advance once more on Sebastopol. The French, it appears, are insisting on delay, but the order cannot much longer be delayed, if we are to reap the fruits of our victory. The Russians are routed and demoralized and a combined assault, by land and sea, must surely be successful. . . ."

CHAPTER EIGHT
>>> • <<<

IT WAS NOT UNTIL the 23rd September that Marshal St Arnaud agreed, at last, to continue the advance on Sebastopol. The marshal, a desperately sick man, had heard that the passage to the next river in their path, the Katcha, was likely to be strongly resisted, and that the one beyond, the Balbec, was defended by formidable earthworks.

But at last, on a fine, sunny morning the two armies re-formed and marched down from the blood-drenched Heights of the Alma into the valley of the Katcha. They met with no opposition, finding in front of them only the litter of abandoned stores and equipment of a fleeing army. The fleet made contact again at the river mouth and Alex joyfully recorded in his letter to Emmy that the 1st Royal Dragoons were landed there from the *Pride of the Ocean* and the Scots Greys from the *Himalaya*—first of the Heavy Brigade to rejoin the Cavalry Division. The Balbec proved to be innocent of earthworks and devoid of Russian troops. As the two armies marched up the far side of the valley, they were able to look down on Sebastopol, four miles below.

Alex wrote: "Sebastopol looked very peaceful in the afternoon sunlight. It is a beautiful town, the buildings a dazzling white, sur-mounted by domes and cupolas of green copper. One could identify many of the buildings . . . the Admiralty, the Naval Bar-racks and, of course, the Star Fort, which appears to be of immense strength, with gun embrasures facing north and south, as well as out to sea. The harbour cuts the town in two; ships lie at anchor in the roadstead but, according to rumour, block-ships have been sunk at its entrance, so that they cannot leave. On the other hand, our ships will not be able to enter . . . even if not prevented from doing so by the guns of the forts.

"Yet it does not look as if the resistance it could offer would be insuperable and, as we observed the town from above, there were few signs of the garrison or, indeed, of the presence of any troops. Lord Raglan is believed to be in favour of an attack from the north, supported by a naval bombardment from the sea, but the French are opposed to this and General Burgoyne—to whose views his lordship pays much attention—has apparently advised a march inland and around Sebastopol. The attack would then pre-sumably be launched from the south and there is talk of basing the fleets on the harbour at Balaclava.

"But I cannot vouch for the truth of this, as Lord Raglan

continues to confer with Marshal St Arnaud and may yet persuade the French to his way of thinking."

But Lord Raglan's final interview with Marshal St Arnaud on Sunday, 24 September, resulted in his yielding to the French wish to turn inland at once. St Arnaud sat stiffly in his chair, contributing little to the discussion, and as they left, a British staff officer remarked on how regally he had behaved. "Did you not observe him?" Lord Raglan said sadly. "He is dying."

Within a few hours, the marshal was reported to have collapsed with an attack of cholera but in spite of this, next morning at 8:30, as had been agreed, the two armies started the march inland. This time, the British led and the French soldiers cheered them as they passed.

The march was to be accomplished as rapidly as possible, for neither commander relished the prospect of being cut off for too long from his fleet. The country over which they must march was dense and virtually trackless woodland and brush, of which few maps were in existence, so that the main body of the British army was ordered to strike south-east on a compass bearing. But they accomplished this successfully, save for an unfortunate incident in which the cavalry, under Lord Lucan, being misdirected by their guide, failed to rendezvous with Lord Raglan and, as a result, the British commander-in-chief was in danger of capture by a Russian force leaving Sebastopol. He was saved, to the cavalry's humiliation, by a troop of the Horse Artillery, under Captain Maude.

After meeting only token opposition, Balaclava was entered. The French left Lord Raglan the choice of taking Balaclava or the neighboring harbours of Kamiesch or Kazatch as his base, waiving their claim to the right of the line, when the two armies swung round to face Sebastopol. On the advice of Admiral Lyons, he chose Balaclava, which was deep, hemmed in by massive cliffs and possessed of great natural strength. It also possessed, however, two great disadvantages; it was small and landlocked and all supplies had to be carried from the ships in harbour up a narrow, rutted track, to the camps on the plateau above it. Additionally the British right flank was open to attack and had constantly to be guarded.

On 25 September, the dying Marshal St Arnaud relinquished his command of the French army to General Canrobert. Next day he was carried on board the battleship *Berthelot,* where he died the following afternoon. Lord Raglan resumed his council of war with the marshal's successor, but found him even more reluctant than St Arnaud had been to agree to an immediate assault on Sebastopol. An assault without siege-guns would, Canrobert stated emphatically, be suicidal and Sir John Burgoyne agreed with the French view—the siege trains must be landed and the heavy guns got into position to bombard the Sebastopol defenses, before an attack could be contemplated. To this, Lord Raglan was reluctantly forced to agree although General Cathcart, whose 4th Division was on high ground overlooking the very heart of the Russian defenses, protested that he could walk into the town, with scarcely the loss of a man.

The assault was delayed, in deference to the French concept of war and, as the days passed into weeks, the inhabitants of Sebastopol built up their defenses. Men, women and children worked night and day to raise great mounds of earth in front of their city and to man these with guns, building them into an extended system of formidable strength . . . eventually four miles long. When the expected Allied attack failed to materialize,

Prince Menschikoff responded to Admiral Korniloff's urgent demand for reinforcements and, by 9th October, had sent him nearly thirty thousand men.

The British army, to whom—on the hills above Sebastopol—these frenzied defensive preparations were no secret, waited in growing frustration and impatience. It was taking much longer than anyone had anticipated to drag the heavy siege-guns into position and now the guns of Sebastopol were subjecting them to increasingly heavy counter-fire. The crowded harbour at Balaclava, where all supplies, guns, ammunition and reinforcements had to be set ashore, was turning into chaotic shambles, with ships packed so closely together that none could move. The port lay outside the Allied perimeter and was connected with the camps by a narrow gorge, up which everything required for the siege had labouriously to be carried.

Alex wrote briefly to Emmy, a few paragraphs dated 4 October, from bivouac on the heights overlooking Sebastopol:

"We now have tents for the officers, and a few for the men, although we are told that more are on the way from Balaclava. We are just out of range of the guns but there are frequent raids by the Russians on our perimeter; in consequence, we have to furnish pickets for outpost duty and are always under arms. It is becoming increasingly cold, unpleasantly so at night. Cholera is, alas, again on the increase and the men grow weary of this waiting. The siege train has been landed and the guns are being got into position but it is slow work, for they must be manhandled up the cliff from the harbour. The navy is landing guns and the sailors work magnificently, fifty men to a gun, dragging their eighteen-pounders up the pass to the plateau lashed to drag ropes. The army is hacking out emplacements and digging trenches on the high points, with infinite labour, for the ground is rocky and difficult to prepare. . . ."

On 6 October he wrote still more briefly:

"General Scarlett and the rest of the Heavy Brigade landed two days ago, and Colonel Beatson with them. They are encamped at the eastern end of what is known to us as the South Valley and today I sought them out and received your most welcome letter from the colonel's hands. I am glad to learn that Lord Cassell has recovered and I pray that you and he may both soon be with Charlotte in Therapia or, at least, on your way there. Your letter has given me much joy, my dearest Emmy. I am reading it now for the third time and will endeavor to answer it when I have fully taken it in. . . ."

On 8 October, Alex wrote:

"Yesterday morning, Colonel Sterling, the brigade major, went to post an outlying picket at daybreak, and I accompanied him. While there, we saw a considerable body of Russian cavalry in the valley below, which advanced to within two miles of Balaclava, their skirmishers in front. They drove in a small picket of our Dragoons and then we heard the British trumpets sounding 'to horse' and Lord Lucan rode out, with the Cavalry Division, and they formed up and advanced.

"Meanwhile the Russians galloped up and down, trailing their coats, as it were, and inviting an engagement. I waited, my heart in my mouth, watching for the charge which both Sterling and I were certain would be ordered. But the order never came . . . the 17th Lancers rode up, escorting some Horse Artillery, which unlimbered and opened fire and the Russians withdrew out of range, jeering at our men.

"Later, Phillip told me, there had been a very ugly scene between Lord Lucan and Edward Nolan, in which the latter accused Lucan of neglecting his duty by his failure to attack the enemy. Everyone in the division is bitterly angry, not least Lord Cardigan who missed the affair—as he is sick and aboard one of the ships in the harbour. But he accused Lucan openly, saying he had mishandled the division and he has told the officers of the 11th, to their faces, that they are a set of old women for not having ignored Lucan and charged in spite of him!

"Alas, the poor cavalry, that they must suffer such a commander! Will their chance to show their true worth never come? I find myself wondering whether I should not be wiser to remain where I am, with a commander I can wholeheartedly respect, than attempt to rejoin General Scarlett's staff and thus, perforce, come under Lucan's command. Like Edward Nolan, it is quite heartbreaking to me to be compelled to witness our Cavalry Division being used only for defense and never being permitted to attack . . . although it is said that Lord Raglan is responsible for these instructions to Lucan. But William Beatson urges me to return 'where I belong,' as he puts it, and my loyalty to him binds me strongly, for we have been through much together, he and I. . . ."

The next part of the letter was dated 14 October:

"Today," Alex wrote, "Lord Raglan gave the command of Balaclava and responsibility for its defense to Sir Colin Campbell, although Lord Lucan retains independent command of the cavalry.

"I am to ride with Sir Colin and Captain Shadwell to the village of Kadikoi this morning, so that he may inspect the positions. His command is very inadequate, or so it seems to me. It comprises the 93rd Highlanders, numbering under seven hundred men, a hundred or so invalids and convalescents newly returned from hospital in Scutari, Barker's troop of Horse Artillery, two battalions of marines with artillery, and about fourteen hundred Turco-Tunisian auxiliaries, of whom I have heard little that is good. This force is disposed in a semicircle north and east of Kadikoi, and redoubts, with naval guns, have been constructed to command the Woronzoff Road. Not all the defense work is yet completed and Sir Colin is anxious to have it speeded up, lest there should be a sudden attack.

"Shadwell and I are going with him on his tour of inspection and no doubt, after this I shall be better able to assess the strength of our defenses. . . ."

Alex was compelled to cut short his letter in midsentence, for Sir Colin Campbell was impatient to begin his tour, after which— while he now had a clear picture of the position, he no longer had the heart to enlarge on the defensive strength it possessed in his letter to Emmy. Defensive weakness, he thought wryly, would have been a more apt description. . . .

The Woronzoff Road ran south-east out of Sebastopol and, crossing the Plain of Balaclava, it followed a narrow ridge of high ground, known as the Causeway Heights, finally dropping down to the Tchernaya River, which it crossed by a bridge below the village of Tchorgoun.

The Plain was some three miles long and two wide, enclosed on all sides by hills, and it was divided into two by the ridge which carried the road, the Causeway Heights. Two valleys ran on either side of the Causeway. The North was shut in on one side by the Causeway itself, on the other by an irregular range called the Fedioukine Hills. The South Valley, along which ran the three-mile-long track—for it was little more—from Balaclava to its junction with the Woronzoff Road, was also contained by hills. In this, at the head of a gorge a mile above the harbour, was Kadikoi, where the 93rd Highlanders were encamped, with the Cavalry Division camp to their front.

Strategically it was vital for the British army to retain possession of the Causeway Heights. Sir Colin Campbell at once realized this and, with the limited means at his disposal, he concentrated on its defense, for it was the key to Balaclava and to the army's line of communication with the harbour and the ships. To lose the Causeway Heights would be to lose the only good road to the infantry divisions' camps and the siege-works overlooking Sebastopol, which must be kept supplied with ammunition . . . whatever else they went without. The alternative to the Woronzoff Road was a number of rough mountain tracks, unworthy to be called roads, up which supplies could only be hauled with extreme difficulty.

Of the six redoubts in the course of construction, No. 1 was not on the Causeway Heights at all but on a hillock, known as Canrobert's Hill, to the east. This was the strongest, with good entrenchments and earthworks, and its three naval twelve-pounder guns were manned by a battalion of the Tunisian auxiliaries. Of the remaining five, all positioned on the Causeway Heights and beside the Woronzoff Road, No. 4 occupied the best position, being immediately below a plateau on which General Bosquet was posted, with two French divisions, forming a *corps d'observation,* with which he could dominate both the road and part of the Plain below. Nos. 2 and 3 were about half a mile apart and 5 to 6 separated by nearly a mile, each containing one naval gun. In every redoubt, Sir Colin Campbell posted British artillery N.C.O.s to direct the Tunisians' fire. "And," as he remarked dryly to Alex, "also it is to be hoped, to steady them!"

He was reluctant to use the Tunisians for so vital a task as the guarding of the Causeway Heights, for he mistrusted them, but was left with little choice. Captain Barker's guns, and the Royal Marines with their artillery, were posted on high ground to the rear of the 93rd, covering the gorge. With the battalion of convalescents, they formed the last line of defense but Sir Colin Campbell, aware that they were very ably commanded, had the highest confidence in their ability to hold Balaclava Harbour . . . and even if the Tunisians failed to repel an enemy attack, they could at least give warning of one. This, he knew, would come from the east, from the Tchernaya valley or over the Fedioukines, but so long as the Tunisians held their redoubts and kept a vigilant lookout, there was no danger of his being taken by surprise.

On 16 October, Alex—who had been working night and day on the defenses of Balaclava—received orders to report to General Scarlett, delivered in person by William Beatson. He bade farewell to Sir Colin with regret but, as he and Colonel Beatson rode into the cavalry camp at the foot of the Heights in the South Valley, he felt his heart lift, and Scarlett's greeting of him was so flatteringly warm that his last regret vanished. To Emmy, he wrote that night:

"I am back 'where I belong' at last, Emmy my love . . . with the cavalry and William Beatson. I have not yet seen Phillip but intend to seek him out as soon as I can. The only news is that Lord Cardigan now has his private yacht, the *Dryad,* anchored in Balaclava Harbour—with a French chef and a civilian friend, Mr Hubert de Burgh, to minister to his comfort. He had obtained Lord Raglan's permission to sleep aboard and his brigade does not see him until after he has enjoyed a late breakfast, we are told.

"Edward Nolan waxes bitterly cynical on the subject of 'Lord

Look-on' and 'The Noble Yachtsman' and William Beatson tells me that they are called 'the cautious ass'—Lucan—and 'the dangerous ass'—Cardigan. But, thank heaven, General Scarlett is liked and trusted by all."

The following morning the bombardment of Sebastopol was started by the Allied siege-guns, supported by a naval bombardment of the sea forts. This was to be, at long last, the prelude to an assault on the town . . . or so it was rumored. The naval bombardment did not, however, achieve the success that was hoped for it, although it went on for more than three hours. A heavy loss of life, together with a heavy toll of ships, caused Admiral Dundas to give the signal to the British fleet to haul off soon after 5:30 that evening. The French fleet did no better—wooden ships had been pitted against stone forts and the damage done to the latter was almost negligible, despite the fire-power of the combined fleets.

The Allied land batteries, by comparison, did well although they too suffered severe casualties. But the bombardment was ceaseless and it smashed the defenses of Sebastopol one by one. The garrison now considered an attack virtually certain but, despite Lord Raglan's urging, the French held back. Their batteries on Mont Rodolphe, being nearer than the British to the Russian counter-fire, had sustained many more casualties and made much less impression on the opposing enemy position in the Flagstaff Bastion. A French magazine and an ammunition dump had received direct hits and exploded and General Canrobert insisted on a further 24-hour delay.

Next day, the British land-based guns kept up the bombardment alone; the French were silent and, during the hours of darkness, both sides worked frantically to repair the damage to their defenses. The following morning, the French guns were firing again and both sides continued the bombardment from dawn to dusk. But no orders were issued for the long-awaited assault and, as quickly as they were destroyed, the Russians rebuilt their earthworks and they also brought in more troops and more guns. It was now they, and not the Allies, who made plans to attack. . . .

On 21 October a false report from a Turkish spy caused preparations to be made to meet a Russian attack. The 4th Division, under Sir George Cathcart, was brought down from its position on the heights overlooking Sebastopol, and the Cavalry Division stood-to throughout the night . . . but to no avail. The Russians did not attack. To Sir George Cathcart's fury, his division was in a state of extreme exhaustion when, after an arduous march up steep slopes, it regained its camp, and the cavalry endured a miserably cold night, losing an officer of the 17th Lancers from exposure.

In consequence, when a second and very similar report reached Lord Raglan on the evening of 24th, it was taken seriously by no one except Sir Colin Campbell and the Turkish commander, Rustem Pasha, from one of whose spies it had originated. This report stated that a force of twenty thousand Russian infantry, with artillery and five thousand cavalry in support, under General Liprandi, was about to launch an attack on Balaclava. Lord Raglan, remembering the previous false alarm, having read it, made no acknowledgement of his message to the anxiously waiting Sir Colin . . . and he issued no orders, beyond the request that he should be informed if "anything new came in."

Sir Colin, on his own initiative, informed Lord Lucan of the report, doubled his pickets, ordered the 93rd to sleep in line, armed and with their greatcoats on, and kept the Tunisians at their guns throughout the night. It was all he could do, and when Lucan's request for more Horse Artillery was refused by Lord Raglan, he released Barker's troop from his own command.

The morning of 25th October—the anniversary of Agincourt—dawned obscurely. The mists of the Crimean autumn hung over the heights and uplands and rested over the beleaguered city of Sebastopol like a pall. Under its cover, Cossack *vedettes* from the Tchernaya valley reconnoitered the positions of Lord Lucan, General Bosquet and finally that of Sir Colin Campbell. They reported an "ostentatious weakness" in the latter and also the fact that the high ground at Kamara, which overlooked Canrobert's Hill, was destitute both of guns and pickets.

Prince Menschikoff ordered General Liprandi to attack the British flank and rear, in an attempt to capture Balaclava and destroy its ships and stores.

The battle of Balaclava started at half past six that morning, with an attack on the Turkish redoubt on Canrobert's Hill.

CHAPTER NINE

⋙ • ⋘

THE CAVALRY DIVISION turned out, as usual, an hour before daybreak, in accordance with Lord Lucan's practice of inspecting them at this hour. Alex, attending General Scarlett, joined the small cavalcade which followed the divisional commander on his early morning tour of inspection.

It was still dark and cold and the mist swirled and eddied about them as they left the Heavy Brigade lines and trotted on to the Light Brigade camp, where Lord George Paget was waiting for them. Lord Cardigan, on the plea of an attack of dysentery, slept late on board his yacht and, in his absence, command of the Light Brigade devolved on Lord George, who had his men "standing at their horses." The inspection over, they started to lead their animals out to water, grumbling a little in low voices, for this early morning stand-to was unpopular with the entire division.

It was just like any other morning since he had rejoined General Scarlett's staff, and Alex had no sense of impending disaster as the cavalcade approached the most easterly of the Turkish redoubts on Canrobert's Hill. But, as they did so, the first grey light of dawn brightened the misty eastern sky and, with a sudden quickening of his pulses, he saw that something unusual was afoot. Two flags, instead of the single crescent and star, flew from the flagstaff behind the redoubt and, aware of what this signified, he was about to draw attention to it when Lord George Paget also observed the strange signal. Reining in his horse, he gestured in the direction of the flagstaff and said, in a puzzled voice, "Hullo—there are two flags flying, are there not? What does that mean?"

One of Lord Lucan's aides replied, "Surely, my lord, it means that the enemy is approaching?"

"Are you sure—" Lord George began, only to break off as his question was dramatically answered when a gun in the redoubt opened fire. It was met with a thunderous cannonade from the high ground to the right and a round shot came hurtling down toward the little group, scattering some of the staff officers and passing between the legs of Lord George Paget's horse.

Lord Lucan took in the situation and started to issue orders. An aide was sent galloping back to warn Sir Colin Campbell, and a second despatched to Lord Raglan's farmhouse headquarters, six miles away, urgently requesting infantry support. As the mist cleared, a very large body of Russian infantry could be seen, advancing in two columns south of the Woronzoff Road. They were preceded by skirmishers, with cavalry on both flanks, escorting their guns.

Lucan conferred with his two brigade commanders and Alex, waiting expectantly, saw General Scarlett motion to him. As he drew level, he heard Lucan say, above the now continuous roar of gunfire, his tone resentful and bitter, "Since Lord Raglan failed to act upon the communication sent to him yesterday by Sir Colin Campbell and myself, and since he has left us here altogether without support, I consider it our first duty to defend the approach to the town of Balaclava. The Turks will have to do the best they can—we are in no position to help them. The defense of the harbour will, of course, depend chiefly on my cavalry, so that I shall be compelled to reserve them for that purpose." When Scarlett muttered a protest, he shrugged. "I will see whether I can accomplish anything by a feint—we may, at least, delay them. Lord George, I am placing the Light Brigade in reserve. General Scarlett, you will mount your brigade, if you please, at once. I shall require one regiment to escort two troops of the Horse Artillery— Maude's and Barker's—as soon as you can get them mounted."

General Scarlett met Alex's inquiring glance with a brief nod and, saluting Lord Lucan, he set spurs to his horse. Alex, his fellow A.D.C., Lieutenant Elliott, the brigade trumpeter Thomas Monks and Scarlett's tall orderly, Trooper Shegog, fell in behind him. As they galloped back toward the Heavy Brigade camp, the general glanced from one to the other of his aides and said, a wry smile curving his lips beneath the windblown white moustache, "You heard what his lordship said, Alex, I've no doubt."

"Yes, sir, I did." Alex drew level with his commander.

"I am not one to question the orders I receive from my superior officers," Scarlett observed, his voice ominously level. "But if the cavalry is to defend Balaclava, then I do not understand how it can possibly do so if kept in reserve. And do you, from your previous experience of them, Alex, imagine that the Russians—in their present strength—will be delayed by feints and can- nonading by one of our regiments and two troops of Horse Artillery?"

"Since you ask my opinion, sir . . ." Alex's smile was also wry, "I do not expect them to be." At his back, Elliott's raised brows signified his bewilderment, but he said nothing. He, too, was an Indian army veteran, who had served throughout the Gwalior Campaign and at Ferozeshah with the Bengal Light Cavalry.

"Frankly, no more do I," General Scarlett stated grimly. He turned in his saddle. "When we reach our lines, I shall order out the Scots Greys to escort the artillery. And I shall want Colonel Beatson at my side throughout the day, so find him, will you please, Alex, and ask him to attend me? I had entrusted him with a mission, of a confidential nature, to Sir Colin Campbell at Kadikoi. Ride after him and both of you join us as soon as you are able."

Alex saluted and set off in the direction of Kadikoi. He recognized William Beatson riding towards him when he had covered about half the distance to the village and hailed him with relief. The colonel reined in. "I heard the firing," he said, "and I was with Sir Colin when Lord Lucan's aide arrived with news of the attack. Where is General Scarlett?"

Alex told him and saw his heavy brows meet in a frown.

"They're attacking the redoubt on Canrobert's Hill, you say? That may well mean disaster, unless the Turks hold. You've been with them, Alex—do you suppose they will?"

Kneeing his horse to a canter, in order to keep pace with his companion, Alex sighed. "They are Tunisian auxiliaries, unaccustomed to war and, I should judge, badly officered, sir. They are not likely to hold for long if they are not supported. The odds against them are overwhelming . . . from the sound of the firing and the little I was able to glimpse through the mist, I should imagine that at least eighteen or twenty guns are ranged against their three. And there are perhaps two divisions of infantry, with strong cavalry support—both Cossacks and Lancers."

Beatson's frown deepened. "Are the Tunisians to be abandoned, then? If they're not supported, we could lose the Causeway Heights!"

Alex repeated Lord Lucan's words, his voice expressionless.

"Lucan has asked for the 1st and 4th Divisions to be brought down—he despatched an urgent request to Lord Raglan whilst I was there. But inevitably there must be a considerable delay before either division is able to make the descent from the plateau." He hesitated. "How is Sir Colin faring, sir?"

William Beatson permitted himself a fleeting smile, "As you might expect, being the man he is, he's doing everything in his power to prevent the enemy from entering Balaclava. He had the 93rd lying down in their ranks all last night, in greatcoats but without bivouac fires. Since dawn, he's had them positioned in two lines at the entrance to the gorge . . . on rising ground, with a ridge behind them. An admirably chosen position. To their right, he has two Turkish battalions and some Tunisians, about a thousand men in all. The marines are on the Col behind him, with their heavy naval guns, and the invalids' battalion is in support. Also, while I was with him, he sent a messenger to Bosquet, whose mortars cover the road, to inform him of the situation."

"And Sir Colin himself?" Alex asked, conscious of a sudden sinking sensation in the pit of his stomach.

The colonel shrugged. "When I left him, Alex, he was riding up and down in front of the 93rd and calling out to them, in that rich accent of his, 'Remember, men, there's no retreat from here—ye must die where ye stand if need be.' And such is the Highlanders' love and respect for him, there was not a man said him nay. They'll die, if he tells them they must, rather than permit the enemy to pass them and as I told you, they're well positioned and—" he broke off, smothering an exclamation, and pointed ahead of them to Canrobert's Hill, which had just come into sight. "The Tunisians appear to be running . . . and like a rabble, not like soldiers."

Alex slowed his horse to a trot. He saw a disorderly mob of Tunisians, led by a mounted officer, come leaping and scrambling down the slope from their redoubt. Below them, in the valley, two troops of British Horse Artillery had their guns unlimbered and were directing a spirited fire into the dark mass of Russian infantry which, tightly packed and with bayonets fixed, was advancing toward the redoubt, preceded by Cossacks and skirmishers. But the Horse Artillery were themselves under a withering fire and their six- and nine-pounders were no match for the Russian twelves.

After a while, Alex saw them receive the signal to withdraw out of range. As he watched them limber up, a Russian shell burst among them, killing a number of men and horses and, as he learned later, severely wounding their able and gallant battery commander, Captain Maude. Two squadrons of the Greys covered their withdrawal but, although both troops again unlimbered and opened fire, the Russian advance did not halt. As more Tunisian auxiliaries fled from the redoubt, some of the Cossacks leaped their wiry little horses over its ramparts and the redoubt was carried when the infantry followed them, bayoneting any who were left. Evidently the retreat had been too precipitate to allow time for the guns to be spiked for, a few minutes later, these were firing once more . . . only now their fire was directed against the second redoubt from which, after firing a ragged volley, the Tunisian gunners retreated, screaming with terror.

They flung themselves down the slope and the Cossacks pursued them with lance and pistol, riding many of them down before they had covered more than a few yards, showing them no mercy. Turning away from the unpleasant sight, Alex saw that the Light Brigade was positioned to the left, below redoubts 3 and 4.

The Heavy Brigade—towards which he and Colonel Beatson now made their way—was some distance in front of the Light, below and slightly to the right of the captured redoubt on Canrobert's Hill. Slowly and inexorably, the Russians continued to advance, flanked by two large bodies of cavalry. They were evidently not deceived by Lucan's attempt at a feint attack and, as the Greys and the Horse Artillery fell back to the position occupied by the Heavy Brigade, it, too, started to withdraw, menaced by the Russian cavalry.

William Beatson exclaimed, in a shocked and angry voice, "In the name of God, Alex—look at that! Lucan is falling back. He'll lose us the Causeway Heights if the Tunisians realize what he's doing."

He had scarcely spoken when, as if in answer to his words, the Tunisians in all save one of the remaining redoubts—obviously believing themselves abandoned and about to be sacrificed —gave up any pretence of further resistance and beat a hasty and disorganized retreat. They flung down their arms and accoutrements as they ran and, as before, little groups of Cossacks spurred after them in relentless and vengeful pursuit, strewing the slopes and the plain below with their dead. In spite of this, a considerable number managed to reach the 93rd's position, where they rallied uncertainly and ranged themselves on the right flank of the other Turkish battalions.

No. 4 redoubt, however, still held out, delivering a rapid and precise fire into No. 3 as the Russians entered it. From above, General Bosquet's mortars put an end to the Cossacks' slaughter and forced them to retire up the slope once more. But the respite was short lived. A bayonet charge on No. 4 redoubt sent its defenders rushing for safety and most of them deservedly reached it, although the Cossacks, braving the mortar fire from overhead, galloped after them with savage yells.

When Alex and Colonel Beatson at last reached General Scarlett and reported to him, the cavalry position had become untenable. The abandoned redoubts were all in Russian hands and only in No. 4 had the guns been spiked. Both brigades were within musket-shot of one or more of these and their gradual withdrawal had brought them into the 93rd's line of fire. Sir Colin Campbell himself rode over and, on his advice, Lord Lucan ordered the cavalry's withdrawal along the length of the South Valley to the slopes of the Causeway Heights. Here they would be out of the Highlanders' line of fire and, should Sir Colin's force fail to hold them, they could attack the Russian flank.

Strategically this was a wise move but the order, when it was received by both Heavy and Light Brigades, was misunderstood. The officers openly questioned it, their men—thirsting for action—heard it with bewildered dismay. Ever since the Russians had opened the attack they had, it seemed, done nothing but fall back ignominiously before them, with Lord Lucan apparently at pains to avoid an engagement. Were they now, they asked each other, to abandon the 93rd and Sir Colin Campbell, with a few thousand unreliable Turks and Tunisians, to certain attack and probable annihilation, at the hands of the Russian cavalry? Even Alex, although he was aware from whom the suggestion for the order had come, felt bitterness well up inside him.

At his side, William Beatson was looking anxious and Elliott was cursing angrily beneath his breath. But the order, unpopular though it was, had to be obeyed. No support was yet forthcoming from either the Duke of Cambridge's 1st Division or Sir George Cathcart's 4th and an A.D.C. had been sent by Lord Raglan to make it clear, both to Lord Lucan and Sir Colin Campbell, that the cavalry must wait and act in conjunction with those two divisions, now marching down from the heights. Lucan had no choice but to order the withdrawal, by alternate regiments, of both cavalry brigades. Alex was despatched by a tight-lipped Scarlett to put these instructions into effect. As he cantered towards the leading squadron of the Royals, he noticed a body of Russian cavalry, some six or seven hundred strong, starting to move in the direction of the hillock behind which the two thin lines of Highlanders crouched waiting, as yet unseen by them . . . all, did they but know it, that now stood between them and the capture of Balaclava. His angry frustration grew, as he repeated the order to withdraw to each of the regimental commanders and each, in turn, listened to him in stunned and horrified silence.

By 7:30, the inglorious retreat down the South Valley was over. Both brigades were in position; waiting despairingly for orders—any orders—which would enable them, instead of remaining uselessly immobilized, to attack the enemy.

Instead, a written order came from Lord Raglan, brought by an aide who had taken over half an hour to reach them. The British commander-in-chief had now established his general headquarters on the heights, at the Ridge, which overlooked the Plain of Balaclava, six hundred feet below. From here, he could see the entire battlefield spread out below him like a relief-map. But, as later events were so tragically to show, he apparently did not realize that those taking part in the battle were unable to see, from one side of the Causeway Heights, what was going on—a short distance away—on the other.

From his point of vantage, Lord Raglan had observed a very large force of Russian cavalry, between three and four thousand strong, supported by artillery, enter the North Valley. He was quite unaware that this force was invisible to Lord Lucan and his staff, in the South Valley—cut off from their sight by the intervening Causeway Heights. His order, laconically phrased as: *"Cavalry to take ground to left of second line of redoubts occupied by Turks,"* was incomprehensible to Lucan, in command of the Cavalry Division. He complied with it angrily and with extreme reluctance since it meant, in effect, that once he had done so, the cavalry would be removed from their strategically useful position, covering Sir Colin Campbell's flank—and if Sir Colin's Highlanders failed to repel the expected enemy attack, then Balaclava would be lost.

The Cavalry Division made its second withdrawal, this time toward the Sapouné Ridge and, reaching its foot, Lord Lucan turned the two brigades in line to face east, looking out along the South Valley. The men's spirits were low, their hopes fading fast. Alex, waiting with Colonel Beatson and Lieutenant Elliott, found his thoughts constantly straying to Sir Colin Campbell and the two thin lines of red-coated Highlanders, of whose fortunes no news had yet been received. Lord Cardigan, he observed, had now made his belated appearance and taken over command of the Light Brigade but how or when he had done so, Alex could not have said. He watched the tall, brilliantly uniformed figure, on the splendid chestnut horse riding arrogantly up and down in front of the Light Cavalry, with increasing frustration. But his frustration turned to relief when a second order from Lord Raglan—brought to General Scarlett by Lord Lucan in person—commanded that eight squadrons of Heavy Dragoons were to be detached towards Balaclava to support the Turks who, the order stated, "are wavering."

The Turks might be wavering, he thought, no one had expected them to do anything else, after their behavior in the redoubts but . . . at last the cavalry was being sent to the 93rd's aid. He and Elliott galloped thankfully over to the regimental commanders to relay this latest and most welcome order and the men in the selected squadrons gave a subdued cheer, as they eagerly formed up, watched enviously by the rest of their comrades, who were still compelled to remain inactive.

General Scarlett's plump, red face wore a smile as he led his eight squadrons off—two each from the 5th Dragoon Guards, the Greys, the Inniskillings and the 4th Dragoon Guards. He said, as Alex took his place behind him, "Lord Cardigan will not be pleased by this—he will think that we are stealing a march on him!"

But Colonel Beatson, Alex noticed, who was riding beside the general, was not smiling. He dropped back after a while, as they came in sight of the Cavalry Division camp, along the edge of which their route to Kadikoi lay and, when Alex greeted him, said in a low voice, "Alex, my friend, I do not like this."

"Why not, sir?" Alex stared at him, puzzled.

William Beatson shrugged his massive shoulders. "It is an instinct, perhaps. General Scarlett is anxious, as we all are, to carry out our orders with as little delay as possible. But . . . we ride as if we were merely exercising our horses, without putting out scouts or maintaining any sort of alert. And"—he gestured to the wide, undulating ridge of the Causeway Heights, some eight hundred yards to their left—"our view is obscured, so that we do not know what is going on across there, in the North Valley."

"But Lord Raglan must surely know, sir," Alex protested. "He is in a position to see both the North Valley and this, is he not?"

"Lord Raglan's orders are taking half an hour to reach us," the Colonel pointed out. "The situation can change radically in half an hour. The Russians have a very large force of cavalry—Lancers and Hussars, as well as Cossacks—and now that we have lost the redoubts, they would meet with no opposition if they entered the North Valley. Or, for that matter, if they crossed the Woronzoff Road. Which is what *I* should do, were I commanding them."

His reasoning was logical, Alex realized; and Elliott; who had joined them in time to overhear his last few words, nodded thoughtfully as he glanced over his shoulder at the Heights. "Alex and I could ride up a little way, sir," he suggested, "and see what is to be seen, if you wish."

"Good," Beatson assented. "Do so at once. I will tell General Scarlett what you are about."

The two A.D.C.s put their horses to a canter. They had covered only a few hundred yards when Elliott, who was in the lead, pulled up suddenly. "Look!" he exclaimed, a slight tremor of excitement in his voice. "There they are. . . ."

At the same moment, Alex saw first a line of lance-tips appearing over the top of the hill and then, starting to descend the southern slope of the Causeway, a massive column of Russian horsemen, swiftly followed by a second. The sight was at once imposing and alarming—although it was evident, from the way they rode and the fact that they had no scouts on either flank, that the Russians did not suspect the close proximity of the British cavalry, any more than the British suspected theirs. They trotted downhill in two lines, each four deep, the light blue uniforms and splendid horses identifying the two leading regiments as Hussars, the cream of the Russian cavalry.

The last vestige of mist had at last dispersed and the sun drew glittering reflections from weapons and accoutrements as the great mass of horsemen came steadily on. There were, as nearly as he could judge, between three and four thousand of them and Alex drew in his breath sharply. Below, even now passing through the tents and the lines of tethered horses of their camp, were a scant five hundred British cavalrymen, quite unprepared to receive an attack from so overwhelming an enemy force . . . he and Elliott, as if by common consent and without exchanging a word, swung their horses round and went galloping back in search of General Scarlett.

The general received their news with commendable calm. His round, red face lost a little of its colour but that was all and he said, his voice quite steady, "We shall have to charge them. Give the order to wheel left into line. And I want the lines exactly dressed—the Greys and the Inniskillings, in front. There is to be no undue haste."

The dressing was meticulously carried out and, as their commander had ordered, without haste. Impeded on the left by the tent ropes, the eight squadrons wheeled into line facing the Heights, the first line composed of two squadrons of the Greys and a squadron of the Inniskillings—three hundred men in all—the second, two squadrons of the 5th Dragoon Guards and the remaining squadron of the Inniskillings. The 4th's two squadrons were coming up, with the Royals, but they still had some distance to cover and Alex was sent to warn them of what was happening. On his return from this errand, he saw that the officers of the leading regiments had ridden out in front and, as if preparing for a peacetime review, had turned to sit their horses rigidly facing their own men. Their backs were to the enemy who, by this time had seen them and halted on the crest of the Heights, in order to change their own formation.

Lord Lucan made his appearance while the slow parade ground movement was being carried out. He dashed up to General Scarlett in a state of visible agitation and informed him that he had ordered up the rest of the division in reserve. Alex heard him say breathlessly, "You will have to charge them, General Scarlett. They must be stopped at all costs."

"That, my lord," Scarlett replied, in measured tones, "is what I am preparing to do. But I will have my lines properly dressed before I do it." He raised his sword, waving it in a reproving arc at the right of the line, where the Inniskillings were attempting to press forward, and the men obediently fell back, to pick up their dressing again. William Beatson rode up and the general asked, without turning his head, "What are the enemy at now, Colonel Beatson?"

"They are drawn up in a square formation, sir . . . and halted." Beatson's voice was as calm as his brigade commander's and now, Alex realized, he was smiling. He supplied a few other details and added significantly, "Their distance is about five hundred yards."

"General Scarlett!" Lord Lucan thundered. "Further delay is hazardous. I order you to charge the enemy!" He signaled to his trumpeter and, his voice shaking with emotion, told him to sound the charge. The clear, thin notes echoed and re-echoed back from the enclosing hills but Scarlett's raised sword restrained them and not a man moved from the now almost perfectly aligned ranks, with the single exception of William Beatson, who had returned to the spur of rising ground from which he could observe the enemy.

"If you will allow me, my lord," Scarlett said gruffly. "I will order my brigade to charge when I am ready."

Lucan nodded, tight-lipped, evidently not trusting himself to speak and from behind him, Beatson's voice called out, "The enemy is advancing, sir. They are descending the slope at a trot. Their distance is now less than five hundred yards but their advance is slow."

"Then we still have time," Scarlett stated, his calm still completely unruffled. He turned to Alex. "Present my compliments, if you please, to Colonel Griffiths of the Greys and ask him if he is now clear of the picket-ropes impeding his way."

As Alex galloped across to obey his order, he saw that the great advancing mass of Russian cavalry had now halted. They had packed into a deep square and flung out two wings, to widen their front. The grey-clad horsemen sat motionless in their saddles, watching what was going on below them, their demeanor confident—as well it might be for, in previous encounters, the British cavalry had never charged them. With their vast numerical superiority, it was very evident that they did not expect the British to charge them now . . . least of all up-hill. They waited, delaying their own charge, as a cat might wait for a mouse to venture too close to it.

General Scarlett had taken up his position well in front of his first line when Alex rejoined him, with the information that the Greys were still impeded by the tent-ropes but ready.

"Thank you, Alex." His smile, despite the heavy white moustache and bristling brows, was suddenly absurdly boyish. Then he turned in his saddle and said to his trumpeter, "Sound the charge!"

The instant it was sounded, he set spurs to his horse and Alex, aware then of a sense of wild exhilaration that exceeded any other that he had ever experienced, spurred after him. For a fleeting moment, he thought of Emmy—saw her face before him, as if it were a vision from the past but it swiftly vanished and, strangely immune to a consciousness of fear, he galloped on at General Scarlett's heels, seeing only the dark mass of the enemy in front of him.

Elliott rode beside him, his face pale and taut beneath the conspicuous cocked hat which, only that morning, Scarlett had ordered him to don; a few paces in the rear, the brigade trumpeter and the huge, phlegmatic Shegog thundered after them. Glancing back, Alex saw the scarlet-clad ranks of the leading squadrons break into a trot, as their regimental trumpeters repeated the call to charge—and they kept their splendid alignment as their pace quickened, although the Greys, as he had feared they must, experienced some difficulty in doing so until they were clear of the tents. The Inniskillings—beside whom they had charged under Lord Uxbridge at Waterloo—waited for them until, their traditional friendship thus acknowledged, they could ride knee to knee once more. Then they broke into a canter and finally, as the whole line gained momentum, into a gallop. But, due to the Greys' difficulties with the tent and picket-ropes, which had unhorsed a few of them, the front line was now fifty yards to their rear and Alex motioned to Elliott to warn their commander of this. His fellow A.D.C. drew level with General Scarlett, shouting to make himself heard about the thunder of galloping hoofs but Scarlett ignored him. Waving his sword above his head, he did not look round and made no attempt to slacken speed.

Elliott dropped back and now, surprisingly, Alex saw the tension go out of his face and its pallor vanish . . . not realizing that his own lips were twisted into an exultant grin, as boyish as their commander's had been, a few minutes before. He did not think of death, although to Lord Raglan and his staff, watching them from six hundred feet above their heads, it seemed that General Scarlett and the four members of his staff who followed him were riding to certain death, fifty yards ahead of the Greys and Innis-killings.

Alex, in that hectic moment, with the drumming hoofbeats loud in his ears, did not even think—as, in the past, he had often thought—of his horror of being seriously wounded or maimed, and he had no thought of personal glory, no dream of heroism. Rather, in common with the rest of the men charging behind him, he thought of wiping out the bitter memories of the humiliation they had endured in their retreat, earlier that morning. He thought of the Cossacks' butchery of the wretched Tunisians, fleeing in terror from the captured redoubts; and, because just then it seemed to him evident that, as the result of that same ignoble retreat by the Cavalry Division, Sir Colin Campbell and his gallant 93rd must have suffered a similar fate . . . he thought of revenge.

And then, as they reached the great packed, motionless square of Russian horsemen and hurled themselves against it, he thought of nothing, save the primitive urge to hack his way into its heart and destroy it. A single Russian officer, sitting his horse in advance of the front line, lunged at General Scarlett with his saber and Elliott, passing by him on the other side, drove his own weapon up to its hilt in his chest. In his effort to withdraw it, he was almost unhorsed but he kept his seat and, side by side, he and Alex drove their way into the Russian horde, intent on giving their commander such protection as they could. Scarlett was fighting like a lion, slashing and parrying the saber and lance thrusts aimed at him with his sword and Alex, in front of Elliott, now, guarded his back, careless of his own safety.

He saw Shegog and the trumpeter close beside him, fighting

for their lives, and heard a familiar shout come from behind him and then William Beatson's giant figure loomed up on his left, as the first line of the Greys and the Inniskillings, with which he had charged, struck the enemy centre. Their battle cries—the wild Irish yell of the Inniskillings and the fierce, moaning wail of the Greys echoed, as the trumpet call had been, by the hills which hemmed them in—could be heard quite distinctly by those watching the engagement from Sapouné Ridge, six hundred feet above.

To all of them, including Lord Raglan, it appeared that the thin line of scarlet-jacketed British dragoons had been literally engulfed by the dark mass of the Russian thousands. But miraculously, and encouraged here and there by an officer, who fought his way into the mêlée and then turned to face and rally his men, the British line kept some semblance of its original formation and the Russian centre began, incredibly, to waver. But it did not break. After the first shock of surprise, the Russians turned on the handful of men who had departed from all the accepted concepts of war and charged them with such reckless valor, to set about annihilating them. Skilled swordplay was impossible with the two opposing forces jammed so closely and inextricably together, and the battle soon became a series of furiously fought individual contests, each British cavalryman being attacked simultaneously by at least two of his opponents. The Russians' greatcoats were so thick that they afforded a high degree of protection against saber-cuts, often turning the British blows harmlessly aside. But their tightly packed ranks prevented either pistols or carbines being used and even the Cossack lances had to be discarded, in favour of sabers.

The second line of Inniskillings and the 5th Dragoon Guards, following their comrades in the first line, struck with even greater impact and drove a wedge in the Russian centre. But then the two wings on either flank started to wheel inwards, to take their attackers in the rear. They might have succeeded had it not been for the remaining squadrons of the Heavy Brigade, which had now formed up in their separate regiments, preparatory to charging in their turn. The 4th Dragoon Guards were on the left, the 1st—the Royals—in the centre, a little behind them, with General Scarlett's old regiment, the 5th—the Green Horse—and a squadron of the Inniskillings on the right. Each regiment charged on its own, two on the Russian right flank, one in the centre on the heels of the Greys, the final charge being made on the enemy's left flank with devastating effect, for the Russians who had wheeled round to encircle and crush the Greys, found themselves being taken in the rear. The Russian mass broke and, with startling suddenness, began to disintegrate, as it was steadily driven back, reeling and thrown into confusion by the disciplined courage of the British attack.

Alex, still at General Scarlett's back, saw him emerge, spent but triumphant and, apparently—save for a few cuts and grazes—unscathed. He was followed by Shegog and his trumpeter, who fell in on either side of him, and then William Beatson hacked and jostled his way through to the general's side. Of Elliott there was no sign; Alex started back to search for him, glimpsed the plumed hat and thrust past a trio of Cossacks with whom, his face covered with blood, Elliott was engaged in desperate and unequal contest. He took one of the Cossacks from behind with his saber; the second turned on him with a ferocious cry but Alex evaded him and two troopers of the Greys, shouting and cursing at the pitch of their lungs, dealt swiftly and effectively with the third. Elliott was slumping, semi-conscious, in his saddle but, as Alex led him to safety, the first line of Greys and Inniskillings burst through, cheering exultantly, and the Russians in the rear files turned in headlong flight.

Soon to Alex's stunned amazement and relief, the whole great force was in retreat, re-ascending the ridge in complete disorder, pursued by a handful of red-coated British dragoons. A great cheer went up from the men of the Heavy Brigade, too exhausted to join in the pursuit, as they watched the beaten enemy streaming away over the Woronzoff Road and across the Causeway Heights in a panic-stricken bid to gain the shelter of their guns in the North Valley. Apart from a few individuals from other regiments, only the Horse Artillery and the 4th Dragoon Guards—who had cut through from flank to flank, with comparative ease, as the Russians were on the point of breaking—made any serious effort to catch up with the fugitives and thus consolidate the brilliant victory by preventing their escape.

General Scarlett removed his battered dragoon helmet and mopped his streaming brow. He said, with finality, "Well, we have done our part . . . we've routed them. We will leave the Light Brigade to do the rest." He turned to his trumpeter and ordered him to sound the recall adding, with tears in his eyes, "Our men have performed prodigies of valor this day."

As the regiments of the Heavy Brigade started to sort themselves out and re-form, after the confusion of the battle, Alex became aware that the Light Brigade had not moved. Throughout the action Lord Cardigan's command had been positioned in full view of it, less than five hundred yards away, in a perfect position for a flank attack. But not only had Lord Cardigan failed to attack on the flank, he was now making no effort to pursue the fleeing enemy. . . the Light Brigade remained motionless. Bewildered by their inaction, Alex walked his tired horse to the edge of the ridge and looked down. Lord Cardigan sat his horse, surrounded by a small group of obviously angry and disappointed officers—amongst whom he recognized Phillip Dunloy—who appeared to be pleading with him. But he shook his head several times, apparently deaf to their appeals and finally, as if losing patience, he turned his back on them and rode out of earshot. One of them—Captain Morris, in command of the 17th Lancers —wheeled round in front of his regiment, slapped his overalled leg with his drawn saber in a display of angry frustration which, even at that distance, Alex had no difficulty in recognizing for what it was. He sighed, in understanding.

A little later, Lord Bingham—Lucan's son, who was acting as his father's aide-de-camp—galloped up and delivered a written message but, although Cardigan read this, with great concentration, several times, the Light Brigade stayed where it was. The Russian cavalry, with their horse artillery intact, gained the eastern end of the North Valley unmolested and established themselves there, behind their unlimbered guns. The Heavy Brigade, whose courageous charge had succeeded against seemingly impossible odds, watched the fruits of their hard-won victory slipping away from them and—many of them with tears streaming down their cheeks—counted their dead and carried their wounded slowly back to their tents.

In the circumstances, their casualties were light. Alex reported them to General Scarlett as under eighty killed and wounded, of whom less than a dozen had been killed. A number, including Scarlett himself, William Beatson and Elliott, had suffered saber cuts but, after receiving medical attention, they refused to be relieved and returned to duty. As General Scarlett was having his wounds attended to, an A.D.C. sought him out, with a written message from Lord Raglan. He read it, beaming and then passed it to his staff . . . the message stated briefly, *"Well done, Scarlett."* To the A.D.C. he said, "I beg to thank his lordship," and to his staff, "Gentlemen, I say the same to every one of you!"

A little later, Alex to his joy and relief, saw Sir Colin Campbell riding towards them. He offered his congratulations to the commander of the Heavy Brigade and, on being asked how he himself had fared, smiled and answered simply, "Balaclava is still in our hands, thanks to my 93rd . . . and the naval gunners and invalids who gave us gallant support." It was not until a long time afterwards that Alex heard the full story of the heroic stand of the 93rd's "thin red line," in the face of a determined attack by four squadrons of Russian cavalry and of how, with perfect disciplined steadiness and complete trust in their commander, the Highlanders had risen from the ground to deliver three volleys of rifle fire into the Russian ranks, before which they had fled.

Sir Colin, very typically, said little of his own exploits. Instead he rode across to where the Greys were re-forming and, doffing the Highland bonnet he had worn since the Battle of the Alma, addressed them with visible emotion, "Greys, gallant Greys . . . I am sixty-one years of age, but if I were young again, I should be proud to serve in your ranks."

The Greys, as deeply moved as he, cheered him to the echo and their commanding officer, Lieutenant-Colonel Henry Griffiths, wrung his hand.

CHAPTER TEN

⋙ • ⋘

THE END of the Battle of Balaclava—which was to write an unforgettable page in British military history and immortalize those who took part in it—was fast approaching.

But to Alex Sheridan, with the now re-formed Heavy Cavalry

Brigade, the position was still as confused as it was to all the other officers and men of the Cavalry Division—including their divisional commander. They were aware that the Russians still held the captured Turco-Tunisian redoubts on the Causeway Heights, but knew that they had been pushed back from Balaclava itself. They had seen the defeated cavalry fleeing into the narrow, mile-long North Valley, presumably—since this was their habit—in order to seek the protection of their own guns. But they were aware of little else, save the exasperating fact that support from the 1st and 4th Infantry Divisions, although promised early in the day, had not yet materialized.

To Lord Raglan, from the lofty vantage point of his command headquarters six hundred feet above the field of battle, the overall situation was a great deal clearer—although he, too, was by this time also exasperated by the slowness with which the two British Infantry Divisions were carrying out his orders. The Duke of Cambridge had not yet completed his descent to the Plain. Sir George Cathcart had, at last, done so but for some reason he appeared to be in no hurry to carry out the commander-in-chief's instructions to *"advance immediately and recapture the Turkish redoubts."* His division marched past the scene of the Heavy Brigade charge and occupied the nearest two redoubts, from whence a desultory fire was opened, at extreme range, on those held by the enemy. The division then came to a halt.

The routed Russian cavalry had been observed by Lord Raglan and his staff to rally and regroup themselves in columns, ranged across the eastern end of the North Valley, with a line of twelve field guns drawn up in front of them. Behind them, still further to strengthen their positions, were massed their infantry; to their right, along the ridge of the Fedioukine Hills and on its lower slopes were four squadrons of cavalry, eight battalions of infantry and fourteen guns. To their left front, across the valley on the Causeway Heights, were the eleven infantry battalions which had stormed and were now occupying the Turkish redoubts, with the naval guns the Tunisians had left behind, together with some thirty of their own field pieces. They were now being threatened, although not yet seriously, by Sir George Cathcart's division.

To Lord Raglan, taking stock, the Russian force in the North Valley, while it occupied a virtually impregnable position, presented no immediate menace. On the other hand, continued occupation by the enemy of the Turkish redoubts meant that his vital lines of communication with Balaclava were threatened, since the redoubts commanded the Woronzoff Road. He decided to deal with this threat at once, basing his decision on the fact that the enemy on the Heights, although strong, were without support and might be expected to abandon the redoubts if resolutely attacked. Accordingly, he issued fresh orders.

The Duke of Cambridge was urged to hurry his division's final descent to the Plain, advance to a point south of the Woronzoff Road and, in conjunction with Sir George Cathcart, to attack the Russians on the Causeway Heights and drive them from the captured redoubts. To Lord Lucan, he sent another written order—ever afterwards, the subject of argument and controversy. This read: *"Cavalry to advance and take advantage of any opportunity to recover the Heights. They will be supported by the infantry, which have been ordered to advance on two fronts."*

Lucan interpreted this to mean that he was to advance and attempt to recapture the Causeway Heights—and the redoubts—as soon as he received the infantry support which the order suggested was on its way to him. He therefore mounted his division, ordered the Light Brigade to take up a position at the western end of the Causeway Heights, facing down the trough of the North Valley, and drew up the Heavy Brigade on the slopes of the Woronzoff Road, behind them and to their right. After this, as he believed that he had been commanded to do, he waited with ever increasing impatience for some sign of the expected infantry support.

When fifteen minutes had passed without any evidence whatsoever of the infantry's arrival, the men were permitted to stand easy. They dismounted, leaning against their horses, the officers sipping rum from their flasks and those who had them eating hard boiled eggs and biscuits. Some of the troopers lit their pipes but were sternly reprimanded for "smoking in the face of the enemy."

Alex, during this lull, received permission to ride over to talk to Phillip, granted quite readily by General Scarlett. As he trotted up to the Light Brigade's position, he could see, a little over a mile away at the far end of the valley, the dark masses of enemy cavalry waiting there. Phillip, when he found him, was also moodily watching the movements in the North Valley and he said, when they had greeted each other, "Well, Alex my dear fellow— you and your Heavies had the laugh on us this morning! Your charge, while magnificent to watch, was also quite heartbreaking to those of us who would have given everything they possessed to have come to your support. Myself included, needless to tell you."

"Why did you not?" Alex questioned curiously. "And why, in heaven's name, did you not pursue the Russians when they broke? Did Lord Cardigan forbid it?"

Phillip shrugged angrily. "He did . . . and there was almost a mutiny in consequence! He had received orders, he told us, to post the Light Brigade where it was and none, from either Lord Raglan or Lord Lucan, to come to the support of the Heavies.

He blames Lord Look-on, of course, and was as bitter as any of us when we had to stand and watch the enemy escape, without lifting a finger to stop them. It was a chance of a lifetime and we were compelled to let it go. Alex, I would have wept! Look at them now . . ." he gestured down the valley at the confused dark shapes of the Russian horsemen and swore aloud. "This campaign has been nothing but frustration for the Light Cavalry . . . frustration and humiliation. We are never permitted to go into action, to charge the enemy, to show what we are made of . . . it is driving us to despair. You, at least, can hold your heads up, after this morning—yours was a superb feat. But we must bow ours in shame . . . dear God, it is past all bearing!"

"Your hour will come, Phillip," Alex offered consolingly, and he added, without any idea of how close that hour now was for the Light Brigade, "Who knows? It may yet come today."

But Phillip shook his head. "The day is all but over," he returned despondently. "And what are we offered? The chance to support the infantry, which is conspicuous by its absence? So we wait and the Cossacks jeer at us . . . even our own infantrymen call us gilded popinjays and worse. Alex, if this goes on, it will break my heart . . . and every man of the 11th feels as I do."

They talked of the day's events, fretting at the delay, as another half hour passed, without sight or sound of the infantry. And then, riding at headlong speed down the precipitous escarpment from Lord Raglan's headquarters on the Sapouné Ridge, there came a lone horseman, in the conspicuous uniform of the 15th Hussars. As he drew nearer, both Alex and Phillip recognized him as Captain Edward Nolan, on duty as General Airey's aide, and they guessed, from the reckless haste with which he came spurring down the escarpment, that the orders he carried must be of supreme urgency. Nolan was renowned for his passionate belief in cavalry as "the decisive military arm," and, at the sight of him, the spirits of the men of the Light Cavalry Brigade rose. His route took him close to their lines and as he galloped past, Captain Morris, of the 17th Lancers—his closest friend—called out to him urgently, "Nolan, what's going to happen?"

Nolan, without slackening speed, shouted back triumphantly, "You'll see, you'll see!"

Up on the Sapouné Ridge, Lord Raglan had watched his messenger's breakneck descent and, according to those about him, his face had, for once, lost its look of composed tranquility. From where he watched, he had seen teams of Russian artillery horses cantering up to the captured Turkish redoubts and, to him, their intention was plain. They were about to remove the captured British naval guns . . . no doubt with the ultimate intention of despatching them, as proof of victory, to the Tsar. Lord Raglan, to whom, educated in the stern military traditions of the Great Duke, this was unthinkable, knew that he must somehow regain possession of the guns. In desperation, he called General Airey to him and bade him write an order to Lord Lucan. The Cavalry Division's long delay in carrying out his previous order still irked him and, after Airey had written as he dictated and had given this order to Nolan for delivery, he called out after the A.D.C., "tell Lord Lucan that the cavalry are to attack *immediately!*"

Nolan saluted and was gone. Within ten minutes, thanks to the consummate horsemanship with which, scorning the circuitous track, he had made his perilous descent, he jerked his blown and panting horse to a standstill beside Lord Lucan, who was waiting, with the members of his staff, between his two brigades, and thrust the order into his hand. The officers, catching Nolan's excitement, crowded closer, as Lucan read it. But his expression, when he had done so, was one of shocked perplexity.

To him, the order was both obscure and impracticable. It read: *"Lord Raglan wishes the cavalry to advance rapidly to the front and try to prevent the enemy carrying away the guns. Troop of Horse Artillery may accompany. French cavalry is on your left. Immediate."*

The signature on it was General Airey's and Lucan looked at Airey's aide-de-camp as if wondering whether he, too, had taken leave of his senses. For he could see no British naval guns being dragged away from the Turkish redoubts on the Causeway Heights ... while these were clearly visible to Lord Raglan on the Sapouné Ridge, they were cut off from Lucan's view, and it did not for a moment occur to him to read this order in conjunction with the order which had preceded it. The two did not appear to bear any relation to each other, and he took it for granted that the earlier one—which, owing to the infantry's failure to appear, he had been unable to carry out—had now been superceded by this second order, just placed in his hands by Captain Nolan.

Yet he was bewildered. The French cavalry mentioned in the order were obviously the Chasseurs d'Afrique, known to have been ordered down much earlier on by General Canrobert ... but now there was no word of infantry support, so what had happened to the infantry? The only guns in any danger of being carried away by the enemy, of which Lucan was aware, were those at the end of the North Valley, behind which the routed Russian cavalry had established themselves ... in a defensive, rather than an offensive position. Lord Raglan could hardly wish him to attack *those* guns, without infantry support, and with only one troop of Horse Artillery—unless he also wished for the annihilation of the entire British Cavalry Division? The mere suggestion seemed to him so preposterous that he did not entertain it and he started to voice a puzzled and irritated protest at the absurdity of the order, when Nolan cut him short. He said, in a deliberately insolent and peremptory tone, "Lord Raglan's orders are that the cavalry are to attack immediately!"

Lord Lucan stared at him, visibly taken aback. He was fully aware that Nolan disliked him—a feeling which he heartily reciprocated—and he knew that, in the past, Nolan had criticized him openly for his handling of the Cavalry Division. But, as a lieutenant-general, he was unaccustomed to being addressed in so disrespectful a manner by a mere captain, even if that captain happened to be an acknowledged expert on cavalry tactics and a favourite with his commander-in-chief.

He turned on the arrogant young A.D.C. with barely controlled fury. The word "attack" had not been mentioned in Lord Raglan's written order and he was still not clear as to which "front" he was expected to advance on . . . "Attack, sir?" he shouted. "Attack what? *What* guns, sir?"

All Edward Nolan's bitter contempt for the man he had nick-named "Lord Look-on" exploded suddenly. Lucan was, in his eyes, entirely to blame for the deplorable handling of the Cavalry Division and its consequent humiliating inactivity. It had always been his own contention that cavalry—and above all, light cavalry—properly led, could accomplish anything. Yet here was Lucan, as always hesitant, questioning the order he had been given and prepared to throw away the chance of glory that, at long last, was his for the taking. . . . Nolan flung out his arm, in a gesture which embraced the North Valley, where the Russian cavalry waited behind their guns, and said, with a provocative scorn he made not the smallest effort to conceal, "There, my lord, is your enemy! There are your guns!"

His words—and that flamboyantly vague gesture—were to send six score men to their deaths. Long afterwards, it was argued that, in making his gesture, Nolan had no intention of conveying the meaning which Lord Lucan read into it. Yet it is doubtful whether this could have been so; Nolan, as an A.D.C. was a mere bearer of messages, he was not in Lord Raglan's confidence. He had simply been given a written order and a verbal message to deliver, but neither had been explained to him . . . and he was ignorant of the contents of the earlier order.

With his deep and heartfelt belief in the invincibility of the British cavalry, to him the task which Lucan's two magnificent brigades had apparently been set would not have seemed impossible. And if, from the Sapouné Ridge, he had noticed the attempt to remove the captured guns, he would not have attached much significance to it, for the infantry had been called down to retake those particular guns. The guns which mattered, to Edward Nolan, were the guns sheltering the Russian cavalry, whom the Heavy Brigade had already routed—guns designed to cover their retirement—and it was to these he pointed, quite deliberately, in the belief that they were indeed the guns his commander-in-chief wished the cavalry to attack.

Certainly, to all those watching the two men—whether or not, as Alex and Phillip were, they were out of earshot and heard neither question nor answer—Edward Nolan's out-flung arm could indicate only one thing. The cavalry's objective was in the North Valley. And, when Lord Lucan dictated a written order and sent it to Lord Cardigan by one of his staff, the last of their doubts were removed. With quickening pulses and, perhaps, a momentary sinking of the heart, the men of the Light Brigade recognized that their hour had come . . . they were to lead the attack. It was they who were to charge the Russian guns, a mile away, at the end of the North Valley. A strange, unearthly silence fell; after an outburst of talking, the men spoke in whispers, as the news passed from regiment to regiment, from squadron to squadron, from man to man . . . and its import sank in.

Phillip's gaze met Alex's and he said, his voice hushed, as the others were, "So you were right, Alex. Our hour has come indeed."

Alex was silent, his throat tight. Edward Nolan rode past them and Phillip asked him a low voiced question, to which the A.D.C. replied smilingly, "Back to the Upland—oh, no, my lord! I'm on my way to seek permission to charge with the 17th."

Lord Cardigan, sitting his horse a few yards from them, had read his brother-in-law's written order in horrified bewilderment, transcending even Lucan's when he had originally received it from Lord Raglan. For cavalry to attack guns in battery, without infantry support, was contrary to every accepted rule of war. He had longed for action, he was not afraid to die, he had the utmost confidence in the courage and splendid discipline of the men he commanded but—this was madness. The North Valley was a mile in length, shut in by hills on either side, and those flanking hills were the site of other gun batteries, besides that at its eastern end, which his brigade was being ordered to charge. He sent his aide, Fitz Maxse, to remonstrate with Lord Lucan and point out these facts, before complying with the order.

Lucan rode over to him, Lord Raglan's original order in his hand. Coldly—for, even now, he could not forget the hatred that, for thirty years had been between them—he read its contents to Lord Cardigan and ordered him to advance down the North Valley with the Light Brigade, while he himself followed, in support, with the Heavy Brigade.

Alex, sitting his horse a few yards away, was a witness of the tense, unbelievably bitter little scene and he listened in mounting horror and dismay as Cardigan, bringing down his sword in formal salute, said with equal coldness, "Certainly, sir. But allow me to point out to you that the Russians have a battery in the valley at our front, and batteries and riflemen on each flank."

"I know it," Lucan returned, his tone bleakly resigned. "But Lord Raglan will have it. We have no choice but to obey."

Lord Cardigan saluted again. "Advance very steadily," his brother-in-law instructed. "And keep your men well in hand."

There was the same icily formal acknowledgement; then Cardigan wheeled his horse and, in a harsh undertone which could be clearly heard by those grouped about him, muttered to himself, "Well, here goes the last of the Brudenells!" After which, outwardly calm, he trotted across to Lord George Paget who, with the 4th Light Dragoons, was dismounted and smoking a cigar. "Lord George, we are ordered to make an attack to the front," he stated, without preamble. "You will take command of the second line, and I expect your best support. Mind . . . your *best* support!" The last sentence was repeated and Lord George reddened resentfully.

"Of course, my lord. You shall have my best support."

Phillip laid a hand on Alex's arm. "I must go." He smiled tightly. "Wish me luck, Alex. I think I may need it."

"You know I do, Phillip. God go with you."

"And with you." Phillip turned and galloped off to where the brilliantly uniformed squadrons of the 11th Hussars were starting to form up and wheel into line. Alex watched them and suddenly it became more than he could bear. His old regiment was going to brave the fury of the Russian guns . . . it was going, perhaps, to its destruction and his place, when it did so, was in support, behind it with the Heavy Brigade. He hesitated but only for a moment and then rode over to Colonel Douglas, the 11th's commanding officer, saluted and, as Edward Nolan had done a little while before, asked permission to accompany the regiment in the charge.

Douglas recognized him and inclined his head. "If you wish, Captain Sheridan," he answered wryly. "You were once one of us . . . by all means die with us."

Alex thanked him and rode over to join Phillip.

The trumpets sounded, in shrill succession, "Stand to your horses!" "Mount!" and the men obeyed them.

The Light Brigade was drawn up in two lines. The first, from right to left, consisted of the 13th Light Dragoons, the 17th Lancers and, slightly to their rear, the 11th Hussars. The 4th Light Dragoons and the 8th Hussars formed the second line. With half a squadron of the 8th acting as Lord Raglan's escort, the brigade had paraded that morning 675 strong. Lord Lucan, looking down the valley, saw that this wide deployment would be too exposed for the coming attack and ordered Colonel Douglas to move the 11th back so as to take position to the rear of the 17th Lancers. They thus formed the second line, with the 4th and 8th acting as the third.

Lord Cardigan rode forward, to take his place in front of the right squadron of the Lancers. He sat his big chestnut horse, seemingly unmoved and perfectly composed, his staff—on his instructions—several yards behind him, as he waited for the troop officers to finish aligning their men. In the magnificent uniform of the 11th Hussars, his long legs encased in the famous cherry-coloured overalls, he sat bolt upright in his saddle, with drawn sword, looking neither to right nor left. His head, in its crimson-and-white plumed busby, was—as always—held arrogantly and, as his sole concession to the fact that he was going into action, he wore his blue, heavily braided pelisse over his tunic, instead of slinging it from his shoulders. In contrast to those of most of the other officers, his uniform—being kept on board the *Dryad* and cleaned and pressed daily by his valet—looked as if it had come straight from a military tailor's.

When the shouted commands of the troop officers died away, there was again a strangely pregnant silence. Lord Cardigan raised his voice and, without any sign of apprehension or excitement, gave his orders. "The Brigade will advance. The first squadron of the 17th Lancers will direct. Walk march . . . trot!"

The three lines of the Light Brigade started to move slowly down the North Valley, followed several minutes later by the Heavy Brigade, led by Lord Lucan. Owing to the nature of the ground, for part of the North Valley was ploughed, the troop of Horse Artillery Lord Raglan had authorized had to be left behind.

To the watchers high above them on the Sapouné Ridge there was, at first, no indication that Lord Raglan's order had been mis-interpreted. It was not until Lord Cardigan had covered some two hundred yards and then—instead of inclining right, in the direc-tion of the redoubts on the Causeway Heights, continued the advance straight on down the valley—that the awful truth began, at last, to dawn upon the British commander-in-chief and his staff. But, by the time Lord Raglan realized how appalling was the error that had been made, it was much too late to correct it.

Even the Russians occupying the redoubts had assumed, until that moment, that their captured guns were the objectives towards which the British Cavalry Division was advancing. The watchers on the Sapouné Ridge saw them retire and, with their support-ing infantry, form up to receive the charge which, they were obviously convinced, was about to be launched against them. It was the ideal opportunity for Sir George Cathcart's 4th Division to make a bid to retake the redoubts but Sir George did not take

it . . . like the watchers with Lord Raglan, he remained a spectator, as bewildered as they by the Cavalry's extraordinary change
of direction.

The Russian gunners and sharpshooters on the Fedioukine
Hills and the forward slopes of the Causeway Heights did not, at
first, divine the purpose of the steady advance of the brilliantly
uniformed squadrons of the Light Brigade. They were also completely taken by surprise and stared down incredulously, unable
to believe that so small a force could possibly be entering the
North Valley with the intention of charging the twelve-gun battery at its eastern end. The gunners expected them to wheel and
escape from the trap before its jaws closed about them . . . but
they did not.

At an unhurried trot, with superb precision and in perfect
alignment, the Light Brigade came on. About fifty or sixty yards
separated the first line from the second; the third was also about
this distance behind the second, the gap steadily widening. Alone
at their head, rode the tall, striking figure of their brigadier-
general, the gold frogging on his spectacular blue and cherry-red
Hussar uniform glistening in the sunlight. He led them into the
range of the flanking guns as if he were either unaware of their
presence or else supremely indifferent to the terrible threat they
offered . . . and nothing, it seemed, could shake his rocklike calm.

The Russian gunners stared at him in stunned fascination,
scarcely able to believe the evidence of their own eyes; the
infantrymen sighted their rifles but did not fire, for they, too, were
stunned by this extraordinary turn of events. Then the first shock
of surprise passed. Officers bellowed frantic orders and, one after
another, the batteries on the Fedioukine Hills opened up, hurl-
ing a deadly cross-fire of grape and round shot and cannister
upon the slowly moving horsemen below.

As the first battery started firing, a single rider detached himself from the 17th Lancers' leading squadron and galloped frenziedly across its front towards Lord Cardigan. Captain Nolan passed ahead of him—an unforgivable breach of military etiquette, which Cardigan observed with outraged astonishment.

Nolan was waving his sword and shouting at the pitch of his lungs as if, at the eleventh hour, he had realized the probable consequences of his taunt to Lord Lucan and was now seeking desperately to avoid them by halting the brigade's advance. But his voice was inaudible above the crash of guns and the drumming hoofbeats of the Light Brigade's chargers and Lord Cardigan wrathfully waved him back. To him, it must have seemed as if the young upstart A.D.C., who fancied himself as a cavalry tactician, dissatisfied with the speed of the advance, were attempting to take over the leadership of his brigade and this, quite properly, he could not allow.

The true reason for Nolan's action will never be known. A shell burst to Lord Cardigan's right and a splinter from it struck Nolan in the chest, killing him instantly so that—by an ironic twist of Fate—he who was the cause of the tragic misinterpretation of Lord Raglan's order, became the first to pay the price of it. The sword fell from his hand but the hand remained raised, high above his head, and a ghastly scream broke from him, echoing above the thunder of cannon-fire and the crackle of musketry. Yet, even in death, he did not fall from his horse. The animal wheeled round in terror and, although his body slumped, it was still in the saddle as his charger passed through the ranks of the oncoming 13th Light Dragoons, only slipping from it when, at last, the Light Brigade had passed him by.

The advance continued, its pace quickening a little now as, from three sides, the awful hail of fire opened great gaps in the ranks, mowing down men and horses, who had no defense against it. Alex, at Phillip's side, felt his heart turn to stone as the shells burst among the men of the 11th. Every man's instinct was to end the unendurable ordeal by speeding up the advance but Lord Cardigan sternly restrained them, aware that to do so now would be disastrous. They still had nearly three quarters of a mile to cover before they reached the guns they had been ordered to charge. . . .

To the shocked and helpless spectators on the Sapouné Ridge, it now appeared certain that the five splendid regiments under Lord Cardigan's command were riding to their doom. Men wept and cried out in horrified protest. General Bosquet, deeply moved by such a display of disciplined courage, was heard to exclaim, *"C'est magnifique, mais ce n'est pas la guerre . . ."* and an old French general, tears streaming down his cheeks, gripped the arm of General Buller's A.D.D. *"Pauvre garçon!"* he said, as if seeking to comfort him, *"Mon Dieu, j'ai vu des batailles, mais ceci est trop. Que vont-ils faire?"*

The dreadful advance went on. The Light Brigade were within the range of the guns which were their objective now and, in a frenzy to come, at last, to grips with the gunners who were wreaking such terrible havoc amongst them, the 17th Lancers began to press forward. Lord Cardigan, without looking round, laid his sword across Captain Morris's chest and called out, above the din, "Steady . . . steady, the 17th Lancers!" Abashed, Morris dropped back.

"Close to your centre!" "Look to your dressing on the left there!" The troop commanders shouted. "Close in! Close in to the centre!"

This was now the most frequently repeated order and both Alex and Phillip echoed it, as the toll taken in men and horses increased and the charging line narrowed, became more ragged and unevenly spaced. Riderless horses added to the confusion; instinct and training impelled them to seek the familiar formation, to return to the squadron lines, after their riders had been killed. Wounded men, too brave to seek safety in retreat, endeavored to keep up with their unwounded comrades and found that their bravery was not enough . . . they fell back, bringing disorder to the line behind them.

Compared with the Heavy Brigade charge in which he had taken part that morning, Alex realized that this slow advance under such an inferno of fire was the greatest ordeal which he, or the men with him, could ever be called upon to endure. The Heavies' charge had taken ten minutes; it had been short, they had come almost instantly to grips with the enemy and had been able to meet that enemy on equal terms, man for man, if not in equal numbers. And they had won a significant victory.

But the Light Brigade could not achieve victory. Here, in this mile-long advance along the North Valley, they had no weapons with which to answer the hail of shot and shell which rained down upon them. Only British discipline kept the men of the Light Brigade from breaking ranks and dashing forward, in disorder, to attack the guns. Only British courage kept the men of the Light Brigade, the men of his old regiment, in their rapidly shrinking lines, still moving forward. It was a matchless courage which, he knew from experience, few other troops possessed and, as he watched the men about him fall and the rest continue to advance, Alex Sheridan felt a glow of heartbreaking pride in these splendid soldiers who were his countrymen, his flesh and blood, to whom he had returned, after the long years of exile.

The wheel had turned full circle, he thought. He was back,

once more, with the 11th Hussars. With them, he had learnt his trade and with them, as a boy of seventeen, he had begun his military career . . . this was his regiment. Now he expected death as, he supposed, they all did—they were soldiers, they could recognize the odds against them. Now he was afraid as, no doubt, they all were—yet he was proud to think that, if death must come to him, it would come in such company as theirs. He was back where he belonged.

For a fleeting moment, he let his thoughts stray to Emmy and he saw her face, as he had seen it earlier that morning, floating before him. But he knew it was a vision, a dream existing only in his imagination . . . a long way from reality.

Reality lay ahead. Reality for him, and for the pitifully few survivors of the Light Brigade, was the guns, shrouded in smoke, belching forth flames. The guns were quite close to them now and the charge became a wild gallop, as the Russian gunners fired their last salvo and then, in terror, when the depleted first line of the 17th Lancers charged them, crawled beneath their guns.

The 17th were followed by the 11th Hussars. Alex, conscious neither of fear nor of pity, found himself at Lord Cardigan's heels, passing right through the battery, hacking and slashing at the gunners as he went, with Phillip, shouting a stirring "View Hulloa!" at his side.

Behind the line of guns were ranged the great, unmoving mass of Russian cavalry. A group of these, in blue Lancer uniform, started to form up to their right and Colonel Douglas, expecting reinforcements and having no orders to retire, shouted to Phillip that they must charge. Wearily, the eighty men of the 11th—all that were left of them—realigned themselves and charged. The Russians broke and retreated before them and they galloped on, still in the belief that reinforcements from the Heavy Brigade must be following behind them.

But none came. Lord Lucan had halted the Heavy Brigade when, coming under even heavier fire from the Fedioukine Hills than the Light Brigade had done, they suffered very severe casualties, Lucan himself was wounded in the leg, one of his staff killed and two others wounded. He said bitterly, to Lord William Paulet riding at his side, "They have sacrificed the Light Brigade—they shall not have the Heavy, if I can help it." He ordered his trumpeter to sound the halt and withdrew the Heavy Brigade out of range of the Russian guns, but he held it, as close as he could, with the intention of covering the Light Brigade's retreat.

Unaware of this, the 11th drove the Russian Lancers back until, realizing at last that the expected reinforcements had not appeared, Colonel Douglas decided that the time had come to break off the attack and retire. But now Cossacks attacked them on the flank, firing their pistols with deadly effect and a second regiment of Lancers loomed up on their left, to harass their retreat.

Joined by Lord George Paget, with the remnants of the 4th Light Dragoons, the 11th continued to fall back, until Alex saw that they were about to be taken in the rear. He shouted a warning and Lord George called on his small, exhausted handful of men to make a stand. "Halt—front!" he bade them hoarsely. "If you don't halt front, my boys we're done."

The men of both regiments obeyed as coolly as if they had been on parade. Faced by a resolute line, the Lancers and Cossacks who had been pursuing them, also halted and finally—inexplicably—drew off. There remained the newly arrived squadrons of Lancers in their rear, which now started to form up, as if with the intention of taking the offensive and cutting off their retreat. Alex glanced at Phillip and said grimly, "We are going to have to fight our way out of this, I fear."

"Yes." Phillip's smoke-blackened face twisted into a rueful smile, which swiftly faded. "I fear you are right."

In response to the urging of their few surviving officers and Lord George Paget, the men of the 11th and the 4th, now reduced to a total strength of less than fifty, again formed as compact a line as they could. They faced about and, as fast as their tired horses could carry them, charged the Lancers who were seeking to cut them off. Their charge met with little resistance. The Lancers wheeled, evidently afraid to meet it and they galloped past almost unscathed, only halting when they reached the silent line of guns against which their original charge had been made.

And now they, with the other shattered regiments of the Light Brigade, had the mile-long gauntlet of the North Valley to run a second time. Now, weary and wounded, many of them on foot, others leading lamed and bleeding horses, they must once again brave the Russian guns—although these had been rendered less effective by the magnificent attack of the French Chasseurs d'Afrique on the Fedioukine batteries, which they had charged and silenced to aid their British allies' retreat.

Nevertheless, for Alex, as for a great many others, the return through the valley was the worst part of the ordeal.

The guns on the Causeway Heights still dealt out their awful carnage; the riflemen massed on the slopes above them poured down a hail of Minié balls from safe concealment, and roving bands of vengeful Cossacks rode down the lame and the unhorsed, the wounded and the disarmed, showing them no mercy.

The whole valley was a shambles, the ground strewn with dead and dying men and hideously mutilated horses. Ahead of them, as the 11th began their painful retreat to their own lines, small groups of men, their uniforms so spattered with mud and blood as to be almost unrecognizable, straggled back, some walking, some leading a horse, miraculously unscathed, on which a badly injured man clung weakly to the saddle. Others, barely able to hobble themselves, dragged a dying charger which they refused to abandon and sought, even in their own extremity, to save.

Alex dismounted beside a wounded sergeant of the 8th and, with difficulty—for there seemed to be no strength in his arms—picked him up and got him, somehow, on to his animal's back. It was then that he realized, for the first time, that he had been wounded himself. His right arm was stiff and soaked in blood and he staggered along, clinging to his horse's stirrup, in a state of dazed half-consciousness and well-nigh unendurable pain.

Phillip, too, was walking now, having yielded his horse to another wounded man and their pace got gradually slower, with Phillip dropping behind. Alex did not see the Cossacks who attacked him, did not hear their approach but he heard Phillip's voice call his name and turning, saw that his brother-in-law was surrounded. He lurched towards them, lunging blindly with his sword-point and, by a lucky chance rather than skill, succeeded in unhorsing the nearest of Phillip's attackers. The rest closed in on them both with the object, he supposed dully—since they did not use their lances—of taking them prisoner.

Phillip was fighting them valiantly but his own efforts, Alex realized, were slow and ineffectual. They ceased altogether when a Cossack lance struck his sword-arm, knocking his weapon from his grasp and he went down under a blow from a pistol butt. Then, recovering consciousness, he was aware of an English voice, close to his ear, begging him to lie still.

"We drove them Cossack swine off, sir, don't you worry. And we'll get you back . . . it's not more'n another quarter of a mile now and there's a regiment of the Heavies coming out to meet us. If you can sit a horse, sir. . . ."

But Alex knew he could no longer sit a horse. He tried to shake his head, to tell these troopers of the 11th who had saved him that they must leave him and go on to seek safety themselves. But seemingly they did not hear him, for he found himself being bundled into the saddle of a big bay and held there by two of them, since he could not sit upright. He tried to look round for Phillip but he was nowhere to be seen and one of the troopers, in answer to his faintly croaked question, shook his head regretfully.

"Them Cossacks got his lordship, sir. I'm sorry, we done what we could. We'll bring his body back, sir, if we can manage it."

After that, their voices and the continued roar of the guns became a meaningless blur of sound, drowned in his pain. . . .

On 6 November the first of the ships bringing the wounded from Balaclava began to unload at Scutari.

Emmy Sheridan stood on the rickety landing stage, a shawl wrapped about her against the cold, and watched apprehensively as the men were lowered into caiques and rowed to shore. Behind her, the great, imposing bulk of the Barrack Hospital loomed majestically, looking from the outside like a sultan's palace. But Emmy, who had been a frequent visitor there during the weeks which had followed her return to Constantinople, was aware that, from the inside, it presented a very different picture. It was dank and dark, a maze of long, echoing corridors and huge, badly ventilated rooms, the floors cracked, the walls streaming with damp. The whole place was filthy and verminous and, as a hospital, it was deplorably inadequate to care for the thousands of sick and wounded men who were now crowded into it. Destitute of furniture, lacking medical supplies, drugs, comforts and proper cooking facilities, it was also short of doctors and surgeons and staffed by untrained, overworked orderlies.

There were no beds; the sick lay in long lines, half naked, on the floor, the majority without bedding, and it was often days and sometimes weeks before they were examined or had their wounds dressed by a surgeon. In addition, there was a shortage of water.

Emmy had been appalled when, coming from Therapia to await the expected arrival of Miss Nightingale and her band of forty, officially-appointed nurses, she had paid her first visit to the hospital.

She had done what she could—little enough, in all conscience —to ease the lot of the unfortunate sufferers who occupied its dark and foul-smelling wards. As a guest of the British ambassador, Lord Stratford de Redcliffe, her visits had been tolerated by Dr Menzies and Major Sillery, who were in charge of the Barrack Hospital . . . but they had not been welcome. And when Emmy had told Dr Menzies of her nursing training and experience and offered her services to him, he had told her flatly that she must wait until Miss Nightingale arrived and make application to her.

"Miss Florence Nightingale," he had said, with restrained coldness, "has been appointed Superintendent of the Female Nursing Establishment of the English General Hospitals in Turkey by the Secretary at War. I cannot authorize you to nurse here. And frankly, Mrs Sheridan, as a lady of quality and the wife of an officer, I can't imagine why you should have any desire to do so. You've seen the conditions under which we are compelled to work . . . how can anyone of gentle birth possibly want to share them?"

So . . . she had waited, with growing impatience and despair, Emmy recalled, and the most she had been able to do for the sick and suffering had been to provide them with a few comforts, paid for out of her own pocket. More than once, she had been tempted to give up the idea of waiting for Miss Nightingale's arrival and return to Therapia, where Charlotte and Arthur Cassell were comfortably established at the ambassador's summer residence, while the latter enjoyed a lengthy convalescence.

But then had come the news of the Battle of Balaclava and she had learned of the terrible casualties suffered by the Cavalry Division. Anxiety for Alex had kept her where she was, waiting, hoping . . . and losing. A hope. She had received a second letter from him, and one from Phillip, both almost a month old by the time they reached her and, since then, she had heard nothing, save a host of rumors—each more alarming than the last.

Emmy shivered, as she watched the first batch of wounded being loaded on to stretchers, for the painful, jolting climb up to the Barrack Hospital, praying that neither her husband nor her brother might be among them. More caiques were now coming up to the landing stage and she peered down, searching for a familiar face, yet dreading to see one.

Miss Nightingale and 38 nurses, who had also heard the news of Balaclava, had arrived the previous day. The nurses included fourteen hospital nurses but the remaining 24, she had been pleased to see, were Catholic and Anglican Sisters. They had been formally and courteously received by Dr Menzies and Major Sillery, but both doctors had made it abundantly clear to Miss Nightingale, as Emmy had since learned, that they considered female nurses in a military hospital "an unwise indulgence, unfavourable to military discipline and to the recovery of the patients."

Miss Nightingale had listened to them with dignified politeness, offering no comment. She had received Emmy's offer of her services at first with a certain understandable mistrust but finally, when she learned more about the new recruit, with gratitude. Yet even this did not mean that Emmy had gained entry to the wards as anything but a visitor. Miss Nightingale, having settled her party into five cramped, virtually unfurnished rooms—which were all that had been provided for them—soon found that in spite of the courteous welcome they had been accorded few, if any, of the doctors intended to make use of their services. "The doctors do not want us," she explained to Emmy. "Therefore we must wait. No nurse is to enter a ward, unless at the express invitation of a doctor. But when they do call on us—as eventually they will have to—we will be ready. Go back to your lodgings, Mrs Sheridan. I will send for you, I give you my word, as soon as there is work for you to do."

And so, it seemed, she must continue to wait, Emmy thought sadly, as she watched another line of stretchers wending its way up the precipitous slope, the Turkish bearers frequently pausing for breath. They set down their burdens roughly, indifferent to the agonized cries of the unfortunate men to whom this rough handling was torture.

Suddenly unable to endure the sight and sound of this suffering any longer, she approached one of the litters and, kneeling in the mud beside it, sought to ease the cramped position of the man who lay huddled upon it. Then, to her horror, she recognized him and smothered a cry.

Sheer, blind chance had brought her to this particular stretcher . . . from a distance, there had been nothing familiar about the face of the wounded man which, in any case, was half-hidden by a bloodstained bandage. Her brother's pain-dimmed eyes looked up into hers as she said his name.

"Phillip . . . is it you? Oh, Phillip, Phillip!"

He managed to twist his lips into a semblance of a smile and then, so faintly that she could scarcely hear it, he whispered her name. "Emmy, it . . . it's good to . . . see you."

He was dying, she realized; in these last months, she had seen death too often not to sense its imminence, and she knelt there, holding tightly to his hand. The Turkish bearers made as if to resume their journey but she shook her head. "No—leave him here. I will take care of him."

They shrugged, only half understanding, and went to squat a few yards from her. She had a flask of brandy, Emmy remembered, and she took it from her reticule, held it to his lips. He sipped it gratefully.

"Thank you . . . Emmy. That . . . helps."

"Does it, Phillip?" She felt tears come to prick at her eyes, as she considered what to do. It was unthinkable to take him to the hospital, yet she could not attend to him here. Although perhaps Miss Nightingale . . . as if he had read her thoughts, Phillip weakly shook his head.

"It can't be . . . much longer, Emmy. I'd like to lie still."

"I could take you to the ambassador's residence—" Emmy began but again he attempted to shake his head.

"No . . . time, my dear. Alex, perhaps . . . you could take him."

"Alex?" Emmy's heart missed a beat, then started to pound in her breast, like a wild thing, seeking release. "Is Alex—was he on board the transport with you?"

Phillip nodded. "With me . . . all the way . . . in the charge down the . . . North Valley. Came back to . . . help me, when the Cossacks attacked. I was almost . . . left for dead . . . then, Emmy. But they brought me in." He accepted another sip of Emmy's brandy and a little colour returned to his white face. "To die here instead," he added sadly. "But at least . . . with you."

"You're not going to die, Phillip," Emmy said, wishing that

she could believe it, hoping that he might, but he only smiled up at her in mute denial of her attempt to offer consolation and then started to give her messages for Sophie, a letter which, on his instructions, she took from the tattered pocket of his mud-caked jacket.

"She'll have a son," he asserted, his voice a little stronger now. "She must, for my sake, to carry on the name."

"I'm sure she will, Phillip dear." Emmy wanted to ask him about Alex and, again as if he had sensed her unspoken question, he answered it.

"Alex is not too bad. He lost an arm but I saw him on the transport. He'll be all right, if you take care of him."

"I will take care of him," Emmy promised. She offered him the flask again but he shook his head.

"No pain now," he told her. "Thank God . . . no more pain. There was a chaplain with us, on the transport. He gave me . . . Absolution. Yesterday, I think, or perhaps the . . . day before."

He was silent and, as she watched, forcing back the tears, the light went out of his eyes and his face began gradually to lose its taut, tormented rigidity and to relax, so that it was the face, not of a desperately wounded man but of a boy. He smiled.

"It was a splendid charge, Emmy," he whispered. "We showed them . . . what we could do. Right up to the guns . . . with Cardigan in front of us. Ask Alex, he'll tell you. He was there, with us, with the 11th . . . riding beside me." And then, with a sudden change of tone, he said, "Say a . . . prayer for me, Emmy. And for my . . . son."

Emmy did not know at what moment his soul slipped away. She knelt, his hand in hers, saying the prayer he had asked for and feeling his fingers relax their grip . . . when she opened her eyes to look at him again, his face was shuttered and at peace.

Blinded by tears, she got to her feet and motioned to the Turk-ish bearers to resume their burden.

It was not until half an hour later, after a long search, that she found Alex. He was in one of the corridors lying, as all the oth-ers were, on a pile of reeking, verminous straw, spread out thinly over the cracked tiles of the floor. The fact that, officially, this was designated an officers' ward made little difference to the condi-tions—they were no better than those of the private soldiers in the huge, barn-like rooms beyond. There were fewer officers, that was all, but to compensate for this, there were fewer orderlies to attend to their needs. Now there was only one, a wizened, unshaven old pensioner, who had found the fresh influx of patients too much for him and, after fortifying himself in the canteen, had crawled away into a corner to seek temporary oblivion in sleep.

Emmy eyed him with disgust and went to kneel at Alex's side, heedless of Miss Nightingale's orders, caring for nothing save the fact that she had found her husband at last and he was wounded and in pain. He recognized her and called out, attempting to raise himself on his one good arm. But the dreadful over-crowding below decks in the sick transport, the wretched discomfort and the lack of proper food had weakened him, so that the effort was too much and he sank back on the filthy straw. He managed to smile at her, as poor Phillip had and this time, try as she might, Emmy could not restrain her tears.

"Ah, Emmy . . . my love, you mustn't cry." His voice was husky with emotion. "I am not as bad as I look, you know."

"Aren't you?" She looked into his pale face, with its untidy growth of stubble, at the stump of his right arm, wrapped in a blood-soaked bandage, at the torn and tarnished lace of his uni-form jacket which had been cut away, in the field hospital, to expose the arm the surgeons had taken off. He was one of the many, she knew, and better off, perhaps, than most but he was Alex and it broke her heart to see him thus.

"You should not be here," he admonished her gently. "We are all in a terrible state, after the voyage. We shall look better when they have attended to us and cleaned us up, I promise you."

Remembering his dread of being badly wounded and helpless, Emmy could hardly speak. In any case, there was nothing to say; she could not tell him that no one would attend to him or dress his wounds or shave him, if she did not. She scrambled up, fighting back the tears. "I . . . I'll come back, Alex," she told him. "I'll only be a little while."

Close to despair, she went in search of Miss Nightingale but she was nowhere to be found. The Mother Superior of the Catholic Nursing Order listened to her story sympathetically and promised her some of their bandages and comforts, if she obtained Dr Menzie's permission to attend to her husband. Finding him in his office, she repeated her story and he gave her grudging permission.

"It is scarcely justice that because one man has his wife here he should receive attention, when the others cannot, Mrs Sheridan. But, on the other hand, since you are his wife, I cannot find it in my heart to refuse you. You may bring him water with which to wash and a razor. But, until the surgeon on duty has examined him, you had better not attempt to dress his injuries."

"I am a trained nurse," Emmy pointed out.

"But you are not a doctor, are you?" he countered.

"No, alas . . . I am not," Emmy conceded, controlling herself with difficulty.

"There are still some professions which remain sacred to the mere male, Mrs Sheridan—in spite of this invasion of our hospitals by female nurses, ordered by the Cabinet," Dr Menzies said.

"However"—he eyed her warily and added, as if he had suddenly recalled the fact—"you are a guest of Lord and Lady Stratford's, are you not?"

"Yes, Dr Menzies. But I am about to enroll as one of Miss Nightingale's nurses," Emmy began. "And—"

He cut her short. "I will send Dr McGrigor with you," he offered. "He shall dress Captain Sheridan's wounds. And, as soon as it is possible, we will discharge your husband into your care. No doubt the ambassador will put a room in his residence at your disposal . . . which Captain Sheridan can occupy during his convalescence."

Emmy did not argue; she had got what she wanted.

With Dr McGrigor and the bandages, hot water and other comforts she had been able to beg from the Mother Superior of the Bermondsey nuns, she returned to the chilly corridor where Alex lay, and together they set to work to make him comfortable. The surgeon was a kindly, conscientious young man; having once started, he showed no inclination to abandon his errand of mercy. He said diffidently, "I shall look at some of the others, since I am here, Mrs Sheridan. And I should appreciate your competent assistance, if you can spare an hour or so to help me."

A doctor had asked for her help, Emmy thought, and, as she willingly assented to his request, her heart lifted. Miss Nightingale's orders had been to wait until a doctor invited the nurses to work with him. . . . "There are others, Dr McGrigor," she told him, greatly daring. "Other nurses who would gladly assist you, if you need them."

He sighed, looking at the long rows of suffering men and then capitulated. "Find me two more as skilled as yourself, Mrs Sheridan, and I will not refuse their aid."

It was Miss Nightingale herself who selected the two nurses and brought them, in person, to the ward—Mrs Roberts, a woman of much experience, from St Thomas's Hospital, and Mrs Drake, from St John's House.

By the time Emmy returned to Alex's side, the whole ward had received attention and Dr McGrigor, with his two assistants, had gone on to the big other-ranks' ward beyond, leaving her in charge of this one.

It was a small victory but it was the beginning of a much greater one. The nurses had proved themselves and, as she looked down at Alex's sleeping face, Emmy felt a surge of thankfulness and relief. Her husband still looked pale and exhausted, but he was enjoying the first real sleep he had had since the retreat from the North Valley and already the lines of pain were being smoothed from his face. She thought of Phillip, as she sank down beside him, and of the others—so tragically many of them—who had died and who would die as the result of this cruel war. But at least Alex was safe and now, with the coming of Miss Nightingale, something would be done to alleviate the agony of the sick and wounded who were brought to this vast, disorganized hospital.

She would take Alex to Lord Stratford de Redcliffe's house, she decided, and there—as Dr Menzies had suggested—she would nurse him back to health. But afterwards . . . Emmy sighed and bent to kiss his white cheek. Afterwards she would come back to work with Florence Nightingale.

Alex stirred in his sleep and, as if guided by instinct, his hand sought hers and his fingers tightened about it.

"Emmy . . ." he murmured but did not waken. "Emmy, my dearest love . . ."

Emmy sat beside him, waiting for the dawn of a new day.